97

Praise for the delectable Culinary Mysteries by Nancy Fairbanks

"A clever, fast-paced tale sure to satisfy the cravings of both gourmands and mystery buffs. Food columnist Carolyn Blue is a confident and witty detective with a taste for good food and an eye for murderous detail. A literate, deliciously well-written mystery."

—Earlene Fowler, author of *The Saddlemaker's Wife*

"Not your average whodunit . . . Extremely funny . . . A rollicking good time."　　　—*Romance Reviews Today*

"An entertaining amateur sleuth tale . . . Fun."

—*Painted Rock Reviews*

"Fairbanks has a real gift for creating characters based in reality but just the slightest bit wacky in a slyly humorous way . . . It will tickle your funny bone as well as stimulate your appetite for good food."　　　—*El Paso Times*

"A fast and funny whodunit."　　　—*The Best Reviews*

"Nancy Fairbanks scores again . . . a page-turner."

—*Las Cruces (NM) Sun-News*

"Nancy Fairbanks writes a delicious . . . amusing amateur-sleuth story."　　　—*Midwest Book Review*

"Humor, entertaining characters, and a puzzling mystery round out the mix . . . a not-to-be-missed read."

—*Roundtable Reviews*

French Fried

Nancy Fairbanks

BERKLEY PRIME CRIME, NEW YORK

THE BERKLEY PUBLISHING GROUP
Published by the Penguin Group
Penguin Group (USA) Inc.
375 Hudson Street, New York, New York 10014, USA
Penguin Group (Canada), 90 Eglinton Avenue East, Suite 700, Toronto, Ontario M4P 2Y3, Canada
(a division of Pearson Penguin Canada Inc.)
Penguin Books Ltd., 80 Strand, London WC2R 0RL, England
Penguin Group Ireland, 25 St. Stephen's Green, Dublin 2, Ireland (a division of Penguin Books Ltd.)
Penguin Group (Australia), 250 Camberwell Road, Camberwell, Victoria 3124, Australia
(a division of Pearson Australia Group Pty. Ltd.)
Penguin Books India Pvt. Ltd., 11 Community Centre, Panchsheel Park, New Delhi—100 017, India
Penguin Group (NZ), Cnr. Airborne and Rosedale Roads, Albany, Auckland 1310, New Zealand
(a division of Pearson New Zealand Ltd.)
Penguin Books (South Africa) (Pty.) Ltd., 24 Sturdee Avenue, Rosebank, Johannesburg 2196, South Africa

Penguin Books Ltd., Registered Offices: 80 Strand, London WC2R 0RL, England

This is a work of fiction. Names, characters, places, and incidents either are the product of the author's imagination or are used fictitiously, and any resemblance to actual persons, living or dead, business establishments, events, or locales is entirely coincidental. The publisher does not have any control over and does not assume any responsibility for author or third-party websites or their content.

PUBLISHER'S NOTE: The recipes contained in this book are to be followed exactly as written. The publisher is not responsible for your specific health or allergy needs that may require medical supervision. The publisher is not responsible for any adverse reactions to the recipes contained in this book.

FRENCH FRIED

A Berkley Prime Crime Book / published by arrangement with the author

PRINTING HISTORY
Berkley Prime Crime mass-market edition / December 2006

Copyright © 2006 by Nancy Herndon.
Cover art by Lisa Desimini.
Cover design by Elaine Groh.

ISBN: 0-425-21308-0

BERKLEY® PRIME CRIME
Berkley Prime Crime Books are published by The Berkley Publishing Group,
a division of Penguin Group (USA) Inc.,
375 Hudson Street, New York, New York 10014.
The name BERKLEY PRIME CRIME and the BERKLEY PRIME CRIME design are trademarks belonging to Penguin Group (USA) Inc.

PRINTED IN THE UNITED STATES OF AMERICA

10 9 8 7 6 5 4 3 2 1

For My Niece, Anne Herndon

Author's Note

Characters and plot elements are fictitious. Many places and dishes are real, but used in a fictitious context. Who wouldn't love the sights, food, and people, not to mention their dogs, of Southern France? The book was inspired by one of our most delightful trips ever, but of course no one got killed, or even injured. Winston Churchill was inspired by a pug dog named Winnie, who belongs to my friend Mary Sarber. Charles de Gaulle was inspired by the late Buster, who belonged to my friend Becky Craver. I have no dogs, but they *are* fun to write about.

Take my word for it: Southern France is a wonderful place to visit, and the natives are very nice, even if you can't understand a word they say. There were no riots when we were there, and while I was writing *French Fried*, the rioting didn't last too long, but that's easy for me to say; no one torched anything belonging to me. None of the places I write about are as perilous as my books might make them seem, so don't obsess about danger; travel if you have the chance.

Books I used for research in writing *French Fried* are Gerard Comeloup, *Lyon: World Heritage Excursions*; Louis Jacquemin, *Traboules & Miraboules*; Gerard Gambier, *Murs peints Lyon*; Louis Jacquemin, *Colors of Lyon*; J. Granier and S. Gagniere, *Avignon*; Alexandra Bonfante-Warren, *Timeless Places: Provence*; Francie Jouanin, *A Taste of Provence*; Gerard Gambier, *The Traditions of*

Lyon's Gastronomy; Andre Domine (editor), *Culinaria France*; Maria Villegas and Sarah Randall, *The Food of France*; Giovanna Gibert, *Provencal Cooking*; Patricia Wells, *At Home in Provence*; Waverley Root, *The Food of France*.

NFH

Lyon

"There is another stretch of wine-covered hillsides, running from Macon almost to Lyons. Here the wine is coarser and the food becomes heavier; the southernmost section, which produces the coarsest wine of all, Beaujolais, has probably affected the cooking of Lyons, too, with its sausages and its potato dishes . . . The cooking of Lyons fits the character of the city—it is hearty rather than graceful, and is apt to leave you with an overstuffed feeling."

Waverley Root, *The Food of France*

"It is no accident that Maurice Edward Saillard, the famous writer on food and drink, known as Curnonsky (1872–1956), referred to Lyon as the capital of gastronomy, considering the city's optimal strategic position, from the culinary point of view . . . Many well-to-do gourmets have lived in Lyon during the course of its history, whether they be Romans, medieval princes of the church, bankers, merchants, or silk manufacturers. Their cooks created exquisite dishes from the rich variety of the ingredients on offer."

Andre Domine, Editor, *Culinaria France*

1
Perilous Pâté

I made the pâté de foie gras, using nothing but the best ingredients, including exceedingly expensive black truffles, minced fine. The four slices had to be irresistible in taste as well as appearance.

My own kitchen was the scene of my preparations, which is not to say that, as a rule, I cook. I have better things to do with my time than to waste it on what, among nonprofessional cooks, is considered woman's work. But any scientist who has worked in a lab can follow a recipe. This one had been in my family for generations. I followed it exactly but for the one tiny addition, which should not change the flavor for the worse. Even if it did, it was only one tiny drop surrounded by several inches of delectable homemade pâté on all sides. This particular compound is over 1,250 times more toxic than cyanide and would begin to do its work rapidly—the more ingested, the quicker the effect.

I made it in my lab. Not an easy synthesis, but it had been done before; in fact, the compound was becoming of interest medically in very dilute solutions. The solution in my small vials was not at all dilute and, therefore, satisfyingly deadly. Having made the pâté in a small roll, I sliced it neatly into four rounds and carefully placed a drop in the middle of each. Then I covered and refrigerated the tray that held the rounds and, after running water into the vials for a half hour each, I crushed them in a towel and disposed of the whole, along with my protective gloves, by putting the "evidence" into a paper bag and throwing it into a public trash container in a suitably distant neighborhood. It was early morning when I returned to prepare the offering of iced champagne and pâté with toast accompanied by the handsome computer-generated note attached to the champagne. Again I wore gloves so that there would be no fingerprints except those of the delivery messenger, who would not be able to identify me because I disguised myself as a messenger in taking the package to him.

I couldn't predict whether both or only one of the visitors would eat the pâté with its unexpected ingredient. But surely at least one would love pâté enough to indulge. If the husband, my vengeance would be direct. If the wife, her loss, for gossip revealed that he was very fond of her, would be devastating and would last as long as he lived. Or as long as I allowed him to live. I had not yet made that decision.

Or perhaps they would both die. By leaving something to chance, my retaliation became the more exciting.

"Wish me luck," I whispered to the ghost who haunted my rooms and my dreams.

2
The Pâté Thief

Robert Levasseur drove his sporty coupe up and down Charlemagne Cour, looking for a place to park and glancing anxiously at his watch. Why the devil had they chosen to stay in the Perrache area? The university had excellent hotels in which to house guests, places convenient to the chemistry department building. In order to carry out his mission, he had to arrive at the hotel before the visitors collapsed into their beds to sleep until the evening's welcome dinner.

Adrien Guillot, senior professor and organizer of the Avignon meeting next week, had assigned Robert the task of taking Professor Blue and his wife to breakfast, but Guillot, in a hurry to escort his own wife to visit her mother in a Paris hospital, had failed to tell Robert when the plane was to land. *Ah! A parking place!* Robert pulled in, locked his car, and strode toward the hotel. Fortunately, Zoe, the adorable departmental secretary, whom Robert very much wished to invite to dinner, had had the name of the Americans' hotel.

He entered and called to a sour-faced young woman sitting at a computer, pointedly ignoring him, "Mademoiselle, I am here to welcome Professor Jason Blue and his wife."

"I'm busy," she snarled.

"They're Americans. Are they here?"

She looked up and squinted at him. "Americans? No, not yet." A sly look came over her face. "But they are troublesome even before their arrival. Already a messenger has come by demanding to take champagne and hors d'oeuvres to their room. You could go up and wait for them there."

"Surely that's not encouraged. It *is* their room."

"Champagne. Pâté de foie gras. Wasted on Americans if you ask me. But where are you from with your strange accent? Are you another American?"

"French Canadian." *Pâté?* Robert's mouth watered. Even the disappointment of having his excellent French pegged as American could not overcome the thought of pâté. "Well, perhaps I will, if that's the way you handle things here."

She rose from her desk to fetch the heavy key from under the glowing counter. "Cover the desk for me," she called to an idle fellow behind the bar. The hotel had a Las Vegas ambiance to it. Lots of neon. Robert had been to a meeting in Las Vegas once and considered the place extremely tasteless.

He did like Jason Blue, whom he had met at an Ottawa conference. The poor man had had to leave suddenly because his wife had been lost on a cruise ship. Although the couple had grown children, Blue still seemed to be in love with her. Why else would he had left before the banquet, which Robert himself had planned and arranged to have flown in so that the conferees would have at least one wonderful meal in the French style?

Here in Lyon most of the couples in enduring marriages had already found lovers with whom they met several times a week—always discreetly, of course. He himself was involved in an affair with Madam Laurent, the chairman's wife, and they were very, very discreet. In fact, the situation terrified him, but Victoire was an intimidating as well as a passionate woman. She wouldn't mind if he managed to get a date with Zoe, which would serve as cover for their affair and irritate her husband, but she would mind if Robert ended his relationship with her before she grew tired of him.

Once in the Blues' room, he sat down in a soft orange chair that was much too small for him and stared longingly at the split of champagne and the four slices of pâté with their mouth watering bits of black embedded—truffles, no doubt. He hoped that when the Blues arrived they would offer to share. Robert thought a really fine pâté de foie gras the finest dish in the world. He had once dreamed that at his death, the priest administering the last rites had offered him a wafer with a bit of pâté smeared on it to go with the communion wine. Dying with the taste of foie gras in one's mouth would be the perfect appetizer to heaven, he had thought on awakening, not a dream that was likely to be fulfilled when his time came.

He turned the chair around and stared out the window at the green-leaved upper branches of the trees that lined Charlemagne Cour. With the drapes pulled partially back by Yvette, the hotel's grumpy receptionist, he would hear the gentle rustling. Very nice. Perhaps the Blues had known what they were doing when they reserved a room here—well, except for the unpleasant Yvette. He had to assume that she was a Parisian. People in Lyon weren't rude to guests.

But no thought could distract Robert from the pâté that rested so close. He sniffed the air, thinking he could detect its rich fragrance, then glanced over his shoulder and swallowed hard. Perhaps they wouldn't mind if he took one slice. They were late arriving, and what a shame to let fine pâté dry out under its glass dome. What could one slice matter? He rose, carefully removed the dome, and with the

small spreading knife, swiped pâté across a piece of toast.
Ah, it was so good! One of the best he'd ever had. In
Canada there was never pâté like this. Something must be
wrong with the geese. In less than a minute he had de-
voured the rest of the slice before forcing himself to sit
down again.

Now the plate looked wrong! Two slices in back, one in
front, and that telltale space beside it. They, as Texans,
might not even like pâté. Perhaps the wife was a native
and, knowing no better, thought foie gras was nasty. Some
Americans said that. If he ate the second slice, there would
still be two left for Jason, should he want them. Obviously,
it was the thing to do. The very thought of letting the pâté
dry out made his lips and the inside of his mouth numb
with dismay.

Robert rose, feeling a bit light-headed. He was salivat-
ing and even somewhat breathless as he made his way to
the desk and prepared four more toasts, but with some difficulty because his hands began to feel prickly. Odd. And
his feet, too. Silly little chair had cut off his circulation.

Still the prickliness didn't prevent him from enjoying
each of the four treats as he popped them in his mouth and
sighed with delight. The pâté was so rich and creamy, so
flavorful. And the toast crunched delightfully between his
teeth as the foie gras melted onto his tongue, laving his
taste buds with its matchless flavor. His eyes were already
on the last two slices. If he ate those, too, would the absent
Americans know the difference? But wait. Who had sent
the mini-feast? He leaned forward to read the card on the
champagne split and almost fell over. Now his legs were
numb and rubbery. "From the Department of Chemistry,"
he read aloud through tingling lips. If he ate the pâté, the
Blues might thank the chairman for the champagne and be
asked how they had liked the pâté. They'd say, "What
pâté?" and his secret pilfering would be—

To catch his balance, he dropped his hand onto the desk with a thud that rattled the tray and its contents, and his wrist gave way like foam so that he found himself propped up on his elbow and wobbling legs. Must sit down. No, lie down. He could straighten out the bedspread as soon as he felt better. Scrape the remains of pâté he'd eaten from the plate. He managed to fall on the bed. *Wipe off the knife*, he thought fuzzily. At least lying down he felt better. A few minutes of rest and he'd . . . close his eyes for a time.

The numbness was spreading in his extremities, and his stomach hurt. Robert felt a distant panic set in. Had he had a stroke? Was paralysis overcoming him? He was too young to . . . How he wished someone would come. Anyone. Even the horrid Yvette. Or the Blues. They'd see he was in trouble and call for help. So what if they noticed the missing pâté?

He had fallen on his side and found his breathing becoming shallow. He needed to stand. To take a deep breath. *Stand up*, he told himself, but when he tried, he ended up on his stomach across the two beds.

Someone. Please come. Help me, the voice in his head called silently. He could no longer speak. His lungs cried for air, and he . . . If only help would come.

But by the time someone entered the room, Robert Levasseur, still marginally conscious, could make no sound but a faint cough, a slight wheeze of failing muscles.

Pâté de foie gras is made from the liver of a goose that has been force-fed until both goose and liver are huge. Archetratus, a famous Greek cook of the third millennium B.C., called that liver the "soul of the goose." Pliny mentions that the force-fed geese of Gaul were herded from Picardy to Rome, where they were refreshed with honey and figs to make them fatter and sicker but, therefore, all the more delectable to the Romans.

In modern times hand forcing of feed down the goose's throat is giving way to electric force feeding and even shocking the goose's brain with electricity or chemicals, after which the goose eats madly, grows hugely, and hallucinates. The result is that the foie gras we savor so avidly comes from a goose that is certainly diabetic and probably schizophrenic, and yet its liver is absolutely irresistible to the connoisseur. Personally I try not to think about the process because I'm addicted, too.

Carolyn Blue,
"Have Fork, Will Travel,"
Providence Star-News

3

Welcome to Lyon

Carolyn

Jet-lagged and apprehensive, I stood at the far end of the elevated Perrache Station, high above the district where our hotel was located—in theory. Goodness knows what I'd do if I couldn't find it. "Go down to street level and straight up Charlemagne Cour," my husband had said. "The hotel can't be more than a block or two. Hotel Charlemagne." Then, having already stowed his suitcase in a locker, Jason had hustled off to catch another train, which would take him to the university.

I still had my suitcase. No matter how much trouble trundling it to the hotel might prove to be, I refused to enter a strange hotel in a strange city without any luggage. I made that point to Jason, who replied, "Why not? You don't have to have your nightgown to fall asleep."

I sighed and headed for the curved marble stairs that would take me down to street level. At least the street had tall, leafy trees on both sides, even if the buildings looked somewhat shabby from where I stood. Surely marble was unusual in an el station that had very hard-used wooden floors where we got off and seedy-looking shops selling newspapers, unappealing souvenirs, and hot dogs—hardly the fare to be expected in a city reputed to be the cuisine capital of France. Maybe the hot dogs were actually sausages. Lyon was famous for those. *I don't even like sausages*, I thought grimly, as I bumped my wheeled suitcase down the first marble step and followed after.

Bump. Step. Bump, bump, bump. Whoops. The weight of my suitcase pulled it down several steps and almost took me with it. I managed to catch my balance and my bag on the fourth step but had to stop, hand pressed against my pounding chest. I felt like sitting down right there to indulge in a bout of exhausted tears, but a man stopped beside me, lectured me sternly in French, slammed down the handle of my wheeled bag, and carried it away.

"Here, you! Give that back! Help! He's stealing my suitcase!" I chased him down the curved stair to the next level while people from a newly arrived train galloped down around me, paying my predicament no mind. How very French of them! When I caught him, the thief was standing in front of heavily scuffed, red-brown doors, pushing a button.

As they opened, he said, "Elevator," and shoved my bag inside. As if I was going to get on an elevator with a strange French luggage snatcher. Evidently that wasn't his plan, for he nodded to me and stalked away. I had no idea what button to select, and before I could decide, a woman pushing a stroller crowded in and sent the elevator down to a floor that didn't look promising. She and her wailing child exited, and I stayed on. When the doors whipped open again, I yanked my suitcase out hastily, lest it be carried off by the impatient elevator, onto which an impatient Frenchman had directed me.

After looking confusedly in all directions, I spotted a door with a light above it, so I headed across the grungy, white-tiled floor and stepped out into—what was it? A smelly tunnel with cars, vans, streetcars, and buses whip-

ping by. I must have gone down a floor too far, but I could
see daylight toward my right, and there was a walkway, so
I took it.

Alas, the walkway ended when I emerged, and I was
confronted with a maze of crisscrossing tracks and road-
ways. Beyond that an even larger street, lined on one side
by grimy, industrial buildings, disappeared to my left. That
couldn't be Charlemagne Cour. To my right what I took to
be the end of the station jutted out, and the leafy-tree street
led away from the entrance. Charlemagne Cour. But how
was I to get to the street when everywhere I looked vehi-
cles were cutting me off? Gritting my teeth, I stayed as
close to the curving wall as I could. When I heard a motor
hurtling toward me, I stopped and closed my eyes. A lot of
honking went on, no doubt at me, before I arrived, trembling, at the front, or back, of the station.

There I waited for a light and trudged across while cars
slammed on their brakes and honked at me. Evidently I
hadn't chosen a light meant for pedestrians. Once across, I
leaned against the window of a shop and took deep, calm-
ing breaths until the shopkeeper frightened me half to
death by tapping loudly on the window behind me.

Needless to say, our trip to Lyon and Avignon did not
start out well. We had been invited by Adrien Guillot, a
chemist we met at a meeting in Sorrento. Jason was to give
talks at Professor Guillot's university in Lyon, after which
we would travel to Avignon for an international meeting, at
which both men would be speakers. Naturally I had been
quite excited at the prospect, Lyon being so well known for
its food and Avignon for its history. It had been the resi-
dence of the papacy for a hundred years, and the general
area was the seat of the Albigensian heresy and the result-
ing crusade of the Northern French against the Southern
French. All very fascinating, not to mention the delights of
the Provençal cuisine to be savored in Avignon.

My enthusiasm had begun to wane when Jason rejected, as too expensive, the hotel recommended by the Guillots. He'd gone on the Internet and found the Hotel Charlemagne. Since he liked the price, the hotel was bound to be less than comfortable, but as he pointed out, his attempts to find me in the spring, when my cruise ship went missing, had been very costly. True, but the money was well spent. I had been so very happy to see him on the deck of the destroyer when the United States Navy hauled me up from my lifeboat.

How gallant and chivalrous my dear husband had been, and what a lovely summer we'd had together in New York while he was consulting for Hodge, Brune—a sort of second honeymoon, although our daughter Gwen was sharing the apartment, and son Chris came down from Boston on the weekends. And, of course, Jason insisted that we live as economically as possible, which is hard to do in New York. What with eating two desserts at every opportunity because the situation was so stressful, the ten pounds I gained during the cruise had to be shed, but the family wasn't at all appreciative of my experiments in "diet gourmet." In fact, by the end of the summer, Jason declared that he never wanted to see another salad.

Still, we got along wonderfully, which, sadly, hadn't been the case earlier that year. Jason had hinted that our problems might be due to menopause, but I am *not* menopausal! I'm only in my forties. I attributed our problems to—well, no matter. She wasn't in New York, so that took care of that. We had a lovely summer.

And maybe our Lyon hotel would be nicer than I expected, although a second bad omen had occurred as soon as we landed at the airport. Our hosts, Adrien and Albertine Guillot, were not there to meet us. We were paged and informed that a family emergency had taken them out of town, but they hoped to be back before departure for Avignon. Naturally, Jason was disappointed. He and Adrien had been planning a joint research project.

Albertine was to show me around Lyon, but without bringing her dreadful dog, Charles de Gaulle—I hoped. Now I didn't have to worry about the dog. No doubt she had taken him with her to the emergency, but her absence left me to find my way around Lyon, and it's a very large city with a very intimidating airport. Not the inside; that was fine. But once we went outside to look for ground transportation, the terminal building loomed up like a black and silver bird with gigantic wings upraised. In my sleep-deprived state, I had the shocked perception that the bird building was about to pounce on me.

And the final blow fell here at Perrache, where Jason deserted me. It was bad enough that he refused to take a taxi to our hotel. Too expensive, he insisted, and quite unnecessary when he'd bought a map and plotted our way by bus and subway. What other husband, jet-lagged and exhausted, would be so besotted with chemistry that he felt it necessary to rush off to a university, where he probably knew no one?

Lost in morose thought, I had been limping along, tugging my heavy suitcase behind me, when I spotted, across the street, the sign HOTEL CHARLEMAGNE. Wouldn't you know that I'd chosen the wrong side of the street? Well, I was not walking to a corner so that I could cross safely and sensibly.

"Never make eye contact with a foreign driver," someone had told me in Italy, so I tried it in France, peeking from the corners of my eyes and barging into traffic when it appeared that oncoming cars could brake before hitting me. They did brake, and I walked straight through the door of the hotel without catching a single eye of a single outraged French driver. If jaywalking is a crime in Lyon, I became a criminal on my very first day. Fortunately, no gendarmes were about to arrest me, and weren't they lucky? I was in no mood to put up with annoying French policemen. Bad enough that drivers for two blocks in every direction had seen fit to honk their horns at me.

4
Goldilocks at the Hotel Charlemagne

Carolyn

Actually, the Hotel Charlemagne was nicer than I expected. Potted, ball-trimmed trees and sizable stone lions guarded a rounded glass-and-metal door that led into a modern lobby. Inside, colorful abstract paintings, leather couches, and handsome contemporary rugs greeted me. In a raised section, large, healthy cacti provided privacy for groups of tables served by a rounded bar, while the reception counter, made of glowing, lighted glass, was backed by a deep red wall. All very chic. What I didn't see was a welcoming presence—no bellhop, no receptionist, just a woman working at a computer. I had to clear my throat twice before she said something snippy in French.

When I replied irritably in English, she said, "I am busy."

"Fine," I replied. "We've prepaid our room; just take my passport and give me my key. I've had a long trip, and I want to go to bed."

She scowled and informed me that she was in charge of billing, not reception. Much I cared. I scowled back. After relenting and checking me in, she told me that my room was on the fourth floor and that the bellhop was otherwise engaged. Then she pointed me toward the elevator and handed me one of those huge keys that are so heavy they *have* to be returned before one goes out. Surrounded by so much modern décor, I couldn't imagine why they didn't provide key cards, but with no bellhop, I wouldn't have to tip, so I headed in the direction of the elevator.

Like the key, the elevator didn't fit the interior decoration. It was so small there was barely room for my bag and me. The room provided another unpleasant surprise, not that it was unattractive. Cream walls slightly tinged with orange, a modern painting overhanging twin beds, yellow patterned spreads contrasting with dark gray headboards and lamp tables, most of one wall covered with gray-and-pale-orange-striped drapes, partially opened, and on the left against a pale green wall a gray desk and mirror, a gray chair upholstered in orange, a wall TV, and the opening to a hall that evidently contained bath and closet facilities—quite nice, I decided in passing.

The surprises included a dark-haired man sprawled across both beds, asleep on his stomach and making a strange rattling-wheezing sound. He obviously had a sinus condition. On the desk sat a split of champagne in an ice bucket and a plate with two delicious-looking slices of pâté de foie gras in back, two slices obviously missing in front, a smeared knife, and toast in a small bowl. The envelope attached by a ribbon to the bottle was addressed to Jason and me.

I glanced at the sleeping man and then tiptoed over to open the envelope. The chemistry department had sent us this welcome snack, which was very thoughtful, except that the strange man had come into our room, slathered foie gras onto toasts with the little knife, and eaten it, after which he had evidently fallen asleep across our beds. Who

did he think he was? Goldilocks invading the house of the
three bears? Well, I, as Mama Bear, resented having my
pâté filched. I could call downstairs, but in doing so, I
might awaken the man. No telling what he'd do.

Accordingly, I wheeled my heavy suitcase into the hall
and closed the door quietly behind me. I was so tired, and
now I had to convince that rude Frenchwoman that there
was a pâté thief sleeping on my bed. When she again ignored me, I said loudly, "There's a stranger in my room.
He ate half of the pâté sent to my husband and me and then
fell asleep on the bed." She raised her eyebrows before
returning to her computer. "I demand that you call the
manager."

"Our manager, madam, is having his midmorning snack
in the dining room and cannot be disturbed."

"Very well, then," I replied. "Go up there and deal with
the intruder yourself. Otherwise, I shall have to call the police. He is occupying a room for which we paid and has
eaten food that was sent to us. That makes him a thief. I'm
quite prepared to sign a warrant for his arrest."

That got her attention. She plucked a page from her
printer, folded it neatly in thirds, and popped it into an
envelope. Then she slotted the envelope carefully into a
cubbyhole and, sighing, rose from the desk. "Louis," she
called to a fellow polishing glasses behind the bar, "you
must watch the desk for me while I investigate this report
of an interloper. It is, without doubt, another guest who
wandered into the wrong room."

"Why would another guest have the key to my room?"
I demanded as I trailed her to the elevator, still dragging
my suitcase.

"Leave the suitcase here, madam. The elevator will not
hold the three of us," she instructed.

"Nonsense. We can squeeze in, or I'll ride up with my
suitcase, and you can walk," I retorted, at that point

thoroughly irritated by her haughty attitude. We did manage to edge in, but the elevator emitted alarming groans as it labored upward. I stared at Yvette, as her nametag identified her, just waiting for her to make some unkind remark about the weight of Americans. She stared at the ceiling, lips pursed primly. Her attitude convinced me that I should insist the hotel replace the pâté missing from our welcome gift.

Since this hotel was Jason's unfortunate choice, it seemed only fair that, once the pâté thief was taken away, the two remaining slices should be mine, not to mention as much of the champagne as I felt like drinking before I went to bed.

Yvette plucked the key from my hand, inserted it in the door, and told me to wait outside while she investigated. Fine. There was a sofa in the hall, and I sat down, glad for a little rest. "Please come in now, madam," she called from inside. "This man is not asleep. He is dead." She was standing with arms crossed over her chest, staring with disapproval at the figure sprawled across our beds.

"Nonsense. He was snoring when I left." I looked, too. He was no longer snoring, but that hardly meant he had died.

5

The Death Warble

Carolyn

While Yvette went to call the police, I curled myself on the hall sofa and fell asleep with my head on the padded arm. Sometime later I awoke suddenly to find three Frenchmen staring down at me while they conversed among themselves. "Are you the American lady discovering the deceased person in her bedroom?" asked one.

"No, he was alive when I found him," I replied, giving them a surprise. They were an ill-assorted lot—a stout, middle-aged man with a mustache and a full, unwrinkled face; a tall, thin, dark-skinned man, wearing a black turtleneck and black pants and carrying a suitcase in one hand and a camera in the other; and last, the man who had spoken to me in English. He was of medium height, fashionably dressed, and had very tidy fingernails, possibly buffed. I do like tidy fingernails. When Jason and I became engaged, my first suggestion was that he take better care of his nails.

"I am Inspector Theodore Roux," said the English speaker. "Please meet my colleagues, Doctor Alphonse Petit and Collector-of-Evidence Kahled Bahari."

Alphonse was the portly fellow and Kahled probably

Algerian or Moroccan, although he sounded very French. I shook hands with each.

"Doctor Petit asks why you think the deceased was alive when you discovered him," the inspector asked.

I replied that the man had made a noise—a sort of snore-cough. I was asked to imitate the noise, an embarrassing request. I didn't even remember it very clearly, but the doctor insisted so I gave a little cough, thought a minute, tried a wheeze, and then, unsatisfied with the result, attempted a gargling sound. The last was unsuccessful because one can hardly gargle without liquid. They all frowned; Kahled shrugged and went into the room, from which the flashes of his camera could be seen almost immediately; and the other two talked between themselves in French, imitated my imitations, and rolled their eyes.

"He must have had a sinus condition," I explained, tracing a finger along the path of my own sinuses and then pretending to blow my nose. After providing me with a handkerchief, the doctor turned back to the inspector for more indecipherable discussion.

Finally the inspector said the doctor thought I might have heard "a death—how would you say?—a death—warble?"

"Warble?" I repeated. *The bird sound?*

"The sound a dying person makes in the throat," Inspector Roux explained. "Before or after death."

I had never heard the sound a dying person makes. I hadn't been allowed to sit with my mother when she died, but I doubted that she had warbled before or after the cancer killed her. Then a terrible thought occurred to me.

"If he was dying, I should have administered artificial respiration, but I had no idea," I assured them. "How terrible to think that I might have saved his life, but if I had performed artificial respiration, and he was simply asleep, he would have awakened to find a strange woman apparently kissing him. And first I'd have had to turn him over, and he might have grabbed me." I was picturing the whole dreadful scenario.

"*Non, non,* madam," exclaimed the inspector. "Do not cry. No woman should kiss the sleeping stranger. You were quite right to go for help." He was patting my shoulder while I sniffed into the doctor's handkerchief. "Do not be frayed in the nerves, madam. A strange man in the room! Who would not be distressed? Can we say you do not know the deceased person?"

"Well." I thought about that. "The back of him did not look familiar."

"*Bon.* We will all go in. Do you need the assistance? You will not mind to look at the deceased once Kahled has taken the pictures and the evidence necessary to our investigation. We do not yet know why the deceased is died. Perhaps only autopsy will tell the cause. Eh?"

Since he was holding out his hand, I had to make an effort to rise. Oh-h! A bad idea! Both men hastily took my arms when I wobbled to my feet. "Jet lag," I gasped. I was so very tired.

Regardless of my condition, I was led into the room, where Kahled announced, "Robert Levasseur," and some things in French.

"So you know Monsieur Robert Levasseur, the French Canadian, madam?" asked the inspector, as if, having come from the same continent, the dead man and I should have been acquainted. I shrugged helplessly. "Now we turn the body. Eh?" With some difficulty, due to the large size of the man, they rolled him toward the center of the two beds and gestured for me to look. I'd never seen Robert Levasseur before. He was a nice-enough-looking man, probably in his thirties, but a stranger to me.

Doctor Petit proceeded to examine the body, first for signs of life, but there seemed to be none. Then he looked at eyes, mouth, which he sniffed, and even fingernails. While this was going on, Kahled politely brushed fingerprint powder off a chair and indicated that I should sit down. I did, although it was not a chair in which one could easily doze off.

Inspector Roux donned rubber gloves and went through the billfold of the late Robert. He was interrupted when the doctor straightened and spoke to him in French, after which the inspector said to me, "Doctor Petit says, because of cyanosis showing in blue fingernails and eye pupils of fixedness and dilation, maybe the deceased died of overdose."

"An overdose of pâté?" I asked, bringing looks of shock and anxiety to the faces of the two Frenchmen, but not Kahled. "I have read," I continued earnestly, "that people have strokes after eating a large quantity of very fatty foods. Mr. Levasseur evidently ate two slices of pâté that were sent to my husband and me as a gift, as he could have seen had he bothered to read the card on the champagne. Not very nice of him, I must say."

The doctor looked very much offended and said something angry in French, which the inspector translated. "Doctor Petit wishes you to know, madam, that pâté does not kill. Many millions of Frenchmen eat pâté as often as they can afford and live long and healthy lives. Please do not assume that this man died by our fine Lyonnais pâté. Should such opinion be published, it would do great harm to our reputation as the culinary capital of France."

The doctor again spoke with impatience, and Inspector Roux informed me that pâté did not cause dilation of the pupils. Various illegal drugs and poisons did that. Did I have any of them in the room?

"I have nothing in this room," I replied. "I never got to move in. My suitcase is in the hall."

"Are illegal drugs and poisons in your suitcase, madam?"

"Certainly not. And if I may make a suggestion, you should put that card in an evidence bag. Just in case the pâté killed him, you'll want to find out where it came from. In fact, perhaps Yvette downstairs can describe the messenger who delivered it."

"Kahled knows the collection of evidence, madam. He is a Frenchman, although Algerian."

"I was not questioning his competence because of his ethnicity," I protested. "In fact, being Algerian would make him less likely than you and Doctor Petit to ignore the possibility of killer Lyonnais pâté. Now, please contact the front desk and tell them another room must be assigned to me. I do not wish to sleep—"

"We must get first your information, madam," said the inspector.

"—in a room where this man died. And I want another room that has trees outside the window. I like the trees, but I don't want to have to talk to that woman at the desk again. She was very unpleasant."

"This is true," the inspector agreed. "But you must not judge we of Lyon by her. We are a very friendly people, madam. She is probably from Paris."

6

Brasserie Georges

Carolyn

We went downstairs, leaving the dead man sprawled across the beds with the door carefully locked by Inspector Roux. While he and I sat behind a cactus drinking coffee from the neon bar, he took my name and personal information, looked at my passport, and then questioned me about my reasons for being here, my discovery of the dead man, everything I did and touched thereafter, my interactions with Yvette before and after the discovery, and everything she said. I was even asked to provide my fingerprints for comparison purposes. Naturally I agreed and allowed Kahled to ink my fingers and roll them on cards. Afterward he provided little packages of detergent wipes so that I could scrub the ink off, which was very thoughtful. I couldn't remember seeing that amenity offered by American policemen on television at home.

When we finished the interview, the doctor, who had talked to Yvette and supervised the removal of the French Canadian, joined us at the table and said, through the inspector, that the hotel would not have a substitute room with trees ready for several hours. That was certainly bad news. By then I was so tired that I was experiencing difficulty in focusing my eyes.

"I must now interview Mademoiselle Yvette," the inspector murmured, after expressing sympathy for my sleepless plight.

"And I must have a nap, even if it has to be on a sofa."

"But of course," cried the inspector. "I can show you to one of sufficient length, madam." He led me to a three-cushion leather sofa and plucked a decorative cushion from a chair for my head. I was dozing as soon as my head touched the pillow with its Mondrian-inspired color blocks. I did hear, as if in a dream, the raised voices of the inspector and Yvette as their combative interview ensued, but I found it comforting and sank down into deep sleep, from which I was aroused later by Inspector Roux saying, "Madam, it is at least another hour until your room is ready. Perhaps you would join Doctor Petit and me for a meal. An excellent brasserie of culinary and historic interest is close by."

I blinked dazedly, wanting to fall back into sleep but also aware that I'd had nothing to eat since the continental breakfast served before landing in Paris. Culinary and historic interest? I should go for the sake of my column. So I dragged myself into a sitting position, regretted my rumpled appearance, and agreed to their kind suggestion. Brasserie Georges was, of all places, situated down the industrial side street to the left of the Perrache Station. However, once inside, I found a bustling nineteenth-century establishment with white tiled floors, gilding and draperies, framed advertisements for products no longer made, and a large menu.

Hoping to spend the afternoon asleep in my new room, I chose a soup recommended by the doctor—tomato, shrimp, and ginger, an interesting combination, and very tasty. With it, I ordered a nice white wine, also recom-

mended by the doctor, whose rumpled suit made me feel
less self-conscious about my own travel-worn appearance.

Meanwhile we held an interesting bilingual conversation. Yvette had revealed, grudgingly, information previ-
ously withheld. The inspector began by asking if she'd
informed me that she had sent a man to my room. Imagine
my astonishment. "Yvette claims he was a friend who
came to see you. You are certain, madam, that you do not
know Monsieur Robert Levasseur?" asked Inspector Roux.

"Certain," I assured him, "and she never said a word
about sending him to our room. Why would she do that?
No matter what he told her, she had no right to offer our
room to a stranger. And look what happened. He ate our
pâté. My husband and I love pâté."

The inspector and the doctor, who evidently understood
some English but did not speak it, agreed that all sensible
people loved Lyonnais pâté and that Yvette's behavior was
suspicious.

"Perhaps he was a friend of hers, and when she told him
about the gift in our room, he wanted to have it," I suggested. "Then he became ill before he could remove the
evidence of his theft. Jason and I would never have known
the difference if Monsieur Levasseur had consumed both
the champagne and the pâté and disposed of the evidence."

"But if that is the case," said Inspector Roux, "why
would she send you to the room when she knows the friend
was there enjoying your repast?"

I thought about that. "To frighten me? She seems a very
spiteful woman. And what did she say about the person
who brought the pâté to the Charlemagne? Could she describe the delivery man?"

"Just as a messenger in the green uniform, she said. She
could not remember more."

Our first courses arrived at that point, and I dipped hun-
grily into my soup, a thick tomato broth, fresh-tasting and

tangy with the exotic flavor added by the strings of ginger.
Ginger is another of those many foods once thought to be
an aphrodisiac, although professors at the medical school
in Salerno during the Middle Ages stated in verse that it
was good for all sorts of things. Maybe I should try writing recipes in verse for my columns. Or maybe not. To this
pairing of tomatoes and ginger, the small, salty shrimp provided a lovely contrast. And there was crusty French bread.
Even as exhausted as I was, I wouldn't have missed that
soup. "The identity of the messenger may be important if
Monsieur Levasseur is found to have died from pâté."

Both men protested such a blot on the culinary es-
cutcheon of Lyon, but I pointed out that someone might
have added poison to the pâté. Where once such a thing
would never have occurred to me, I had recently encoun-
tered so much crime during my travels that I easily conjured
up that scenario.

"But madam, if that should be so, then you or your husband are the intended victims. Have you enemies in Lyon?
At the university?"

"We hardly know anyone here," I protested. *Albertine
Guillot!* I thought. *Can she be harboring a grudge over her
poodle, Charles de Gaulle, who made such a pest of himself in Sorrento that they had to put him in a kennel? Surely
not. Albertine and I became friends of a sort before the
meeting ended.*

When I finished my soup, the men were being served a
second course. I was so upset at the thought that Albertine
might have sent us poisoned pâté and then skipped town
while we were dying that I called the waitress back and ordered dessert. On my first perusal of the menu, I had noted
wistfully a dish called Crousillant aux Framboises. At that
time I overcame my interest by reminding myself sternly
that I was no longer eating desserts. I had eaten enough
desserts on the cruise to last a lifetime.

But now, with the thought that Albertine might have planned my death by pâté, I needed dessert, and it was delicious, a crispy bag of filo dough, tied at the neck and containing raspberries and almond cream on a plate drizzled with raspberry coulis. Did they bake the cream-and-fruit-filled dough and then run it under the broiler to brown and crisp it? If the men had ordered dessert, I'd probably have had another serving.

"Let us hope the mysterious Monsieur Levasseur died of natural causes," said the inspector, who was enjoying a hearty sausage and potato dish. "If not, madam, I will inform you as soon as the doctor discovers the cause of death. In the meantime you and your husband should take care. Eat in restaurants. Give no one access to your food and drink," he advised. "I am regretful to warn you in this way when you have the culinary delights in Lyon awaiting you, but in this situation you would be wise to—"

"Yes, yes," I agreed, not much worried because the only people in Lyon who knew us were now out of town. "Thank you for your concern." I finished my Crousillant aux Framboises without a qualm. After all, I doubted that the inspector or the doctor would have any interest in poisoning me.

Tomato Soup with Ginger and Shrimp

- In a heavy saucepan over medium heat, sauté *2 large diced yellow onions* in *¼ cup olive oil*. Add *1 tablespoon finely diced orange zest* and *20 small ripe tomatoes, quartered*. Stir occasionally for about 20 minutes.

- Puree soup in food processor and strain through medium mesh sieve placed over large, clean saucepan. Discard peels and seeds.

- Peel and cut into strings *6 tablespoons fresh ginger* and add to soup. Reheat over medium-low heat, add *¼ pound of tiny cooked shrimp,* and season with *salt* and *pepper.*

- Add *½ to 1 cup heavy or light cream* to taste. Season again and serve.

Carolyn Blue,
"Have Fork, Will Travel,"
Minneapolis Post

7

Resurrection

Jason

Most experts advise the jet-lagged traveler to stay up until bedtime in the country of destination for a faster adjustment to the new time zone, but my wife prefers to fall directly into bed, sleep until dinnertime, eat, and get a full night's sleep. I'm always amazed that it works for her, but she is a very grumpy companion if forced to stay up until bedtime on the first day in Europe. We've tried that.

So I expected her to be rested when I called about the welcome dinner planned by the chairman. I'd have returned to get her, but I'd stayed too long talking science with new colleagues since the man I had specifically gone to see, in the unexpected absence of Adrien Guillot, hadn't been there. "It's Jason," I said into the chairman's telephone. "We're invited to dinner at a restaurant highly recommended for its local dishes. I knew you wouldn't want to miss that, sweetheart. Did you have a good sleep?"

"Don't ask," she muttered.

So I didn't. "Look, could you get dressed and meet us over here? It's an easy trip from the Perrache Station. I'll give you—"

"You want me to go by myself? On the train? During

rush hour? I'll get lost and end up in Toulouse, maybe even Spain."

I laughed at the idea that Carolyn would end up in Toulouse, which is quite some distance from Lyon.

"It's not funny, Jason. I'm tired and upset and—well, maybe I should just stay here."

"Sweetheart, we're the guests of honor. If you're worried about getting lost, you'd better take a cab." *God knows what that will cost*, I thought. "You'll need to change dollars for francs at the hotel. And you might as well go straight to the restaurant. Say at seven-thirty." While Carolyn looked for pen and paper, I consulted the chairman, who estimated the length of the cab ride and suggested that she meet us at eight instead of seven-thirty.

"Your wife will wish enough time for all the necessary feminine preparations before a night out in Lyon," he said rather pompously.

"Dress up," I advised when she got back on the line. Then I told her the name of the restaurant, and she wanted me to spell it. French spelling is not my forte, but I made a stab at it and was quickly relieved of the telephone by the chair, Professor Laurent, who introduced himself to "dear Madam Blue," and proceeded to dictate the name and address, a lengthy process because the French pronounce the letters differently, and many letters required whole conversations to convey.

The chairman seemed irritated by the end of the process, so I could imagine how Carolyn was feeling. *Not the best beginning for the evening*, I thought with misgivings as I took the phone back to say good-bye.

"Who in the world was that?" she asked. "He's almost as bad as the woman down at the reception desk. And, Jason, I have the most amazing story to tell you. When I got here—"

"Carolyn, it will have to wait until later. If you're to make it to the restaurant by eight—"

"Oh, all right, Jason. I'll start getting ready. Did you mean formal, as in long dress and—"

"No, no. But the men will be wearing suits. See you at eight, love. I'll let you go now." I hung up before she could tell me that she didn't like the hotel. She'd had her doubts when I made the reservation, so I assumed her story was about the Charlemagne's deficiencies. At least I could count on her enjoying the dinner. Carolyn always responds happily to new culinary experiences.

I'd had *my* doubts when she became a food writer, mainly because she grew more interested in eating out than in cooking at home, but her new occupation did avert the onset of empty-nest syndrome when our youngest left for college. Carolyn even makes some money with her writing hobby, not to mention the tax advantages. What man could object when his wife was able to deduct all her travel expenses? We ate in restaurants we could never have afforded before.

Carolyn

Our replacement room was much like the first, same décor, same leafy trees outside, and the bed was luxuriously comfortable. I'd slept soundly until Jason called. I hadn't even showered or unpacked before falling into bed. Consequently, I didn't discover the drawbacks of the bathroom facilities until I began to prepare for dinner. On one side of the hall off the bedroom were a small closet and a room holding a toilet, bidet, and sink. On the other side were another closet and another room with a skimpy, curtained shower and another sink. It had looked fine on my brief visit before going to bed.

When I actually used the shower, I discovered the problems. While turned on, it sprayed everything in the room—the sink, the shelf for cosmetics above the sink, the towels, the bath mat, the wastebasket under the sink, even the wall socket into which one could plug a razor if one had a razor that worked on French current and was unconcerned with the danger of being electrocuted.

Imagine stepping from the shower onto a wet tile floor and soggy bath mat, then trying to dry off with a damp towel. I left footprints across to the other half of the bath, and then down the hall into the bedroom, where the telephone began to ring while I was donning my robe. If Jason was calling to hurry me up, I had a thing or two to tell him that couldn't be said at the dinner table.

"Madam Blue," said a French-accented voice. "This is Inspector Theodore Roux. I have very strange news for you."

What now? I wondered, sitting down in the orange chair.

"The man you found in your room. It seems that he is not deceased, as we thought."

"But Doctor Petit declared him dead! They carried him out in a body bag."

"That is true, madam, but our good doctor was so curious about the case that he scheduled Monsieur Levasseur for immediate autopsy."

I shuddered, loath to hear what came next. Something ghoulish seemed likely.

"Most embarrassing. After all, the gentleman had no signs of life until Doctor Petit made the first cut. You may not be familiar with the practices of autopsy—"

"Nor is it something I really want described to me."

"And I do not wish to upset you, madam. To make short my story, Monsieur Levasseur, upon being cut with the dissecting knife, bled. The dead man does not bleed. Certainly not several hours after being declared dead. Doctor Petit and his assistant were horrified."

"I should think," I replied weakly, wondering how many more bizarre happenings I was to encounter on my first day in Lyon. "What did they do?"

"They cancelled the autopsy and checked again for signs of life. There were none. Then they bandaged the cut and sent Monsieur Levasseur to the hospital, where he is being examined. We will hear when anything is determined."

"Well," I said in a shaky voice, "let us hope he recovers from—whatever it is that makes him seem to be dead. Have you ever heard of such a thing, Inspector?"

"Only when the wrong person was sent to autopsy, but that mistake was discovered *before* the procedure began. However, Doctor Petit is much intrigued. He has turned his duties over to others and gone into a medical library to search out similar cases."

"Romeo and Juliet come to mind, although I've never heard exactly what potion it was the priest gave Juliet."

"That is fiction, madam," said the inspector sternly. "This is reality. We must now determine why Monsieur Levasseur appeared to be dead and how this deception was caused."

"You think he was playing a trick?" I asked.

"Or perhaps he attempted suicide. But never have I heard of pâté sending a man into a coma so deep that he appeared to be dead. I think you can assume that no attempt was being made on you or your husband, madam. So I wish you happy dining."

"Thank you," I replied. "And you will let me know how this strange affair turns out?"

"But of course."

"And you should have the pâté tested. Just in case."

"Certainly, madam. The pâté is safe in our laboratories, ready to yield up its secrets, if any."

8
Lyonnais Bistro Delights

Jason

Because our group had a private room at the bistro, I had to abandon the wine and pâté prelude to look for Carolyn. No one in the restaurant, other than my scientific colleagues and their wives, seemed to speak English. If she came in, didn't see me, and couldn't inquire, she might head back to the hotel. Carolyn arrived fifteen minutes late and looking very pretty in a blue dress topped by a delicate shawl she had bought on the Amalfi Coast.

"You've missed the pâté and wine, sweetheart." Much to my astonishment, Carolyn turned pale and expressed relief.

"I had to take a call before I left," she explained.

"For me? You don't know anyone in Lyon."

"For me, and it's a story you should hear."

"Unfortunately, we don't have time." I hustled her into the private dining room, offering her a taste of my wine on the way. "I think they said it was Saint-Peray."

She nodded and sniffed. "I read that it's grown on steep vineyards in cool weather. Notice how flowery it smells."

Carolyn passed the goblet back, and I sniffed, but if it was flowery, I couldn't tell. "Maybe I can get you a little foie gras," I offered, knowing how much she loves it. Her willingness to miss pâté could probably be chalked up to some weight she gained on a cruise last spring, for which we'd all suffered during her summer diet. However, as always, she looked wonderful to me.

"I'll pass," she replied, and surprised me again by taking back the Saint-Peray and draining it. "And, Jason, I really need to warn you about—"

"Ah, Professor Laurent, my wife has finally arrived," I said to the chairman. "Carolyn, may I introduce Professor Jacques Laurent and his wife, Victoire."

Carolyn smiled and shook hands, while Laurent said, "Madam Blue, your husband tells us that you write about food. Consequently, I changed our reservations so that you can savor the real food of Lyon, a famous Lyonnais bistro dinner."

"That's so thoughtful of you," said Carolyn, looking somewhat dismayed.

Was there something about bistro food she didn't like? The chairman seemed to think we would all be bowled over with whatever was coming.

"Fortunately, they serve fish if one doesn't like workers' food," said Victoire Laurent. She was a woman a good deal taller than I, silver-haired, and fashionably dressed in a black suit with colored braid decorating the lapels, as if she were a female member of some eighteenth-century army. She was as thin as her husband was blocky, her face almost emaciated, his perfectly square.

"Professor Charles Doigne and his wife, Gabrielle, my wife, Carolyn. And Professor Catherine de Firenze." Both Gabrielle and Catherine were dressed entirely in black, and I remembered Carolyn remarking that French women seemed overfond of the color. "Professor Raymond Girard and his wife, Sylvie, my wife, Carolyn." They were the youngest of the group, and the very tiny Sylvie was attired

dish of trout tartare wrapped in cured salmon and drizzled with lemon cream sauce.

"A safe choice," said Victoire.

"It is an appetizer," protested Professor Laurent.

"All the better," said Carolyn. "I had a large lunch, so a light dish will be perfect, and so exotic. I've never had raw trout, but sushi is delicious, don't you think?"

"I do not eat Japanese food," said Laurent.

"I'll have the Salade Lyonnaise," said Victoire. "What will you have, Professor Blue?"

"The red mullet looks good," I replied, "but what's a mangold tart, other than something wrapped in leaves?"

"A *salad*?" exclaimed Laurent. Then he turned to Carolyn and muttered, "My wife eats *nothing*. She becomes more skeletal each year."

"Skeletal is chic," snapped his wife, "not to mention healthful. You should order salad yourself."

While dining in a Lyon bistro, a fellow diner, on a diet, ordered Salade Lyonnaise, which looked lovely and struck me as a fine thing to serve at a brunch. It is a Canut, or poor silk worker's, dish. Historian Felix Benoit admired the food of these workers, who used cheap ingredients to produce tasty food. He said, while eating a dandelion salad that might have been the ancestor of what the lady ordered: "Donkey snout and other crude cuts, in a spring salad with some grilled bacon, could bring a saint to damnation."

There is a story about Louis XIV as a rather ill-mannered young man. His favorite pastime at dinner was throwing fruit and bread pellets at the ladies-in-waiting. One such young lady, having been hit by an apple, rose and dumped a whole bowl of lettuce with vinaigrette on the playful king's head. As I watched the lady at our table eat her Salade Lyonnaise, I imagined her dumping it on her unpleasant husband's head. The thought of the dressing and yolks from the poached eggs dripping off his very large nose was quite satisfying.

Salade Lyonnaise

- Rub *1 cut clove garlic* over the bottom of a frying pan. Pour ½ inch oil into the pan. Cut *5 slices crustless white bread* into ½-inch cubes and fry until golden brown (1 to 2 minutes). Drain on paper towels and wipe pan.

- Heat *¼ cup olive oil* in pan and cook *3 chopped scallions* and *3 slices bacon cut in short strips* for two minutes. Add *⅓ cup red wine vinegar* and *3 teaspoons whole grain mustard* and boil 2 minutes to reduce by a third. Pour over *7 or more ounces curly endive, other lettuce, and fresh herbs.* Arrange on serving plates.

- Poach *4 eggs* for 3 minutes, remove with slotted spoon, and drain on paper towels. Place on leaves and sprinkle with croutons. Serve at once.

Carolyn Blue,
"Have Fork, Will Travel,"
Syracuse Ledger

9
The Empty Chair

Carolyn

What a bossy man! Jacques Laurent tried to insist that I order that nasty sausage. And his nose! Not to mention hair so black it looked dyed. His wife's silver hair was lovely, but she was as sharp-tongued as he was pushy, not that he paid attention unless she disagreed with him. And I'm happy to say that my trout tartare was very tasty. They'd flavored it with lemon, olive oil, and fresh herbs. "It was so thoughtful of the department to send us the foie gras and champagne," I said to the chairman.

He looked up from his sausage and Lyonnais potatoes fried in goose fat (Think of the cholesterol count in that meal!). "I'm not aware that we sent anything. Why wasn't I told?" He looked offended. "I'll have to ask the departmental secretary."

"It was waiting for me at the hotel." I didn't mention that it might have had a terrible effect on the pâté thief, serious enough to bring on the aborted autopsy. And what would the thief think when he regained consciousness and discovered the cut on his chest?

Jason was asking Sylvie Girard if there were any special rules for runners in Lyon. Goodness, but she was pretty with her curly black hair and elfin face! At least she wasn't a chemist, so Jason wouldn't become infatuated. And obviously he planned to take his usual morning run tomorrow. Given the problems I'd had just walking to the hotel, the thought of my husband loping along in that traffic was terrifying.

Professor Laurent answered the question for Sylvie. "Our law officers tend to suspect runners of being criminals escaping the scene of their crimes. Unless, of course, they are running on designated paths."

"I didn't see any running paths as I took the train over to the university," said Jason. "I want something close to the hotel."

"If you go early in the morning, you shouldn't have a problem," said Catherine. "Where is your hotel?"

Jason told her, and she suggested a route he might take before traffic became heavy. She was a handsome woman, although rather aloof.

"It is most unfortunate that Adrien and Albertine had to leave Lyon before your arrival," said the chairman. "I believe Albertine had plans to show Madam Blue the city. Is that not so, Victoire?"

"She mentioned the murals, the churches, and the traboules, all sights visitors to Lyon would wish to see. Unfortunately, I have too many engagements to assume those duties myself. Perhaps you can hire a guide, Madam Blue."

Jason frowned. Doubtless he thought a guide would be expensive, but what did he expect me to do? Sit in my room at the hotel watching the leaves blowing on the slender branches outside. For excitement I could eat hotdogs at the Perrache Station and visit newspaper kiosks.

"I would be happy to show Madam Blue around Lyon." Sylvie flashed me a merry smile. "We could go to see the murals first. You will find them so exciting."

I thanked her, while pondering the fact that Sylvie had

a British accent, but spoke what sounded like excellent French. Her husband warned me that I would have to put up with her endless picture taking.

"Indeed, our Sylvie is worse than a Japanese tourist," said Madam Laurent.

"And you must ride in a car with no top," her husband continued. "An ancient Austin Healy."

"Still, the weather is fine, Raymond, so why would one need a top? Anyway, I am having a new one made. Perhaps it will be ready tomorrow."

I agreed to ride in the topless car and then discovered that Jason would have to bring me to the university with him tomorrow to meet Sylvie, which meant getting up very early after so little sleep this afternoon. However, that trip would give me the chance to question the secretary about the pâté. And a local guide with a car was not to be passed up, unless, of course, rain was predicted.

Following Sylvie's offer, Gabrielle Doigne decided that she would be the best person to show me the major churches of Lyon, although Sylvie was welcome to drive, and finally Madam Laurent offered to devote a morning on the third day to showing me the traboules, passages cut through private property so that pedestrians could cross from one street to another. They dated from the days when residences crowded together, sharing walls, for long distances. Even in the company of the chairman's acerbic wife, I longed to see the traboules; they had courtyards, towers, and ornate winding staircases inside.

"I will drive that day, too," said Sylvie. "The traboules are—"

"Garçon," commanded Laurent, evidently tired of the plans to entertain me. He burst into a stream of irritated French, and the waiter promptly removed the one chair that had sat empty beside Catherine.

"Robert didn't tell you that he would be absent from the dinner?" Madam Laurent demanded. "That is unlike him."

"He has been absent all day. But wait." The chairman turned to Jason. "Did he not meet you at the airport, Professor Blue?"

"Levasseur?" Jason asked, and his question gave me a start. "I haven't seen him. We received a message saying the Guillots had to leave town. In fact, I left Carolyn at Perrache because I hoped to talk with Robert today."

"Very strange," muttered the chairman. "Levasseur was to meet you at the airport and drive you to your hotel."

"Oh dear," I said. "This professor's name is Robert Levasseur? Is he, by any chance, French Canadian?"

Jason said he was sure he had mentioned Robert to me after the Canadian meeting. "Well, if you did, I was much too upset to remember after being rescued from the lifeboat," I retorted. What a terrible story I had to tell these people about a member of their department. "I'm afraid I know what happened to your professor. When I entered my hotel room, I found him seemingly asleep across our beds, having eaten half the pâté delivered to us as a welcome gift. I took him for a thief and had the police summoned."

"A *thief*!" exclaimed Madam Laurent.

"Well, he did eat our pâté," I replied defensively, "and I didn't know who he was. He was lying there on his stomach making funny noises, and then the horrid hotel woman said he was dead."

"Dead?" they exclaimed in a ragged chorus.

"If you didn't know who he was, why was he in bed in your hotel room?" demanded Victoire, as if I had arrived for an assignation, only to find his body.

"I really couldn't say," I replied. "I'd never seen the man before, or even heard his name until today. You'd have to ask a very unpleasant woman at the hotel desk. She's the one who let him into our room. Maybe he was a friend of hers." Madam Laurent looked exceedingly angry.

"As I was saying, when the medical examiner arrived, he agreed with Yvette that he was dead, so Professor Levasseur was taken away in a body bag."

"My God, not another corpse!" muttered my husband.

"Actually, he wasn't dead," I protested, "and if he had been, it wasn't my fault. After I had lunch with the inspector and the doctor, Doctor Petit went off to perform the autopsy. At that time it was discovered that your friend wasn't dead after all."

"Then where is Levasseur?" demanded the chairman.

"In some hospital. They sewed up the autopsy cut and sent him off, according to Inspector Roux, who called me with that information tonight. That's what I was trying to tell you, Jason, when I arrived."

All the members of our group then burst into agitated conversation in French while the waiter served a dessert that the chairman had ordered for the whole table, something to do with the Red Cross—a red tart, a red fruit, some white strips, and something that looked like a chile relleno with sugar sprinkled on it. I approached the dish with great caution, while Jason stared at me accusingly, as if I had personally endangered his friend.

10

"Who, in Lyon,
Would Want to Kill *Us*?"

Jason

We were both so tired that we dozed until the cab driver woke us up at Perrache and then the hotel. Much to my surprise, the Charlemagne was nicely decorated. We were given a large key at the desk, after which we squeezed into an incredibly small elevator. When I mentioned that the hotel seemed better than expected, Carolyn admitted that it was, except for the bathroom, where the shower sprayed water everywhere, especially on the floor because there was no curb between the shower stall and the bathroom floor. She also assured me that we were not in the room where Robert had fallen ill.

Feeling conscience stricken that I had left her to face such a trying situation, I apologized. Then, while I had a shower in the dripping bathroom, Carolyn returned a phone call. When I waded out, wrapped in a damp towel, she told me that Robert was now dead.

More bad news. "It's hard to believe that a medical examiner could make a mistake like that," I said, accepting the pajamas Carolyn had retrieved from my suitcase, which the cab driver had, for a tip, retrieved from the locker at Perrache.

"Doctor Petit thinks it's significant that your friend appeared dead when he wasn't. He's having the lab follow up on an idea he has about what might have been in the pâté, and of course, he'll have toxicology done on the stomach contents."

"Poor Robert. He was an excellent scientist and very personable. Why do they think the pâté killed him?" I asked, as we climbed into twin beds and turned off the lights. "It could be something else entirely, something that sent him into a coma."

"A stroke? He looked too young for that," said Carolyn, "and Jason, I wish you'd take the pâté theory seriously; that pâté was meant for us. If I'd eaten it, you'd have found me dead when you got home."

A terrible thought. What kind of food poisoning would one find in pâté? Something the goose had eaten that ended up in its liver? Or perhaps something put into the pâté, part of a recipe? "Did it have mushrooms in it?" I asked.

Carolyn thought there might have been truffles because it had looked so delicious, and she had been furious that the man, whom she hadn't known was a friend, had eaten our gift.

"If the black specks were toadstools mistaken for mushrooms—"

"Why would the department send us a welcome present made at a place that can't distinguish mushrooms from toadstools?" she asked.

"We don't even know who sent the gift. Maybe Robert brought it."

Carolyn said he hadn't according to Yvette, and would I at least consider being careful, in case there *was* someone who wanted to kill us?

"Who, in Lyon, would want to kill *us*?" I asked her.

Carolyn muttered something about Albertine and her wretched dog, and I had to laugh, which did not go over well. Acting on a better idea, I gave my wife a good-night kiss, and we both drifted into exhausted sleep.

All that trouble to synthesize the compound secretly in my lab, and I killed a perfectly innocuous colleague with whom I had no quarrel. Poor fellow, a victim of his own gluttony and my incompetence in the art of vengeance. I wonder how he planned to explain why he had eaten the pâté from their gift platter. Fortunately, I had devised another plan and hoped to fare better the next day with my mission. "Tomorrow," I whispered to my ghostly companion.

Jason

Having been awake for two full days, excluding uncomfortable airplane naps, I was tempted to stay in bed an extra hour and skip my morning run, or perhaps wake Carolyn and devote the time to her. She looked so pretty, curled up in the bed next to mine with her blond hair tangled on the pillow. Still, once one starts skipping daily exercise, middle-aged spread sets in. As long as my knees held out, I hoped to keep running. There's nothing like a cool dawn and a brisk workout to start the day.

Accordingly, I slipped out of bed and searched my suitcase for running clothes. In short order I was on Charlemagne Cour. As I ran, I thought about Robert. What could have happened to him in our room?

I had turned to my left outside the hotel to run along the sidewalk until I had used up half the allotted period. Then I crossed the street and ran back toward the hotel, enjoying the sound of trees rustling in the light breeze and the friendly greetings of shopkeepers, who were sweeping off

sidewalks in front of their stores and arranging merchandise on racks. A very friendly city—Lyon. I don't remember being greeted on the streets of Paris.

During the return trip I picked up a companion, who
came out of a side street and joined me with tail wagging
enthusiastically. I'm not sure what kind of dog he was, but
his coat, blotched in brown and white, reminded me of the
huge cows we'd seen grazing in the pastures of Normandy.
He looked well cared for, no doubt someone's pet, and
gave me a friendly bark from time to time as he tipped his
head up to inspect me.

We both had picked up the pace, so I decided to run as
far as Perrache, then back to the hotel. As we started down
the last block, a car, motor revving loudly, suddenly pulled
out of the road that circled the station and accelerated
toward me. Without thinking, I dove into a recessed doorway. That proved to be exactly the right thing to do, for the
car jumped the curb. I slammed up hard against a door and
crumpled to the cement. The dog, too, tried to evade the
racing car and landed on top of me, but the poor beast had
been clipped, and whimpered against my shoulder, its hind
leg bleeding on my trousers. While the car swerved to
avoid the building and accelerated away, I managed to sit
up and lean against the wall, my heart beating violently.

Had the person driving that car meant to hit me? Or had
he lost control and hit the gas rather than the brake? Since
he hadn't had the decency to stop, I'd never know. I staggered up and discovered that I wasn't badly hurt. Then,
with the injured dog in my arms, I limped cautiously
across the street and entered the hotel, where a cheerful
lady with dark brown hair and a tipped nose met me at the
desk.

"Jason Blue," I said. "Room four-twelve. I was almost
run down by a car, and the dog *was* hit, so I brought him
in. Perhaps you could suggest what can be done for him."

"He's not yours? Oh, poor dear," said Simone, as her nametag read. She rounded the glowing counter and took the dog from me. "He's bleeding. Where shall I put him? Not on a sofa. The manager would object." The dog laid his head on her breast and whimpered. "Monsieur, you must go to the dining room and take a tablecloth from one of the tables. We can fold it on a chair and put this poor creature there."

I followed her directions to the dining room, talked a doubtful busboy into giving me a tablecloth, and returned to help care for the dog.

"He has a tag," said Simone. "His name is Henri. I shall call his owner. And the police—because of the car. Did you see it? Or the driver? It is not allowed for cars to run into pedestrians and dogs."

Simone called Henri's owner. I called Carolyn to explain the situation, and she insisted that Simone contact Inspector Theodore Roux, who should know that another attempt had been made on us. At that point, with my bones aching, I didn't feel like objecting. As ridiculous as it seemed, perhaps there was someone out there who meant to cause us harm.

11
The Dog, the Vet,
and the Inspector

Carolyn

The first day someone tried to poison us. The next some-one, probably the same person, tried to run Jason down, yet we were in a strange city, where one of the three people who knew us was now dead. That left the Guillots, re-ported to be visiting Albertine's mother at a Paris hospital. I tried to imagine Albertine sneaking back here, putting poison in the pâté and speeding down Charlemagne Cour to run over Jason, whom she had no reason to dislike. She might resent *me* because of her dog's behavior in Sorrento, but not Jason.

These thoughts got me as far as the miniature elevator, into which I pushed my way, although there were two peo-ple inside—Germans, who said, I think, unpleasant things about me in German, a peculiar language. As if someone made it up as a joke.

"Jason, you're hurt," I cried, as I got out and spotted my husband. When, close to tears, I threw my arms around him, he told me to be careful of his knee, which had been bruised in his attempt to avoid the car.

"Carolyn, this is Simone, who's been looking after Henri."

Simone had come out from behind the counter to shake my hand. How glad I was that Yvette had the day off. Imagine my husband having to deal her when he arrived, hurt and in pain.

"We are so sorry for your husband's injury," said Simone. "Such a good-of-heart man. Even hurt himself, he brings in Henri, who is injured more. I have called this inspector and the owner of Henri. Both will soon come. And yesterday. *Mon Dieu.* In your time of bad fortune, you must deal with Yvette. Please excuse her. She likes not the English."

"I'm American," I corrected, unwilling to forgive Yvette.

"Speakers of English, I should say. Yvette is engaged to our assistant manager, and he runs away with an English woman guesting in our hotel. How humiliate is Yvette to be replaced by an English woman! Please know that I shall do everything to make you a happy stay."

"Thank you, Simone. You're very kind."

"Henri!" A wizened man wearing a beret and waving a cane burst through the round glass doors. His voice set off a cascade of yipping from behind the counter. Then a brown-and-white dog came limping out, trailing a bloody tablecloth.

While dog and owner reunited with human murmurs of dismay and canine whimpers, while Simone beamed at them and comforted the owner in French, another person joined the group, a large, fat man wearing a shredded brown sweater. He took the dog, carried it to a sofa, and proceeded to examine it. "The manager, he will be furious if Henri bleeds on the sofa," Simone whispered to us. "Monsieur Blue, you look pale. Please sit. I will bring the

rest for your leg." She bustled off to take care of Jason
while I put my arm around his waist.

"I can walk," he grumbled.

"Oh, that is very fine to hear." It was Simone, carrying
a footstool. "Breakfast is serving. If you can walk so far,
you can have some while the inspector is coming."

"I've already been there to get the tablecloth," said
Jason, and we headed for the breakfast room. Simone
propped his leg on the footstool at a table while I went to
the buffet and gathered croissants, raisin rolls, coffee, ham,
cheese, and kiwis. Ah, those kiwis. They were the best I've
ever had. So sweet, just the slightest bit tart. Of course, we
had to peel off the hairy skins and put up with the black
seeds, which lodge in the teeth, but still, kiwis go so well
with cheese.

As upset as I was, I enjoyed the breakfast and congratulated Jason on his genius at choosing reasonably priced
hotels. Then I asked if he was in pain and needed Advil,
which I carry in my purse. I do like to be prepared for the
exigencies of travel. Jason declined and even took his leg
off the footstool. "I didn't want to hurt her feelings, but she
got the footstool before I could say I didn't need one."

"Yes, she's much nicer than Yvette, who sent the foie
gras to our room and then your friend Robert. He'd still be
alive if she hadn't. On the other hand, we might be dead."
Jason frowned at me, but I just had to say, "I hope, after
your terrible experience, that you don't still attribute these
things to happenstance."

"I don't know what to think," said Jason, "but I could
use another cup of coffee."

"Don't move, darling. I'll get it for you." I jumped up to
do so, which is why I wasn't at the table to make introductions when Inspector Roux arrived to take Jason's statement. But before the statement, he helped himself to a roll
and coffee at the buffet—reminding me of the police in

Sorrento, who had always been more interested in the hotel buffet than in corpses found upstairs. I recommended the kiwis and cheese, so he took some of those, too, and we went back to join Jason.

"Professor," said the inspector, putting slices of cheese and kiwi on his raisin roll and taking a bite, "what enemies do you have in Lyon?"

"None," said Jason. "My only friend, except a couple who left town, died last night. I don't know anyone else but academics I met yesterday."

"Very puzzling. Madam, have you enemies?"

"I only know the two who left town," I replied, "plus the people who took us to dinner last night." I was unwilling to implicate Albertine until I'd done some investigating. First, I'd call Albertine's Lyon number to see if she answered.

"Hmmm," said the inspector, sipping his coffee and taking another bite of roll. "Then please tell me with much detail, Professor, what happened this morning. Did you recognize the car?"

Jason gave him a exhaustive description of his run, the itinerary, the people who greeted him, the point at which the dog joined him, and finally the car that sped around the circle, jumped the curb, forced him into the recessed doorway, and injured the dog before speeding off without stopping to offer aid.

How terrifying it must have been. I wondered if I could have jumped out of the way as Jason had. Probably not. But then I wouldn't have been running up and down the street at dawn. "You're going to have to give up exercise, Jason, until we're home. Or at least until the inspector catches the culprit."

"Can you describe the car or the driver? Did you see the license plate, Professor?" asked Inspector Roux.

"Lord, man, I was knocked down in the entry way with the dog on top of me. I couldn't see the license plate. The car was black. The driver looked tall and was wearing a soft cap with a bill. A man. I had less than a minute to look and get out of the way."

Inspector Roux sighed. "Not much information. Perhaps Doctor Petit will discover what killed your friend, and we can find the murderer in that way."

"If there is one," Jason replied.

"There is. Lyon pâté does not kill. Lyon drivers do not run down tourists. Perhaps the murderer is from Paris."

I had to stifle a giggle. Everything bad came from Paris according to the inspector.

"Happily the dog will recover. It has a cut on the leg, so there may be blood on the car, but how will we find the car? Are you much hurt, Professor?"

"A bruised knee," said Jason.

At that moment the owner came in carrying Henri, followed by the fat veterinarian. "Henri thanks you, monsieur, for bring him to safety." He leaned down, and Henri, tail wagging behind his owner's arm, licked Jason on the nose. Then the vet shook Jason's hand and informed him, through translation, that he had a better opinion of Americans for having met Jason.

I went to the buffet for another kiwi. They were *so* good. If I stayed alive long enough, maybe I'd write a column on kiwis, New Zealand's gift to fruit lovers. Actually, France grows its own, and the average Frenchman eats three pounds a year. That's a lot of kiwis.

I couldn't believe it. How many people decide to commit murder and fail twice? Twice! First I killed Robert. Then I waited two hours to spot Jason Blue, and what did I accomplish? I missed him and injured a dog. But I'm not done. I need a new plan, one that won't fail.

12
Sylvie's Suspects

Carolyn

Jason dropped me at the chairman's office, where Professor Laurent was absent, but his secretary, Mademoiselle Zoe Thomas sat at her contemporary black and silver desk, her fingers flying over her keyboard and a telephone tucked under her chin, while she spoke rapid-fire French. I dropped into a black chair with a fan back and a hard seat, wondering if these contemporary designers ever tried sitting in their creations. The office looked very smart, but not very welcoming.

The secretary, on the other hand, was a pretty woman with curly brown hair, her face and figure softly curved, not as fashionable as the gaunt Victoire Laurent, or as chic as the décor of the office. Perhaps the chairman had chosen Mademoiselle Thomas for her gently feminine appearance as well as her typing skills.

She replaced the telephone and addressed me in French, to which I replied apologetically in English. "No necessity for apologies. The English is easier to understand than the French of Americans. You are Madam Blue, yes? Who has asked about pâté? It did not come from our department. No pâté ordered by me would sicken or kill. But if the pâté is innocent in the death of our Robert, then you and Professor Blue missed a treat."

"Maybe someone else in the department sent it to us. Can you think of—"

"Perhaps the Guillots, but they were to meet you at the airport, so why send the gift? And they are gone. No, I think it was a mistake. You will find that Robert died of something else. America is such a violent country. But do not fret, madam. You are safe here."

I was going to tell her about the attempt on my husband, but Sylvie, wearing a black-and-white polka dot dress, breezed in and whisked me away to her little sports car, a gleaming, silver blue, missing only the top. I'd never have known the car was very old if she hadn't told me.

Before we could climb in, I was introduced to Winston Churchill, a small pug dog who greeted me by racing around my ankles and jumping up on my legs. "You know Albertine Guillot and her dog Charles de Gaulle?" Sylvie asked as she picked up Winston Churchill. "Winnie met Charles de Gaulle when he was a puppy and Charles a horrid adolescent, to whom Winnie took an immediate dislike. Immediately I decided that I'd call my dog Winston Churchill. Not very nice of me. But Albertine and I are not compatible. She says unpleasant things about Winston Churchill, both the prime minister and my dog.

"My camera equipment is in the backseat, so you won't mind letting Winnie sit in your lap, will you? If he does something you don't like, just say 'No' or *'Non'* loudly. He'll stop." She opened the door for me and, without waiting for my consent, plopped her dog on my knees. Winnie licked my hand, which I really didn't like, but before I could say *no*, he circled once, curled up, and went to sleep. "He loves to sleep in the car, just like a baby," said his mistress affectionately.

I decided that any dog who disliked Charles de Gaulle

was a dog I could tolerate, but if he licked me again, I'd certainly say *no* loudly.

As she drove away from the university, Sylvie explained that her father had once had just such a car as hers. His wasn't new even then, but she had loved to ride in it along the cliffs overlooking the sea in England, and she was his helper in the many repairs that had to be made. Her father had been English, her mother French.

"So imagine my happiness when an elderly widow in our neighborhood inherited this car. It had been her husband's, but she herself could not drive it, so I fixed it up for her and took her for a ride several times a week. It made us both happy, and then she died and left it to me. Of course, Raymond wanted me to sell it since it is old and always breaking down. But why would I do that? My own car, and I know how to fix it, so you mustn't be alarmed, Madam Blue, if it stops unexpectedly. I am an expert mechanic, at least for this car, and I carry tools and spare parts.

"Now as I drive through these streets, look at the ends of the buildings. They all have murals. This is the project of Tony Garnier, the architect."

I peered at the sepia-toned murals depicting neighborhoods, buildings, and towers. Occasionally, Sylvie whipped the car to a curb and took a picture of me in front of a mural holding Winston Churchill's leash. She must have had a very fast camera, because the dog would not pose. He never stopped moving, tugging at the leash, or barking at me in a friendly manner. You had to like him, even if he was hyperactive, for he did mind. Perhaps a bit of Ritalin would do him good.

Since she seemed the least likely person to attack us, I told her about Jason's experience that morning and confessed that I thought we were being stalked but couldn't imagine by whom.

"Ah, well," said Sylvie, "Albertine is capable of anything. She told us of your problems with Charles de Gaulle. And then he was so tiresome when they got back to Lyon. He bit a policeman. The Guillots had to hire a lawyer to keep the dog from being put down, and then they had to send him to school to learn better manners. You may find him a nicer dog, but Albertine is the same always. She says she is not angry with you, but she probably is."

"But why would she try to attack Jason?" I asked.

"Maybe it was Victoire. What color was the car?"

"Black," I replied. "But why would Madam Laurent—"

"She has a black car. Ah, here it is, *Le Mur des Canuts.* Canuts were those who worked the silk looms, very skilled. They contributed much to the wealth of the city, but they were so poor themselves."

Ahead of us was a long stairway between two buildings, leading up to a grassy area and a stone wall. We left the car, with Winston Churchill bounding along, tugging on his leash, but when we got closer, Sylvie handed the leash to me and instructed me to walk over to the man studying a map and pretend that I was talking to him while she took a picture. "Won't he find that strange?" I asked, reluctant to approach the tourist.

Sylvie burst into laughter. "You see how fine our murals are. He is a painted tourist." So Winston Churchill and I had our picture taken beside the painted tourist. I think the pug was fooled as well because he barked at the picture. Then I moved back to study the mural. It wasn't just the steps that were painted. The buildings to both sides were part of the mural. There was a pigeon on the ledge of an upper window so realistic that I expected to see it fly away.

We stopped in a café for a snack of bread, cheese, wine, and, of course, sausage—Cervelas de Lyon. Sylvie said it had been brought here by the Italian silk merchants and bankers and contained delicious parts of the pig. *Cervelas?*— brains, I suspected, and shuddered. "So why would Victoire try to kill Jason?" I asked to distract Sylvie from further discussion of the sausage she had ordered.

"Robert was her lover, and Robert died in your room eating your pâté."

"He actually died in the hospital, and it wasn't *our* pâté. Someone sent it."

Sylvie shrugged and popped a bite of the sausage into her mouth. "Victoire Laurent is a domineering woman. I can imagine her racing her car into someone if she thought the man killed her lover."

"Well, it doesn't make any sense," I muttered, and slipped a piece of my sausage to Winston Churchill, who was happy to get it. He snuggled up against my leg, chewing lustily, but didn't tip off his mistress to our conspiracy. "And thinking that Victoire tried to run down Jason doesn't explain who sent the bad pâté."

"Now you must try the *cervelle de Canute.*" As she pushed the bowl toward me, Sylvie laughed at my expression. "Nothing terrible, Madam Blue. Although the name means silk workers' brains, it is simply a fresh curd cheese with a bit of olive oil and vinegar whipped in with fresh herbs, shallots, and garlic."

"Do call me Carolyn," I said, eyeing the cheese suspiciously, but I couldn't see anything that resembled brains, and it was, in fact, very tasty. I ate that with my bread and wine and continued to slip the brain sausage to the dog.

While out to lunch with a lady from Lyon, I reencountered my own objection to eating brains. She ordered *cervelas*, a sausage I assumed contained brains because of the Latin word *cervelle*, brain meat. Rather than offend her, I cut off pieces and slipped them to her dog. Then she insisted that I eat a cheese called *cervelle de Canute, silk workers' brains.* I couldn't believe my ill luck, but she insisted that it contained simply curd cheese and flavorings. Only later did I discover that the sausage I fed the dog, although it did contain brains in the time of Julius Caesar, now contained only pork with pistachios or truffles. I'd probably have loved it. The dog certainly did.

Cervelle de Canute

- Beat *1 pound curd or farmer's cheese* with a wooden spoon. Add *2 tablespoons olive oil, 1 tablespoon vinegar, 1 finely chopped clove garlic* and beat into the cheese.

- Chop *2 tablespoons chervil, 4 tablespoons parsley, 2 tablespoons chives, 1 tablespoon tarragon,* and *4 shallots.* Mix well into cheese. Season to taste and serve with *toast or bread.*

Carolyn Blue,
"Have Fork, Will Travel,"
Birmingham Eagle

13

An Academic Suspect
and a Japanese Fish

Carolyn

After our snack, Sylvie drove away while Winston Churchill lay burping in my lap. Perhaps the sausage hadn't been such a good idea, but his ancestors must have eaten every part of the animals they killed, including the brains.

"... *Bibliothèque de la Cité*," Sylvie was saying. She planned to take me to a library? Instead of a real one, it was a library painted on the outside of a building. On each floor were books, manuscripts, quill pens, and even a beak-nosed bird reading in a window. Winston Churchill and I had our picture taken in front of the trompe l'oeil library.

Sylvie was illegally parked when her engine sputtered and a policeman stopped to reprimand her. "What bloody bad luck," she muttered and hopped out, calling over her shoulder, "Don't worry. I can fix it." She then turned to the policeman and chatted with him in French while Winston Churchill stood on my lap, barking with excitement.

We'll probably end up in jail, I thought, but it didn't happen. The policeman, obviously smitten with Sylvie,

helped her raise the hood, then came around to pat the dog
while Sylvie stuck her head underneath and banged on
things with a tool from her trunk. "Carolyn," she called,
"try the engine now."

"I don't know how," I called back, having observed that
the car required shifting and depressing a clutch.

The officer filled in. "Voila!" cried Sylvie, slamming
down the hood. Then he, beaming with admiration, waved
as we drove away without a ticket for illegal parking.

"I have had a thought," she said, "about who sent the
foie gras. Maybe Professor Laurent found out that his wife
was having an affair with Robert, so he sent Robert to your
hotel with the poisoned pâté, knowing that Robert could
not resist it. The man adored pâté, even more than he
adored Zoe, the chairman's mistress."

"Mademoiselle Thomas is Professor Laurent's mistress?" I asked, shocked. Was there no end to the sexual
liaisons in this department? The chairman's wife and a professor. The chairman and his secretary. Jason thinks professors should set a good example, which reminded me
that he himself had given me moments of unhappiness over
Mercedes, his doctoral student from Mexico City. He made
several scientific trips with her, although she was not with
him on this one.

"Of course," said Sylvie. "It makes excellent sense. Not
only does the chairman dislike the affair of his wife, but he
also would dislike the fact that Robert hangs around Zoe,
looking besotted. Two reasons to poison Robert."

"But the clerk at the hotel said a messenger brought the
pâté."

"So Laurent had the pâté sent and then dispatched
Robert to greet you. Robert would not be suspicious. He
knew your husband, and the Guillots were out of town.
Yes, either the Guillots or the Laurents are behind these attacks. Poor Robert. I'm sure he'd much rather have had an

affair with Zoe than with Madam Laurent, and now he's dead. Ah, here is La Fresque des Lyonnais."

Bemused by Sylvie's speculations, I got out of the car and studied the new example of Lyonnais building painting. On the first floor was a shop with windows displaying the food of the city, and on the floors above, standing on their balconies were famous citizens from different centuries in the city's history—Roman emperors, painters, poetesses, soldiers, and politicians. They covered the walls, wearing period clothes. Winston Churchill and I had our picture taken in front of Gastronomie Lyonnaise, with its painted sausages and other comestibles.

As soon as Sylvie dropped me off, I rushed up to my room and called Inspector Roux to ask what progress he had made and to pass on Sylvie's suspects. Jason would probably disapprove of my pointing a finger at our hosts, but I did have our safety to consider, not to mention my citizen's duty to be helpful to law enforcement. He wasn't in his office, so I tried his cell phone. All Europeans have cell phones. "Inspector, this is Carolyn Blue, the woman who discovered the Canadian in her room. I wondered if you've made headway."

"We have not found the car, but we found shopkeepers who agree that it did not seem to be an accident and remarked how good it was of your husband to take care of the dog. I hope he has recovered."

"My husband or the dog? And why did no one go to the rescue if they saw the accident?"

"It is a busy time for a shopkeeper, and they said that he rose almost immediately. Has the professor seen a doctor for his knee? I can recommend one, and if we find the driver, the driver must pay for his treatment."

"What about the poison?" I asked, sure that Jason hadn't gone to a doctor. It's harder to get a man to a doctor than to convince an El Pasoan to give up Mexican food. Only a serious medical condition will do the trick in either case.

"Ah, the poison. Doctor Petit chooses tetrodotoxin. The symptoms of the Canadian gentleman support that conclusion, although the symptoms support other conclusions as well."

"How do you spell it, the toxin?" I asked, planning to look it up on the Internet. Our room had a modem connection, and my laptop has a modem. Inspector Roux spelled it for me.

"The problem is, Madam Blue, that the toxin is found in a fish eaten by Japanese. The chances of a French goose being fed a Japanese fish are slim."

"Fugu. My husband has eaten it. Had I been with him, I would have protested, but a well-trained fugu chef is taught to remove all toxic parts but enough to numb the lips and tongue so the customer can enjoy the danger of what he's eating."

"The Japanese are strange people," mused the inspector. "They never commit crimes, but they take the photographs continuously, more often, I think, than they actually look at the sights they photograph. Very strange."

"I imagine the criminal mashed a bit of a puffer fish into the pâté. Since fugu is said to be quite tasty, Professor Levasseur would have noticed only the numbed lips and tongue, not the taste."

"I know of no place in Lyon that serves such a fish. It is probably against the law."

"Don't you have Japanese restaurants? Have you called importers of fish?"

"Lyon has wonderful fish in the area. We have no need to import fish that kill people," said the inspector indignantly.

I sighed. Obviously I'd get no nap. I had to look up

Japanese restaurants and importers and call them, not to mention Googling—what a ridiculous word—the toxin for information. *Perhaps it is found in some French fish that Inspector Roux knows nothing about*, I thought, and said good-bye to him. Obviously he took his work seriously, but his loyalty to Lyon blinded him to some things that should be investigated.

First I looked up tetrodotoxin, so called because the fish has four ugly teeth. I discovered that it is over 1,250 times more toxic than cyanide. Good heavens, it would take only one ovary or bit of testicle harvested at the right time of year to poison a crowd. I hoped that the police hadn't left the remaining slices lying around. If they had pâté lovers in their ranks, policemen would start dying.

14
Lyonnais Cuisine
for the Well-To-Do

Jason

Fast asleep when I arrived in our room, Carolyn had to be rousted out of bed and convinced to dress in clothes suitable for the fancy restaurant to which the Doignes and the Girards were taking us. We were to pay for our own meals, but not theirs. While she was putting on pantyhose, the discomfort of which she seems to blame on all men, including me, and a green dress, and pinning her hair into a chignon, which required her to choose earrings, hair ornaments, and a necklace, she told me about murals and riding in an Austin Healy with a dog in her lap.

"A large dog?" I asked, grinning.

"A pug named Winston Churchill. Sylvie gave it that name to irritate Albertine and her dog, Charles de Gaulle. You do remember Charles de—"

"Of course," I said hastily, not wanting to rehash the Charles de Gaulle fiasco in Sorrento. After that I heard about the repairs Sylvie made to the car en route and the pictures taken of the dog and Carolyn with hair in disarray because of the topless car.

"Sylvie's very nice," Carolyn added. "Have you ever heard of tetrodotoxin?"

"Not that I recall."

"It's in fugu, and Doctor Petit thinks it killed your friend Robert."

"Where would he get any fugu? I doubt that Robert would even want to try it."

"Probably someone put it in the pâté. Now all we have to do is find out—"

"Carolyn, that's ridiculous!"

She glared at me in the mirror as she put on her second earring, picked up her purse, and walked out. I had to hurry to catch the elevator. Fortunately, the Doignes were waiting for us downstairs, so there was no more talk of pufferfish toxin. Gabrielle, evidently a devout Catholic, began to tell Carolyn about the churches she'd see the next day.

Our second restaurant in Lyon was much more upscale and much more expensive. I could see my wife trying to convert the euros into dollars, then giving up and ordering chicken.

"Ah, Friccasse de Poulet de Bresse. An excellent selection, Madam Blue," exclaimed Charles Doigne. "Bresse has the world's finest poultry. I shall have the same."

Carolyn stared suspiciously at poor Doigne when he insisted that she order a salad of pâté on artichoke hearts. No doubt she was afraid the pâté would be spiked with fugu. He never noticed her dismay because he asked a question about my research, which ignited an excellent discussion of the chemistry of toxins and caused poor Carolyn to shift uneasily in her seat. I'm afraid the women hardly got a word in.

However, when Carolyn's salad was served, she interrupted loudly enough to stop us. "Do you, by any chance, like fugu, Professor Doigne?"

He looked confused and replied. "Is that a type of American music?"

"It is the meat of the puffer fish. Very popular in Japan, although toxic. Surely you're familiar with tetrodotoxin?"

Doigne obviously wasn't. "Is that the scientific name? I know of many toxins, but I am embarrassed to say—"

"I was unfamiliar with it myself," I assured him and raised a mouthful of pâté and artichoke to my lips. "Ah!" I exclaimed, "This is truly a wonderful dish, Charles." To my wife I whispered, "And my lips are not numb."

"Give it time," she muttered back and, with everyone waiting for the American food writer to pronounce on a favorite Lyonnais salad, she took a bite and chewed so slowly that I knew she was waiting for a telltale tingle to alert her before she actually swallowed. Then the taste must have hit her, for she smiled at Charles and took another bite. "A salad to die for!" she remarked, but not happily.

Gabrielle's cell phone rang just then, and her husband raised his eyebrows. "Victoire insisted that I keep it turned on in case she needed to call," said Gabrielle. Evidently Victoire Laurent was not to be denied. She had given that impression when we dined with her the night before.

Our entrées came during this conversation, and Carolyn began to eat immediately. She probably wanted to try the chicken before the pâté killed her. Surely Charles's response to her question about fugu should have convinced her that it was not to be had in Lyon and that Robert's diagnosis was mistaken. Probably the doctor wanted to write a paper for a medical journal on an exotic case.

"Jason, you have to try this. It is absolutely the best chicken I've ever tasted," said my wife, as she dropped a piece of the chicken on my plate. Charles beamed at her, and I had to agree. Our mass-produced chicken at home certainly pales in comparison.

At that moment, while I was savoring the poultry of Bresse, Gabrielle clicked off her phone and, tight-lipped, said to my wife, "Victoire has found that she will be available tomorrow

to show you the traboules. You and Sylvie are to meet her at
the department, and she will drive her own car. Victoire advises
you to wear comfortable shoes, Madam Blue."

Sylvie giggled. "Although it is a classic, Victoire would
refuse to ride in my car. She thinks it too small and too given
to breaking down, but that is not a problem, is it, Carolyn?"

"No, it isn't," said Carolyn, looking relieved that she
was to ride in a larger car.

"My wife, the mechanic," said Raymond, bursting into
laughter.

"Why do you laugh, Raymond? I fix your car, too."
Sylvie then turned away. "So, Gabrielle, shall you go with
them tomorrow, or shall I? Even Victoire's Renault will not
hold the four of us and my dog and cameras."

"I shall show Carolyn the churches on Wednesday," said
Gabrielle.

"You'll bring Winston Churchill?" Carolyn asked
Sylvie.

"But of course. Victoire will be delighted. He is such a
cheerful little dog, don't you think?"

"Oh, absolutely," my wife agreed, as she watched
Sylvie burst into giggles. I was forced to the conclusion
that Victoire would not be delighted to host the dog.
Raymond sighed at his wife's laughter. What a strange
department—prickly wives and sexual liaisons. Probably a
French thing. The wives at home seem to get along, and I
hadn't heard gossip about liaisons, other than a few with
students, of which the deans take a dim view.

"Another piece of chicken?" Carolyn offered.

Naturally, I accepted. I'd never have guessed that
chicken could be as good as beef, and my Charolais beef
was very good indeed.

The best chicken I've ever eaten in my life came from
Bresse in France, and the birds are very handsome

with their blue feet, fluffy white feathers, and red crests—colors of the French flag, by the way. The government dictates how they're to be raised. From birth to day thirty-five they live on diary farms in a hen house and eat milk-soaked corn. Then they're turned loose in green grass (by law they must have twelve square yards each) for varying lengths of time from nine to twenty-three weeks, after which they're put in small cages and fattened up on nourishing feed. Believe me, the fat of a Bresse chicken smells wonderful, and the meat tastes even better.

As for foie gras, the writer Toussaint-Samat warns against serving it with salad because the acidity of the vinaigrette will spoil the flavor. He's wrong, but then I was combining it with artichoke hearts, with salad underneath. It worked for me.

Artichoke Hearts with Foie Gras

- Pull, don't cut, the stalks off *4 large artichokes*. With a sharp knife cut off the tops, rotating the knife.* Pull off the side leaves, put immediately into cold water, and cook for 15 minutes or until a fork will go through them easily. Leave in the cooking water.

- To make a vinaigrette dressing, put *1 teaspoon French Dijon mustard* in a bowl plus any of these optional ingredients: *½ teaspoon salt, ½ teaspoon ground black pepper, 1 tablespoon sugar*.

- Whisk in *3 or 4 tablespoons cider vinegar* until the paste is smooth.

- Vigorously, but gradually whisk in *½ cup olive oil* until smooth.

- Use some vinaigrette to season *11 ounces of different lettuces.* Put the artichoke hearts* in the rest of the vinaigrette.

- Divide the salad leaves between 4 plates, place an artichoke heart in the middle of each plate on top of the salad and a *thick slice of duck or goose foie gras* on top of the artichoke heart.

- Serve with *toasted bread.*

* Be sure that the choke has been completely removed from the artichoke.

Bresse Chicken Fricasseed in Cream Sauce

- Divide a *4-pound free-range chicken,* unless you can get a Bresse chicken, into 8 parts and brown in *2 tablespoons butter* in a braising pan. Add *salt, ground pepper, 1 cup Chardonnay wine,* and *2 cups water.* Cover and braise 20 minutes.

- Peel *3½ ounces small onions.* Clean *9 ounces mushrooms* and cut off stalks. Put them with *2 tablespoons butter* in another braising pan. Five minutes before serving, sprinkle *2 teaspoons sugar* on the vegetables and glaze, then add salt.

- Remove chicken pieces to a plate. Reduce liquid to half and pour in *2 cups crème fraiche* (can be purchased at gourmet stores and online). Reduce again and pour on chicken. Garnish with mushrooms and onions. May be served with spinach and rice or noodles.

Carolyn Blue,
"Have Fork, Will Travel,"
Tallahassee Call

15
Traboule Transportation

Carolyn

I couldn't refuse to ride with Victoire when Gabrielle announced the change of plans, but it did worry me. If the chairman's wife had tried to run Jason down, she might do the same to me, or poison me if we had lunch together. I slept badly.

The next morning when Jason and I set out from Perrache, instead of burying his nose in a paper about toxins, he asked whether I'd enjoyed my pâté and artichoke salad, and I had to admit that I had, even though I worried about the foie gras. "Well, it didn't make you sick," he said cheerfully, "so I guess it wasn't poisoned."

"Now, Jason, you're always saying anything can poison you if you eat too much of it, and it's true. Catherine de Médicis thought she was going to die after eating too many artichoke hearts at a wedding feast, those and the kidneys and combs of cockerels."

"Probably the cockerels did the damage," said Jason. "Artichokes seem pretty benign, unless you get a mouthful of the choke."

"And you a toxin expert. I read just recently that if you

keep a cooked artichoke more than twenty-four hours, it develops a toxic mold."

"Really." Jason looked intrigued. "I'll have to investigate." He does love to hear about a new toxin.

When we arrived at the university, Victoire was telling Sylvie that she couldn't possibly allow Winston Churchill in her car. Her own dog would take offense.

"But your dog isn't here."

"You think Colette, who has a very sensitive nose, wouldn't be able to smell your dog? Believe me, the next time we drive together, Colette will be very angry with me."

"What a lovely black car," I exclaimed. "Very chic."

Victoire frowned and replied that, being of French manufacture, it was reliable and well made. Then she glanced at Sylvie's convertible and shuddered.

"I always think that the color of one's car is significant," I began, improvising as I searched for information. "For instance, couples who have been married for years often have cars of the same color. Jason and I do." We didn't, so I'd have to warn him in case the subject came up. "I'll bet Professor Laurent has a black car, too. Am I right, Madam Laurent?"

"No. This *is* my husband's car."

Ah! So the chairman is probably the one who tried to run Jason down, but why would he do that? Jason wasn't chasing after Mademoiselle Thomas, or showing undue interest in Victoire, as far as I knew. "Then what color is your car?"

"We have only one," she replied. "The cost of purchasing and running a good car is high." Again she looked disdainfully toward the ancient, British-made Austin Healy. "We see no need—"

"But how do you manage?" I protested, as if shocked to hear their one-car status. "Yesterday you had appointments. Did Professor Laurent have to take a bus to work?"

Madam Laurent looked exasperated. "I can't imagine why you are so interested in our transportation arrangements, Madam Blue, but since you insist on knowing, I had appointments with friends who provided transportation, and my husband drove this car to work. This obsession with cars is obviously some American oddity. At least I am happy to see that you took my advice and wore comfortable shoes. I know Americans choose to drive if they have only a few meters to travel, but we French are walkers, which is why obesity is not a problem here."

So it was her husband. And is she saying I'm fat? I've taken off the cruise pounds. "I always wear low-heeled shoes," I replied.

"Very sensible. Of course, on festive occasions, one wishes to wear a higher heel, but then your husband is short. Perhaps he would object. I pay no attention to Jacques on that subject."

While this conversation was proceeding, Winston Churchill forsook his interest in Victoire and bounded over to me. I said *no* immediately, so he didn't jump on me, and I rewarded him by scratching his ears, which made him wiggle with delight, fall to the cement, and roll onto his back with all four legs waving.

"Goodness, Carolyn," said Sylvie. "Now *my* dog is in love with you. First Charles de Gaulle, now—"

"He is not!" I protested. "Perhaps he has a cramp in one of his legs."

Giggling, Sylvie informed me that Winston Churchill wanted me to scratch his stomach. Then to the chairman's wife, she said, "Victoire, the obvious solution is that we go in my car. But you must choose whether to sit in front with my dog on your lap or in the back with the cameras."

I was reluctantly scratching the dog's stomach because he looked so silly with his legs wiggling in the air. Victoire had to take the backseat because Winston Churchill, when he was placed in Victoire's lap, jumped out and snuggled up to my ankles like a cat.

"Maybe you put out a pheromone that dogs like," said Sylvie, looking puzzled.

"You mean I *smell* like a dog?"

"Well, he's friendly, but he doesn't usually take immediately to strange women. And that pleading look he's giving you. As if he expects you to . . . You fed him the sausage, didn't you?" she asked accusingly.

Caught in the act. "I'm sorry, Sylvie. I hope it didn't make him sick."

"Of course it didn't." Sylvie burst out laughing. "No wonder he loves you. He probably thinks you'll be a source of sausage forever, but why would you give him your—"

"I just couldn't face eating brains," I admitted shamefacedly.

"No one puts brains in Cervales de Lyon anymore. Once they did, but now—you should have said something." Then she turned to the chairman's wife, still sitting in the front seat. "Victoire, it seems that Carolyn has bewitched my dog with sausage. Either we'll have to take your car, or you'll have to sit in back with the cameras. For some reason, Winston Churchill throws up if we put him in back, and we can't let him vomit on our guest."

Looking quite grim, Victoire swung her long legs out and managed to squeeze herself crossways into the back. Then the dog and I settled down, and off we went to visit the traboules, while he looked up at me soulfully, waiting for more sausage. When it didn't materialize, he went to sleep.

We only had to stop for repairs twice. A spoke needed replacement on one wheel, and then the car stalled at a busy traffic light. We gained quite an audience of young men to watch both repairs. Victoire stayed inside each time trying to restore order to her hair. Knowing what to expect, I had simply taken the scarf that tied my hair back and tied it under my chin.

When we arrived at our destination, Old Lyon, and set out on foot, I became nervous again and watched every black car on the street as if Albertine might be behind the wheel, unless, of course, the chairman, who knew where we were going, had followed us. But his wife would surely recognize him and the family car. No, he wouldn't take that chance. Would he? Maybe Laurent wanted to run *her* down, too, because of her affair with Robert, whom he had managed to poison with the fugu toxin.

"You know what I'd like to have for lunch," I said impulsively. "Japanese food." If there was a local source of fugu, I needed to find it. "Do you have Japanese restaurants?"

"Madam Blue," said Victoire in a long-suffering voice, "one does not come to Lyon, a city known for its French cuisine, and ask to eat at a Japanese establishment."

"I don't think there is one," added Sylvie.

"And if there were, I certainly would not want to patronize it," said Victoire.

Another dead end, I thought. I'd have to search the Lyon telephone book. It had occurred to me that Madam Laurent could be lying about her appointments yesterday. What if she had rented a black car and used it to attack my husband, and before that had poisoned the pâté and sent it to our room. Having poisoned her own lover by mistake, she would be furious with both of us, as well as unwilling to admit knowing a source of tetrodotoxin. But that didn't explain why she'd send the poisoned pâté in the first place. Her lover was still alive, not dying on my bed, before the poison was added to the pâté and sent to us.

16
Trabouling and Puffer Fishing

Carolyn

Victoire **gave us** the shortest possible history of Lyon: It had been a Roman city, Lugdunum; then a Christian city, ruled by the church in the Middle Ages; and after that a city of trade, finance, and manufacture in the Renaissance when Old Lyon came into its own. "The Renaissance Association has been restoring the buildings and preserving them since 1947," said Victoire. "Many have been turned into public housing, and some were privately purchased and restored with the help of the city. Catherine has a place here, although why she would want to live among lower-class neighbors is a puzzle."

"Because she's descended from Florentine bankers, who came here when they couldn't compete with the Medicis in Florence," said Sylvie, while her dog made forays of friendship toward passing canines.

"Yes, of course," said Victoire. "Much of the architecture is Italianate. Shall we enter a traboule?"

Actually, I hoped to see more than one and wondered if the tour would be as short as the history lesson. I could have provided that much history myself. We ducked into a narrow archway and began. The traboules were delightful, a world unto themselves, sometimes narrow and dark before we'd burst into a courtyard with balconies soaring above our heads and pots of flowers draping over the metalwork, reminding me of the falling flowerpot in Paris that almost hit me and did hit a fellow tourist, although he deserved it.

There were gorgeous circular stairways curving up from floor to floor with twisted marble sides that reminded me of Gaudi buildings in Barcelona or wrought-iron railings on stairs and balconies reminiscent of those in the French Quarter of New Orleans. In some courtyards we'd see arches holding up ornate windowed tiers rising toward the light. And a lovely rose tower with large windows climbing around and upward to the top floor. Some traboules had long inner flights of stone stairs that lead past residences on either side to a street at a higher level. In one place I saw a rugged well, over which a shell-carved ceiling supported the upper reaches of the building. These interior walkways were shabby or lovely or eerie, but all fascinating, and Victoire walked at a fast clip and told us nothing about any of them.

Sniffing into every ancient corner, Winston Churchill tugged so often on his leash that I often had to call out so I wouldn't be left behind. Sylvie, of course, was taking pictures of everything from door knockers—Winnie tended to bark at the ones with lions' heads—to stairs, to the three of us, although Victoire was reluctant to be photographed for the same reason I had been yesterday: windblown hair. I began to resent the fact that Sylvie got to take all the pictures, while I, encumbered with her rambunctious dog, got to take none. I'd have to buy a book or postcards if I wanted remembrances of the traboules.

I also wondered how Sylvie, who had ignored the advice on wearing low-heeled shoes, managed to keep up. The pavement and cobblestones were rough, and Sylvie was wearing very high heels. Victoire remarked in an undertone that Sylvie would develop those "unsightly lumps" on her feet before she turned forty. I, on the other hand, was more worried about dangers in the present. I thought it a wonder that Sylvie didn't break her ankle, but she didn't even watch her footing, whereas I had to watch my step, the dog, and the scenery as I was dragged along.

Eventually we emerged in front of a church that I'd love to have visited, but Victoire assured me, rather sarcastically, that Gabrielle could be counted on to show me every church of note in the city. Perhaps Victoire was one of the nonreligious French. I've heard there are many. And after all, the French Revolution had been antichurch and destroyed all sorts of wonderful things.

"Now if you two wish to look for a Japanese restaurant, I'll just take a cab home," said Victoire.

Remembering that I needed to track down sources of puffer fish, I said that jet lag was catching up with me, because of which I wouldn't mind returning to the hotel.

"What, no one wants to have lunch?" cried Sylvie. Winston Churchill looked disappointed, too. No doubt he'd expected another under-the-table feast with me as caterer.

So I still have the same suspects, I thought as I took the elevator to my room, *the Guillots and the Laurents.* I kicked off my shoes and located the Lyon phone book, but then I felt hungry and glanced at my watch—after one. I called room service for a salad, reminding myself that last night's dinner must have been high cal. Surely a chicken so tasty was full of fat and cholesterol.

Then I began to scan the business listings. I had no problem finding the restaurant section, but telling Japanese restaurants from non-Japanese was difficult because the restaurant names were in French. I was trying the Internet for French translations of Japanese foods, like fugu, when my salad arrived.

After lunch, I connected with what I took to be two

Chinese restaurants, three Vietnamese restaurants, and one Korean establishment. At the Vietnamese restaurants they spoke French and Vietnamese. At the Korean restaurant the owner spoke English and gave me a lecture on Japanese depredations in Korea. I gathered that some now-deceased relative of his had been kidnapped as a sex slave. At any rate, he served no Japanese dishes and thought people who ate fugu were—I didn't actually catch what such people were, but it sounded bad.

He offered me a reservation, but I didn't want that; I wanted to find out where our enemy had bought the fugu, and the Korean proprietor couldn't name any wholesaler that carried such a dangerous item. I think at one of the Chinese restaurants I got a lecture on the rape of Nanking by the evil Japanese Empire, and the man to whom I was speaking claimed never to have heard of fugu and warned me that Japanese food was bad for the digestion.

Then finally I had a stroke of inspiration. I would call the Japanese consulate. There had to be one here in Lyon, which was a large, business-oriented city. For that number, I called the desk, got the helpful Simone, and mentioned that we were looking for a Japanese restaurant.

"There are none," she replied, astonished. "Even the Japanese tourists and businessmen eat Lyonnais food here in Lyon."

"But what if a Japanese businessman yearns for the food of his native country? He would call his consulate for help, wouldn't he?"

Reluctantly Simone got me that number, and I called, waiting twenty minutes for an English speaker to come on the line. "My husband and I want to eat Japanese food," I explained. He knew of clubs for Japanese nationals in Lyon, but we could not join one because they were private.

Why didn't that surprise me? I remember reading that, when the Olympics were held in Japan, many restaurants closed so they wouldn't have to deal with Westerners. "Then perhaps you can tell me where we can buy fugu, that delicious fish that only the Japanese can prepare."

He agreed that only Japanese could prepare fugu, and I could not. Therefore, I shouldn't even think of buying it. "But my husband and I—" He interrupted me to say that fugu was not available in Lyon and hung up.

So how had the pâté poisoner got hold of fugu? The only answer was that Dr. Petit had failed to identify what had killed Robert. I called Inspector Roux to pass on the news, and he admitted sadly he was making little headway in finding out how or why the professor had died, but he assured me that the case was still open and he would contact me if he had news. I, in turn, gave him the name of the hotel in Avignon where we would be staying.

Not my most promising afternoon of investigation. I snuggled down on the bed to think about the attempts on our lives and fell asleep until my husband called to tell me that he had made it safely through the day, and that we were going to dinner with Catherine de Firenze and several faculty members I had not yet met, people who would pick me up at the hotel instead of expecting me to make my way by cab to another restaurant.

"Do any of these people seem to dislike you?" I asked Jason.

"Actually, I'm finding the Southern French very pleasant," Jason replied.

"Yes, yes," I agreed, "but does it seem that any of those we're eating dinner with tonight might be harboring a grudge. For instance, have you had any arguments about toxins?"

"Carolyn, scientists don't kill each other over matters scientific," said Jason in the long-suffering tone I really hate to hear, especially from my husband.

17
A Peugeot Full of Gourmets

Jason

I took the elevator to fetch Carolyn while Bertrand and Nicole Fournier rushed off to study the hotel menu. They were both short, thin people, although they had talked of nothing but food since we stopped to pick up Nicole. I have to admit that I was glad they were coming along. The others attending the dinner were Catherine de Firenze and her Norman graduate student, Martin le Blanc, a very tall, muscular young man with a head of bushy red hair. With two such towering dinner companions, I found it something of a relief to recruit a couple shorter than I.

Of course, Carolyn would be delighted to meet the Fourniers, Bertrand with his encyclopedic knowledge of French wines, and Nicole, a gourmet cook who had, according to Bertrand, studied in Paris just so that she could give dinner parties that were the envy of Lyon. Too bad they hadn't invited us to their house. I shuddered to think what tonight's culinary adventure would cost me. Both Fourniers had competed to tell me what to order from the menu, all dishes that sounded expensive.

"You must not eat in the restaurant of this hotel, Madam Blue," cried Nicole, as soon as Carolyn and I stepped off the elevator. "I have looked at their menu, and it is—how would you say?—mundane."

"With a wine list that has only several entries I could recommend," added Bertrand. "We are the Fourniers, lovers of fine food and wine, as you are, Madam Blue." They both embraced my wife and, holding her face in their small hands, kissed her on both cheeks; Carolyn took this greeting with aplomb, although she raised an eyebrow in my direction when she was released.

"We know that Americans like to use baptismal names, so do not stand on ceremony. Call us Bertrand and Nicole," Bertrand insisted.

"I assume you cook," said Nicole. "We must exchange recipes. I would have been happy to cook for you, but Bertrand says it is too close to the conference for elaborate dinners. Still, you will love the restaurant. The handling of sauces there is an art in itself. So beautiful, so colorful, so innovative."

Bertrand went into raptures over the sauces as he helped us into the car, an ancient Peugeot with seats covered in white hair from some animal that did not accompany us, thank God. Nicole insisted on sitting in the backseat with Carolyn so that she could hear about Carolyn's newspaper column, but Carolyn gave that subject short shrift, saying only that she wrote about food, food history, and restaurants. She then asked Nicole the color of her car. Of course I realized that Carolyn was still searching for the black car that assaulted me. It wasn't this one, which, whatever color it had once been, was now mottled, but never black.

"I do not have a car!" cried Nicole. "We live in an area with wonderful shops. Each day I walk to the markets to pick out the freshest vegetables and fruits, the best fish or meat, and the finest bread from a lovely patisserie only a block from my door. People who shop from cars are tempted to buy too much. Only food purchased on the day it is to be eaten is worth cooking. Don't you agree, Carolyn?"

"Of course," said Carolyn, who had never been grocery shopping two days in a row. "And tell me, Nicole, do you cook Japanese?"

Bertrand chuckled merrily in anticipation of his own joke. "Japanese are not sold in our markets. Nor would it be legal to cook and eat them. Surely, Carolyn, you do not eat Japanese in America, even considering that they, many years ago, were so dishonorable as to bomb your ships without first declaring war."

I could hear my wife sigh. "I was thinking of Japanese fish," she replied politely. "They are so rare and tasty."

"But a Japanese fish would have to be frozen and flown here," protested Nicole. "We eat the fish of our region. The fish of Dombes, for instance. It is so interesting how these fishes are caught."

"Yes," Bertrand agreed enthusiastically. "From shallow, freshwater lakes in huge nets spread by tractors and then pulled in by fishermen, who wade into the water and haul in the carp and pike for immediate consumption or shipment. At the restaurant I shall point to you some fine fishes from Dombes."

"Yes, I read that some of those breeding ponds were established in the twelfth century," said Carolyn. I think she gave up at that point on the Fourniers as murderers. Their car was the wrong color, and the idea of eating Japanese fish was obviously appalling to them.

At the restaurant, which had no sign outside, only an ornate and possibly aged door and heavily draped windows so that we could not see inside, we had to knock to be admitted by a man who greeted both Fourniers with a torrent of French and embraces, which extended to hand-kissing in my wife's case. He didn't greet me at all, evidently taking me for some hanger-on with no culinary credentials.

The restaurant itself was small with elaborately set tables and yellow brocaded walls and chairs, but we were led to the bar because the rest of our party had not yet arrived.

"I know that Americans love cocktails before dinner," Bertrand said and helped both ladies onto high stools facing an inlaid wooden bar with an elaborately etched mirror behind it. Carolyn whispered that the décor was Art Deco, while Bertrand ordered a round of Hypermetropes. I had no idea what was coming, but of course the Fourniers were anxious to tell us in detail about this mixture of green Chartreuse and Vertical Vodka, both made by the monks of the Chartreuse, and served very cold, so cold that my test sip made my teeth ache. I sensibly failed to mention this problem to Carolyn, who would whip out a toothache remedy she carries in her purse. She'd evidently once forced it on a Catalan homicide inspector in Barcelona.

"How interesting," said my wife after her first sip. "I knew it wasn't crème de menthe."

"Heaven forbid," cried Nicole, and she launched into the history and distillation of the two ingredients.

Chartreuse liqueur is made in a monastery founded by Saints Bruno and Hugo in the eleventh century. The recipe for an herbal elixir was given to the monks in 1605, but they were busy mining and smelting, so didn't get to perfecting it until 1764, when it was considered a medicinal stimulant and distributed free to local peasants. Later the monastery distilled a liqueur, 55 percent alcohol, from it. Only three Carthusian brothers ever know the recipe, which contains 130 different plants.

Through avalanches, revolutions, wars, and expulsions, the secret has been kept, but the brothers are now back in their French monastery, gathering and drying the herbs, soaking them in alcohol, and mixing in honey and other things, then aging the product for eight years in wooden casks before you can buy Chartreuse in green or yellow (yellow developed for the ladies) or mix up a Hypermetrope (the cocktail, not the eye disease) of green Chartreuse and Vertical Vodka (also made by the monks), shaken together, ice cold from the freezer. The cocktail is very inebriating.

Carolyn Blue,
"Have Fork, Will Travel,"
Amarillo Ledger

18

Scenic Sauces

Carolyn

After a few sips of my Hypermetrope, I grew to like it. I think it was all the alcohol that made it so palatable. I was feeling quite merry by the time Catherine and her student arrived. But good grief. He was huge. And Norman, according to Nicole, which explained the red hair.

When we were introduced, I said, somewhat the worse for having drained my cocktail, "You must be a descendent of William Rufus." Silence followed that remark. "The son of William the Conqueror, the second Norman king of England."

"Are you inferring something about my sexual orientation, madam?"

Oh dear, I'd forgotten those rumors about William Rufus, who had never married and—well, I hadn't meant that. "Certainly not, Monsieur Le Blanc. William Rufus was redheaded and very large, a man much given to the practices of chivalry, even if there *were* rumors about him, not that there's anything wrong with being a homosexual." I really needed to get off that subject.

"You may remember when the youngest son, Henry Beauclerc, was holed up with his knights on Mont-Saint-

Michel, while his brothers William Rufus and Robert, Duke of Normandy, besieged him. Henry sent a messenger asking that he and his men be allowed to ride ashore with all honors, and William, so charmed with the chivalric honor that would accrue to him by granting the request, agreed."

"Not only does the lady know her Norman history, but she obviously meant to compliment you, Martin," said Catherine sharply.

Martin le Blanc immediately rearranged his expression and shook my hand. Then we all went to our daffodil brocade chairs and had our meals chosen for us by the Fourniers. I had to have Dombes pike, dragged in a net fresh from one of a thousand or more ponds and shipped to me in a tanker that very day. Pike in butter sauce and Gratin Dauphinois, a dish of thinly sliced potatoes baked in a very rich sauce. It was quite nice, although Catherine said she preferred the potatoes with poultry or lamb.

"But Carolyn has not yet sampled it," cried Bernard.

"A terrible mistake on the part of her previous hosts," said Nicole. "What could Gabrielle have been thinking? Carolyn could have had the Gratinois with her Bresse chicken last night."

I assured them that I was happy to accompany my fish with the potatoes, which had an excellent texture. That earned me a lecture on Bintie potatoes, an old Netherlands variety with an oval shape, a yellow skin, no eyes, and the excellent ability to stay meaty after cooking. I made note of all this for future columns.

"And did you enjoy the traboules today?" Catherine asked, perhaps feeling it only polite to bring up something I could talk about.

"They were fascinating," I said. "Sylvie told me that you are from an old Florentine family and that you live in that district."

"Yes, I own an apartment in a tower. When it came on the market, I bought it immediately because family papers indicate that my ancestors once lived there. I am myself from Avignon and have a flat there as well, but it is not so charming as my home here in Lyon."

"How lucky you are to live where your ancestors once lived," I said enviously.

Catherine smiled. "Would you like to see it?"

"Goodness, yes, if it wouldn't inconvenience you."

"Unfortunately, I cannot show you through. I know you are going to see the churches with Gabrielle tomorrow, which will no doubt take you into the afternoon, while I must drive to Avignon tomorrow. However, I can leave a key for you with Madam Ravelier, who lives on the first floor. Simply knock on her door and then climb the stairs. You can let yourself in and look around, then return the key to my neighbor."

"That's so kind of you, Catherine, but I couldn't let you—"

"Not at all. Just be sure to lock up afterward. I'll write down directions. Madam Ravelier will be home after three in the afternoon." She wrote directions in English on a piece of paper that showed me how to get from Charlemagne Cour to her apartment by public transportation and on foot. I was quite excited at the prospect of seeing a tower apartment, and thanked her with all my heart. What a generous woman, although I'd initially thought her rather reserved.

Bernard interrupted us by launching into a description of Antonin Careme, a nineteenth-century chef who created pureed sauces from sugar and fruit or nuts and then turned them into beautiful, if ephemeral, designs on dessert plates by using the a knife blade.

"This is a talent still practiced here in Lyon, especially in this restaurant," Nicole added. Then the chef himself came out with six waiters, each carrying a plate that featured a different design highlighting small balls of colorful sorbets. Mine was a scene with purple mountains, green grass, a tree, and bushes. It was so beautiful that I couldn't bear to eat it, but the chef, after my comment was translated, said that I must. Still, I insisted on being allowed to photograph each creation before anyone ate. The result was that the sorbet began to melt into the decorations, so I didn't feel as bad about eating mine. Then the chef kissed me on both cheeks and presented me with an autographed menu.

Catherine warned me to take care in her neighborhood, which contained public as well as private housing. "You'll be safe," she said. "I've never been accosted, but do keep your eyes open, and be sure to turn on the light on the stairs. It gets rather dark before you reach my door. The switch is to your left as you enter the tower."

I assured her that I would be careful, lock the door, and return the key. It was only after we said good night that I realized that I'd forgotten to ask her the color of her car and whether she liked Japanese food. However, I saw that the car in which she and Martin left was not black, so I didn't worry about my failure to pursue my investigation.

I did worry when the Fourniers announced that they would now take us to see the festival of lights. Goodness knows when we'd get home after such a long dinner, and I had to get up early to meet Gabrielle and Sylvie at the university.

I have to admit that I forgot about bedtime once we began to drive by beautiful buildings spotlighted in gold, blue, and green, their reflections shining in the waters of both rivers. We saw the hospital, Hotel-Dieu, with its cross-topped capitol dome reflected in the Rhône, several old stone forts, the beautiful St.-Georges footbridge over a river with a floodlighted church spire behind it, a mansard-roofed university, and perhaps best of all, the basilica on the hill, aglow in blue light. It was magical. I almost regretted the fact that we would be leaving soon for Avignon.

Jason was regretting the size of the dinner bill. "That meal cost us a fortune," he said as we walked into the hotel.

"But wasn't it delicious?" I replied.

Gratin Dauphinois

- Set oven at 325° F.

- Peel *2 pounds Bintie (if you can get them) or baking potatoes,* wash, and slice very thin.

- Peel and halve a *clove of garlic* and rub it on a 9x6½-inch baking dish. Layer the potatoes, overlapping; season layers with salt, pepper, and grated *Gruyère cheese (½ cup in all).*

- Pour a mixture of *1 cup heavy cream, ½ cup milk,* and a little *muscat wine* over the potatoes. Sprinkle remaining cheese on top. If top becomes too brown, cover with foil.

- Bake 60 minutes. Let rest 10 minutes. Serve.

Carolyn Blue,
"Have Fork, Will Travel,"
Des Moines Ledger

19

A Pious Tour

Carolyn

On our way to the university, surrounded on the tram by students, Jason tried to talk me out of visiting Catherine's apartment, but I refused on grounds of rudeness.

"But she said the neighborhood is dangerous."

"No, she said to keep my eyes open, but that she'd never had a problem."

"She's an Amazon. What criminal would bother *her*? At least take Sylvie with you."

"Absolutely not. If I take Sylvie, I'll get stuck with holding the dog's leash while she takes pictures. For once I want to take my own."

Jason gave up, and I stared out the window at the modern university buildings, all named after famous scientists. "Don't they have the liberal arts here?" I asked.

"How should I know?" Jason muttered. "I only see chemists and eat in expensive restaurants."

To cheer him up I pointed out a building named for Ampère and told the story of his statue, one of many snatched from their pedestals in Lyon because of a 1941 law requisitioning bronze statues to be melted down to make chemicals for French grape vines and soldering pipes. "Ampère's statue wasn't pulled down until 1944, but after Lyon was liberated by the Allies, they discovered the statue in the Perrache Station. It never was sent away to the foundry."

"Where do you find these stories?" Jason grumbled.

"In a booklet I sent for from the tourist bureau."

With that we left the tram, and I headed for the parking lot where Winston Churchill, Sylvie, and Gabrielle awaited me. Sylvie was carrying a large basket and informed me that we would have a *machon* picnic after seeing the basilica, our last stop. Gabrielle protested that a *machon* was a breakfast. "But eaten in the vineyard," Sylvie retorted.

"What's in it?" I asked.

"Beaujolais, of course." She lifted the napkin. "Good farm bread with *fromage fort* to spread on it, bacon, sausage—but the sausage has nothing nasty in it, Carolyn—and pâté."

"Pâté?" I echoed. Was it Sylvie who had tried to poison us? Why would she? And her car was not black, but maybe Raymond's was. And how was I to explain my refusal to eat her pâté? While she popped the basket into the trunk with her tools and ordered Gabrielle into the backseat with the cameras, I decided that I would eat no pâté that Sylvie did not first eat herself. If she served me first, I could politely pass my portion to Gabrielle. Surely Sylvie would not allow Gabrielle to eat poisoned pâté. Satisfied with my plan, I climbed into the front seat. Winston Churchill then jumped into my lap and went into his I'm-starving-where's-my-sausage routine. I turned my head.

"Where to, Gabrielle?" Sylvie cried gaily, as she started her car and went into a flurry of shifting. "Let's go to St. Bonaventure."

Gabrielle said that church was not on her itinerary.

"But the altarpiece in the Sacre-Coeur Chapel is gorgeous, and that's where the Canuts, who hadn't already been killed for wanting a living wage and rioting, were massacred."

"Since you have planned a picnic and both Carolyn and I have afternoon appointments, we must limit ourselves to the cathedral and the basilica. Please take us to Saint-Jean first. Carolyn, the cathedral was built between the twelfth and the fourteenth centuries with additions at later times, so you will notice a mixture of architectural styles. However, the outside is definitely Gothic and quite lovely with three hundred or more medallions carved into the stone— biblical stories and depictions of medieval life, such as tasks performed during particular months and domestic scenes."

"My favorite is the man beating his wife," said Sylvie. "The church quite approved of wife beating back then. Maybe it still does."

"Unfortunately," said Gabrielle grimly, "the Huguenots tore off all the statues in the sixteenth century. Southern France had a history of heresy that required stamping out."

"Yes, some poor fellow here in Lyon wanted to go back to the original Christian poverty. He left his family, gave away all his money, and started preaching," said Sylvie. "Of course, the church disapproved. He and his followers were taken for Cathars and driven out, and then the king in Paris and the pope got together and launched a crusade against the whole region. Lots of land grabbing and heretic burning came out of that."

"Sylvie," said Gabrielle sternly, as our driver parked, "I hope that once we are inside the cathedral, you will show some respect, no matter what your own heretical views may be. I shall certainly pray for your soul at one of the altars."

"Actually," said Sylvie, "I'll have to stay outside with Winston Churchill. I doubt that they'll let an Anglican dog into a Catholic cathedral."

So Gabrielle and I went inside to look at the thirteenth-century stained glass, the Romanesque apse, the old vaults and choir, and some gorgeous lacework stone carving in a Bourbon chapel. Then Gabrielle knelt at a side altar to pray for Sylvie, and I watched the famous astronomic clock in order to hear the chimes and see the figures that come out on the hour, but it didn't happen. Gabrielle explained that appearances started at noon.

She was very pleased that I had enjoyed the visit. Sylvie was very irritated when Gabrielle refused her suggestion that we walk up the Fourviere Hill so that we could see the Roman sites. "Don't you want her to see the place where the nuns found the teeth of the lions that ate St. Blandine and the other martyrs?" Sylvie asked.

Gabrielle didn't. We took the funicular, I'm happy to say. I didn't want to walk up a huge hill, and Gabrielle insisted that there wouldn't be time to see all the sights of the basilica and eat a picnic lunch on the esplanade if we walked and looked at remains of the heathen Roman era. To tell the truth, I almost liked the basilica better at night bathed in blue light than in daylight when it was a glaring white, bedecked with crenellated towers, carving, statues, stairs, a porch with red granite columns, all symbolic of something, the whole having been built with the donations from Lyonnais Catholics in the nineteenth century. "Like Gaudi's Sagrada Familia in Barcelona," I said.

"Absolutely not," said Gabrielle. "I've seen pictures of that church. It's bizarre. Our basilica is beautiful, and it's dedicated to the Blessed Virgin." On which note we went inside to see the sights. My favorites were the Saint Thomas Becket chapel, which contained part of the original shrine from the fifteenth century. Evidently Becket had fled to Lyon before returning to his martyrdom in England.

Other interesting embellishments were the six historical mosaics, three of which related to proclamations about the

Virgin, one to the battle of Lepanto when the Turks were defeated, one to Sainte Joan of Arc and another to Saint Pothin's arrival in Lugdunum. I supposed he was one of the martyrs thrown to the lions or founded the first Christian church or something.

Sylvie was particularly amused at the depiction of Louis XIII giving France to the Virgin Mary in 1638. "If she didn't give it back then, I'm sure Louis XIV took it back during his reign," said Sylvie, giggling. Gabrielle was not amused and retorted that the burning of Ste. Joan was all the fault of the English.

"I didn't realize that Mary wasn't considered the mother of God until the fifth century," I said to change the subject.

"Of course, she was," snapped Gabrielle. "It was just made official by St. Cyril at the council in Ephesus."

"I've never understood about the Immaculate Conception," said Sylvie.

"I'm sure you haven't," retorted Gabrielle.

"I mean, they didn't decide on that until the *nineteenth* century."

"Well," I interrupted, "it must be time for lunch." Not that I was looking forward to it. I'd have to do some fancy footwork to get out of eating the pâté.

20

A Perilous Picnic

Carolyn

"**You shouldn't make** fun of other people's religions," I whispered to Sylvie as we left the basilica.

"Tell that to Gabrielle. You should hear her on the Church of England and Henry VIII. A couple of years ago I mentioned how much I liked the BBC series about his wives, and she called Henry a nasty, lecherous heretic."

I sighed, not having expected that my tour of churches would turn into a religious war. At least the esplanade beside the basilica had a wonderful view of the city. Sylvie unpacked her basket, which contained food, wine, goblets, plates, silverware, and pretty napkins. The sun was warm, the sky blue, the breeze cool, and the combatants willing to call a truce.

I situated myself so that when the pâté was passed, I could intercept Gabrielle's or pass mine to her. It worked perfectly, except that a fly landed on my pâté when I passed it to Gabrielle, and Sylvie promptly replaced it with another slice. Then she fixed mine, which had perhaps been meant for me in the first place. I couldn't really insist on switching with either of them. I might well be stuck with the tetrodotoxin, I'd simply devour everything else on my plate and declare that I couldn't eat another bite.

Ignoring all my resolutions to gain no weight on this trip, I had two glasses of wine and even enjoyed the dried sausage. The farm bread was lovely and crusty and all the more delicious for being slathered with *fromage fort*. Sylvie said it was made from grated Gruyère, leftover bits of cow and goat cheese, and then mixed with sour cheese and a sauce of leeks and white wine. I ate three slices and everything else on my plate except the pâté, while Winston Churchill sat next to me looking hopeful. *I ought to give him the pâté*, I thought maliciously, but of course, I wouldn't. It wasn't his fault Sylvie might be trying to poison me.

"What a shame about Albertine's mother," said Gabrielle. "I hear the poor woman is in terrible pain. And all from a— what would you say?—a fowl pox?"

I tried to keep the astonishment off my face. A foul pox? The English called it the French pox and the French, the English pox. Either way it was syphilis. "Poor woman," I stammered.

"Yes," Sylvie agreed. "And to think it was lurking in her system all these years."

"Really?" Did they mean she'd caught it as a young woman or even as a child? Perhaps it was congenital. Poor Albertine. This sort of gossip must be terribly embarrassing for her if she was aware of it. To change the subject, I said, "Sylvie, that was absolutely delicious. I'm embarrassed to say I can't eat another bite, and here I never got to the pâté."

"It's really excellent," said Gabrielle. "You must try a taste."

Sylvie hacked off another slice of bread and slathered my pâté onto it. "Eat," she said. "I made it last night, and I am not letting an American food critic escape without tasting my pâté." She grinned at me and actually held the bread to my lips. What could I do? Terrified, I took a bite and assured her that it was very tasty. In fact, it was wonderful, and if I hadn't been afraid of meeting Robert's fate, I'd have gobbled up the rest. "But truly, Sylvie, I can't eat any more. I'll get a stomachache. I have a—a hiatal hernia." Which was a big fat lie.

"My aunt had that," said Gabrielle.

"She just doesn't like my pâté. Or she thinks goose liver is nasty."

"Not true," I protested. "In fact, if you'll give me your recipe, Sylvie, I'll put it in my column and send you a copy." *If I live that long.*

On the downhill funicular I detected a tingling in my lips, one of the symptoms of tetrodotoxin poisoning. By the time we settled ourselves in the car, my tongue was going numb. The drive home brought on tingling in my hands and feet. *It's probably too late for me already*, I thought as I made my way into the hotel and got my key. *Am I going to die on a Charlemagne bed just as Robert Levasseur did?*

Strangely my symptoms had disappeared by the time I reached my room. Perhaps I had suspected Sylvie unfairly, or the fact that I had had only one bite of pâté might have saved me. Was the poison only in the first slice, which was thrown away with the fly, or in another section of the pâté on my bread?

Whatever the answer, I now felt fine and anxious to see Catherine's apartment. Even if I got lost, the lady with the key would be there the rest of the afternoon. I was so relieved to be alive and symptom-free that I managed to get to Old Lyon by train, bus, and foot at three-fifteen. I knocked on the right door, received the key from a grumpy lady, and went in search of the light switch.

It didn't work. Still, I could see to the first turn by the

light from the courtyard. I'd just feel my way that far, and perhaps the bulb on the next stretch would be lit. Once I closed the door to the courtyard, it was very dark, and I had to move slowly, hands brushing the rough stone on both sides and feet feeling for the steps. After twelve steps my toe reached for the back of the next and moved too far. It must be the landing, but there was still no light. I'd have another flight to climb before I bumped into Catherine's door, and then I'd have to fumble around for the keyhole, which—

Suddenly I was falling backward in the dark, scraping against the walls with my arms and legs, struggling to halt the fall, until there was a burst of pain in my head. Then nothing.

21

Where's Carolyn?

Jason

I'd **talked to** all the people in the department who shared my interests and some who didn't, and now wondered why I wasn't out sightseeing with Carolyn, exploring a good church or two. Still, no one had mentioned dinner plans, so perhaps we could find a restaurant ourselves, where we would be able to choose our own meals, unlike last night with the departmental gourmets.

I was packing my briefcase when Miss Thomas, the chairman's secretary and, possibly, mistress, informed me that the Guillots were back, hoped to take my wife and me out to dinner, and would pick us up at our hotel at eight if that arrangement was acceptable.

I agreed. Adrien and I had much to talk about, and perhaps Carolyn and Albertine would manage to get along. They seemed to have made up their differences before we left Sorrento, but that dog, the cause of the enmity, was in an Italian kennel by then. If Albertine would only leave the creature at home, we should have a pleasant evening.

When I finally reached the hotel after my trip on various modes of public transportation, all crammed with French people returning from work, the clerk, grouchy Yvette, who had taken over the desk from pleasant Simone, insisted that our room key was gone. Perhaps the Charlemagne hadn't been such a good idea.

"Your wife came in at midafternoon," said Yvette, "but she left again without returning the key and has not come back. We do expect the room keys to be returned, monsieur. What if she loses it? Someone could use it to steal your belongings, and you cannot expect us to take responsibility when madam—"

"She understands. I understand. Perhaps she came back without your noticing," I interrupted. *Or perhaps you ignored her when she stopped at the desk,* I thought. "I'll check the room myself."

Yvette shrugged, and I took the elevator upstairs. Our room was locked, and Carolyn did not respond when I knocked. Because I had no key, I went downstairs and asked for one, but Yvette insisted there was only one key, which was why keys had to be returned by guests leaving the hotel.

"Fine," I snapped. "You can use your key to let me into my room." Our argument was broken up by the manager, who forced Yvette to hand over a key. At that point I was so irritated that I fantasized about throwing it at her head when I returned it. With luck Carolyn had been deeply asleep and hadn't heard my knock. However, she wasn't asleep; she and her handbag were gone. As the French are given to providing one with business cards, I had both office and home numbers for the Girards and the Doignes, Carolyn's sightseeing companions that day.

I called Raymond first, and he put Sylvie on. "But I left her at the Charlemagne before three. How weight-conscious your wife is. She was going to pass up the pâté I made for our picnic, but I did get her to eat a bite, which she admitted was superb. I may be the only Englishwoman you ever meet who can make a fine pâté de foie gras."

The very word *pâté* sent a chill up my spine. I had ignored Carolyn's idea that Robert had been killed by fugu toxin in pâté meant for us, but now my wife had been forced to eat some and had disappeared. Where was she? Lying dead in Old Lyon?

Thinking the same thing, but for different reasons, Sylvie suggested that Carolyn had accepted Catherine's invitation to see the tower apartment. "Catherine must have taken a liking to your wife, and why not? She is a delightful person, even if she did disapprove of my twitting Gabrielle about the church. I couldn't resist. It's *so* much fun. Maybe Carolyn got lost. I'm sure she'll be back soon. Does she know that Albertine and Adrien are taking you to dinner?" Sylvie giggled. "Maybe she's delaying her return to get out of it."

Could someone as flighty as Sylvie have poisoned my wife? The desire to tease Gabrielle did show a certain maliciousness, but it took more than that to poison someone. And why would she? I called the Doignes next and spoke to Gabrielle, who complimented me on my wife's appreciation for Catholic history and churches. "She was stunned by the beauty of the basilica and Saint-Jean Cathedral. I wish I could say the same for Sylvie. I'm not even sure she's Church of England. What sect do you and Carolyn adhere to? Protestant I suppose, but still—"

I really had no interest in discussing religion with Gabrielle so I interrupted to ask if she'd heard from Carolyn after their outing.

"She's not home yet?" cried Gabrielle. "I might have known. Sylvie probably had an accident or her car broke down, and the two of them are marooned somewhere. Poor Carolyn. She was worried about getting a stomachache from the pâté and her—what was the word?—hernia. My aunt had one. Very unpleasant."

What hernia? I wondered. Gabrielle wasn't much help. She could only suggest that I call the police to ask for reports of accidents involving two women in a small, foreign car.

I stopped worrying about an accident when I remembered that Yvette had claimed Carolyn came back to the hotel and left again. I didn't know who to call next or where in Old Lyon the apartment was. I should have put my foot down on that score, but it is quite difficult these days to put my foot down with Carolyn. She used to listen when I asked her to do something she didn't want to do. Now I was lucky to find dinner waiting when I got home. I blamed it on my mother. Sometimes I spied that feminist gleam in my wife's eye, the same gleam that had made chaos of my childhood. I was fifteen the first time I had to bail Mother out of jail. Before they divorced, my father had done that.

The telephone rang just then, Yvette calling to say that the Guillots were waiting for me in the lobby, and that she would be very angry if I did not return the room key lent to me at the manager's insistence. I put my suit jacket back on and took the elevator downstairs.

I got her. She'd probably be dead by the time they found her. And her husband, even now, would be wondering where she was and why she hadn't returned to the hotel. By late evening he'd be frantic, but with no identification on the body, he wouldn't be able to find her. He could look for days with no success. Maybe they'd bury her in a pauper's grave, and he'd never know. A just and enduring revenge.

22

I've Been Poisoned

Carolyn

First, I was aware of the terrible pain in my head, pounding, inescapable. It made me want to get away from my own consciousness. Then I realized that I didn't know where I was. Only confusion met my attempts to think. Confusion multiplied a hundredfold by pain. I heard a whimper and thought it was mine. I tried to open my eyes, and the light cut into them like a razor into flesh. I heard a voice, not speaking my language, and wished it away. The hand on my shoulder, although gentle, terrified me because it might belong to the person who had hurt me.

"Madam?" The voice was female and nonthreatening.

Eyes still closed, I whispered, "Where am I?"

More foreign voices conferred softly. Then a man's voice in accented English said, "Madam, you are in a hospital."

"Where?"

"In Lyon, France. Do you know your name?"

Did I? "Carolyn? Carolyn Blue?"

"And you live in Lyon?"

Did I? Memories began to slip through the agony, and I replied, "Charlemagne. On Charlemagne Cour. My hotel."

"You are a visitor to our city?"

More memories leaked in between the waves of pain. "I've been poisoned. Treat me for tetro—tetrotoxin. No. Dotoxin? The poison in fugu. In the pâté at the basilica."

Several people spoke to each other unintelligibly. "My head hurts. Can't you do something? At least make me throw up before the poison shuts down my nervous system."

"Madam," said the male voice, "it is unlikely you have been poisoned. You were found in a stairway. Without consciousness. An injury to the head."

"Someone hit me on the head?" It felt like it, but what about Sylvie's pâté? "Sylvie?"

"She hit you?"

"Made the pâté."

"You may have fallen on the stair and hit your head on the stone wall."

"Catherine's apartment," I mumbled, remembering now that I had been feeling my way upstairs in the dark.

"However, there was no handbag. Did you carry one?"

"Yes. Oh lord, did they take her key?" Even through the pounding, I now feared that my attacker took Catherine's key and burglarized her apartment. "And *my* key? To the hotel room. Did they—" Jason would be very upset if everything was stolen. Our laptops. Our clothes. "And my money and credit cards—are they gone?"

"Your purse was not found. Can you open your eyes?"

"No," I said firmly. Either a criminal had attacked me, something Catherine had warned me against, or this was another attack on Jason and me. "One man has died of poison meant for us. My husband was injured when a car tried to run him down. Now I've been attacked. Call Inspector Theodore Roux. It's his case. And my husband. Jason Blue. At the Charlemagne. Or at the university."

"What university, madam?"

I couldn't remember. Why did these things happen to me? I was a good person. Before I could complain, someone pried one eye open and shone a light in it.

"You have a concussion," said the male voice.

"Then give me some painkillers."

"Not yet," he replied.

"That's mean." I felt like crying, but was afraid it would make me feel worse.

"But we will make the calls. Jason Blue at the Hotel Charlemagne and Inspector Theodore Roux. Yes?"

"Yes. And maybe an ice pack if I can't have any painkillers, but I know why. The French don't like Americans. That's why."

"I assure you, madam, I like many Americans. We will give you painkillers when it is safe." Then the lights dimmed. I could tell through my eyelids, which seemed transparent for all the good they did. "Does that help? The light."

"Yes, but I need a guard so the people who want to kill us—"

"You are safe here. French hospitals are very safe."

"Giverny wasn't. They sprayed chiles on Professor Childeric," I mumbled. "If your flower gardens aren't safe, why should I believe you about your hospitals?" I drifted in confusion and pain, trying to think what could have happened to me. Who knew that I would be at Catherine's apartment that afternoon? Who . . .

Then a hand held mine. Male. Surely the doctor wasn't—"Madam Blue. Carolyn. It is I, Theodore Roux."

"Sylvie poisoned the pâté," I answered without opening my eyes. It was enough to recognize his voice.

"The pâté Professor Levasseur—"

"The pâté at lunch. She made it for the picnic and practically forced it down my throat." My head didn't hurt quite so much now, and I was angry.

"But Madam Blue, the doctor says you have had a bad fall on a stairway, and your head is concussioned. He finds no signs of poison. I will take this Sylvie's name, but—"

"Yes, do. Sylvie Girard. Husband, Raymond Girard. University. You say I fell? Climbing to Catherine's?"

"Did someone push you?"

"Why else did I fall backward? I remember that. Backward."

"Who would know you were to be in the traboule stairway?" he asked. "Why were you there?"

"To see Catherine's apartment. She's Italian. From the Renaissance bankers. She knew because she invited me, but she went to Avignon, so it wasn't her. Sylvie and Gabrielle knew because they took me to churches. Gabrielle Doigne. Husband . . . Doigne. Same department. Catherine's student Martin le something. He would have heard her, and he was angry because I said he looked like William Rufus."

"Who is William Rufus?"

"But if Martin pushed me, who poisoned the pâté and tried to hit Jason?" I had to give him Catherine's last name and position, but couldn't remember Martin's last name, even if he didn't like me. "Also the Fourniers. They were at dinner when Catherine made the offer. Nicole and Bertrand." I remembered something else. "It must have been Bertrand. He said I had to have the potatoes with the fish because I might not get another chance. How did he know that, unless he planned to finish me off before I could eat another dinner in Lyon? Catherine said they were better with lamb and—and something, but he said . . ."

The inspector was muttering *potatoes* and *fish*, and I could hear the scratch of his pen. When he'd written down the names of our gourmet hosts and promised to interview them, too, he said, "Of course it could have been a simple robbery. Are any of these people the type to steal your purse?"

"For goodness sake, Inspector, it's obvious that my handbag was stolen to make the attack *look* like a robbery. Can't you see that?" I opened my eyes to glare at him for his lack of professional reasoning. The eyes were a bad idea. Such a little light to hurt so much.

"Poor madam. You are in pain. I will call the nurse."

"Why? They won't give me anything. Just go out and find who did this. You can hit them on the head for me, if you like. And try to get my credit card back so Jason won't be upset, and Catherine's key and the hotel key. If Yvette is on duty, she'll have a fit because I forgot to return the key. She's so mean." I paused, drawing a breath against nausea. "Can't talk anymore. My head hurts. So do a lot of other places. But not as bad as my head."

"Bonsoir, madam," said the inspector softly. "I shall begin questioning suspects immediately. Even if I have to wake them up. And a guard at your door. I will get to the top of this."

"Bottom of this," I corrected, wishing that he'd go away and leave me in peace and quiet. Talking and listening were painful. Even thinking was. And the worst was his cell phone, which rang close by and sent a wall of blackness right over my head.

23

Lost Reservations

Jason

Adrien **apologized for** missing our appointment. "Albertine's mother gave us a fright. She was in such pain that we had to go. Now we must fit enough planning in tomorrow and during the meeting to get our project under way. No?"

Albertine, for her part, assured me that she had secured a reservation, even on short notice, at a restaurant that would delight my wife. "My wife has disappeared," I replied. "She left the hotel around three and hasn't been seen since."

Mouth pinched in her dark, thin face, eyes flashing with anger, our hostess said, "So Carolyn has hidden herself in order not to see us. I even left Charles de Gaulle at home, although my poor dog has had a terrible time since he met Carolyn. So have Adrien and I, but here we are to welcome you, and she has not seen fit—"

"She didn't even know you were back," I snapped, "and I can't say that I give a damn about your dog. It's my wife I'm worried about. I've called the people she was with this afternoon, and they don't know what happened to her. If she went to Catherine de Firenze's as she planned, she hasn't come back. I'm almost convinced that, as Carolyn thinks, someone really is trying to kill us."

"Indeed?" Albertine raised her eyebrows in a supercilious way. "Isn't that a bit paranoid? Well, no matter. We can talk during dinner—unless we miss our reservation. It took a lot of influence to get a table. We'll just leave a note for your wife."

"You think I'm going out to dinner when I don't know what's happened to Carolyn?"

"Do you expect us to skip dinner because she's wandered off?"

People in the lobby, including Yvette, were staring at us. "Go off if you want to, but leave me the address of Catherine's apartment. At least I can see if Carolyn managed to get that far. If not, I'll . . ."

The Guillots had to admit they knew only that Catherine lived somewhere in Old Lyon. "She hasn't been particularly sociable since her husband died, and that's been ten years at least," said Albertine. "Really, ten years and she hasn't returned our dinner invitation."

"She's in Avignon," said Adrien. "Perhaps we can reach her by phone and get the address."

"After dinner," his wife added.

"Now," I insisted, and Adrien, thank God, agreed and went off to call information for a number in Avignon. He got it, but Catherine didn't answer. Then he insisted that his wife get out her address book and call everyone in the department to see if they had Catherine's address or any word of my wife. He was so forceful that she agreed, and they split the list and called everyone they could think of. Nobody knew Catherine's actual address, just that she had restored, with a loan from the city, an apartment in a Renaissance building.

"Obviously we can't knock on doors in every Renaissance building," said Albertine.

"I'll try Catherine again." And this time Adrien got her. She was evidently quite astounded to hear that Carolyn had not returned from her visit to the apartment, but gave us the address, after which we set off in the Guillots' black Renault to find the place.

On Catherine's instructions, we knocked at the door of a woman on the first floor, who answered wearing a robe and a hairnet. Yes, she said, an American woman with blond hair had called and taken the key at three-fifteen. We asked if she had seen Carolyn leave. The woman then burst into an angry tirade in French.

"She says that when the woman did not return the key, she, Madam Ravelier, went upstairs with a flashlight to find the woman, whom she felt might be stealing Professor de Firenze's belongings." Adrien stopped translating and began to look dismayed, as did Albertine.

"What's she saying?" I demanded.

"She says she found the woman's body on the stairs, unconscious with a bloody head, so she called the ambulance service, and they took her away." The neighbor added a few angry remarks. "And the key was gone," Adrien continued, "so she went up to Catherine's door. It was ajar, possibly burglarized judging by the condition of the apartment."

"Poor Catherine," said Albertine. "She'll be very upset to hear that she's been robbed, probably of family treasures brought to Lyon from Florence. We'd better call her right away with the news."

I couldn't believe Albertine was more worried about Catherine's possessions than my wife's well-being. "Where did the ambulance take Carolyn?"

"The woman doesn't know," Adrien replied. "I think we'd better call the police."

The woman said something else, and Albertine translated: "She called the police herself when she found

Catherine's door unlocked, but they said they doubted that they'd find the teens who committed robberies, that the stolen items had probably already been sold for a fraction of their value. What a shame!"

"As if I care," I snapped. "Obviously Carolyn's right about someone being out to get us. There's an Inspector Theodore Roux who's looking into Robert's death and the attempt to run me down. Maybe we can get hold of him. Ask the woman if we can use her phone."

Madam Ravelier refused and slammed the door.

Instead we went to the police station, where I demanded that they find out to what hospital my wife had been taken and also that they get in touch with Inspector Roux and ask him to call back on Adrien's cell phone. However, the local police felt they should ask me thousands of questions about our problems in Lyon; to most answers they expressed astonishment and said that the city was very peaceable, even their district. A few burglaries and robberies certainly, but very little violence. My wife must have fallen down the stairs, after which some boy had happened upon her and taken her handbag, or perhaps it had gone with her in the ambulance.

And through all the questions Albertine was complaining that they'd never get another reservation if they didn't keep the one they had.

I wanted to strangle her.

24

Only One Visitor at a Time, Please

Carolyn

Why was he still in my room, saying, "Yes, I'm with her now," and giving the name of a hospital. "She has the concussion, but her doctor says she will recover." It occurred to me that the man who was after us, who probably thought he'd killed me, was in league with Inspector Roux. Now that he knew I was alive and where I'd been taken, he'd try again, and the promised guard would never arrive to watch my door. I opened my eyes and stammered, "How could you betray me?"

Closing his cell phone, the inspector looked at me curiously. "Betray you, Madam Blue?" he asked. "That was your husband, who has been searching for you. You do not wish to see your husband? He is on his way and is most relieved to know that you are alive."

"Jason?" My voice wobbled. Was the inspector telling the truth? "You're sure it was Jason?"

"He said so. Who else would be looking for you, madam?"

"The murderer," I replied and burst into tears. My nurse bustled into the room and reprimanded Inspector Roux, who announced that he had to leave so I could rest and he could continue his investigation.

"Is the guard outside?" I whispered to her, and she nodded. I was so relieved that I drifted immediately into sleep.

The next voice to awaken me was Jason's. "Sweetheart, how are you?" he asked, sounding very worried.

"I hurt all over, my head and everywhere else, and if you say, 'I told you so,' because I went to Catherine's, I'll never forgive you." Tears were rolling down my cheeks.

"*Mon dieu*, Carolyn, there is no reason to weep. I have just questioned your doctor, and you will recover, although perhaps not in time that we can drive you and Jason to Avignon."

I couldn't believe my ill luck. It was Albertine Guillot, right here in my room. She'd probably brought Charles de Gaulle with her. "Where's the dog?" I asked.

"If you mean *my* dog," she said stiffly, "he is at home. Poor Charles de Gaulle has had a difficult year and is much subdued after being harassed by the police, taken to court, and sentenced to death. It was terrible."

"What color is your car?" I was not about to be diverted from the possibility that she was our attacker. Obviously she still resented me.

"My car? What has my car to do with anything? My car is green."

"What color is Adrien's?" Jason had been smoothing the hair away from my brow. "Stop touching my head," I said, angry that he had brought the Guillots when I felt so terrible.

"My car is black," said Adrien soothingly. "What color is your car, Carolyn?"

"Ah ha! Black! I knew it."

"My poor love," said my husband. "You're so upset." Actually, he looked as upset as I felt. "Maybe Adrien and Albertine can come back tomorrow to visit." I saw him give them a look, as if to say, "She's not herself, as you can see."

All Jason cared about was his research proposal with Adrien. He'd never believe that the Guillots wanted to kill us. "Which one of you came back from Paris in the black car?" I demanded.

"We both did," said Adrien. "Of course, we're so sorry to have missed the opportunity to welcome you, but Albertine's mother—"

"Oh, yes. Her hospitalization for syphilis."

"*What* did you say about my mother?" Albertine snarled in a voice so loud it hurt my head.

"Only one visitor at a time, please," said the nurse, who had evidently heard Albertine shouting and come to my rescue.

Adrien grabbed his wife's arm and, murmuring over his shoulder, "We'll say good night now and let you rest, Carolyn," dragged her from the room.

"Carolyn," said my husband in a firm voice, "close your eyes and take a deep breath. Your head injury, about which I'll have to talk to your doctor—"

"I'm not crazy. Didn't you hear what they said? They both drove back from Paris in the black car. Probably Albertine poisoned the pâté before they left, and when they heard that we weren't dead, they drove back overnight, and Adrien tried to run you down the next day."

"They came back this afternoon," said Jason, "and invited us to dinner. Albertine made reservations at a fancy restaurant as soon as they got here."

"She's lying. You have to call days, maybe weeks ahead to get reservations at a good restaurant."

"And what's this about syphilis? That's a terrible thing to say about someone's mother."

"Gabrielle told me. Evidently it's common knowledge."

"She said that today? On the church tour? Carolyn, can you even *remember* what happened today?"

"Oh, go back to the hotel, Jason. At least Inspector Roux believes me."

"But darling, I can't leave. I feel terrible that you've been hurt, and that I didn't take seriously enough the threat you perceived, although I did ask you not to—"

"You're saying 'I told you so.' I knew you would. And you don't have to protect me. The inspector gave me a guard. I just want to be left alone. My head hurts." I sniffled.

"Monsieur," said the nurse, who was still in the room.

Jason sighed and kissed me on the cheek. "I'll be back tomorrow morning," he whispered softly.

25

The Angry Suspects

Jason

The Guillots were gone when I left the hospital. And I— so tired, worried about my wife, and disheartened because she'd sent me away—didn't feel like being frugal. I took a cab to the hotel and blackmailed food from Yvette by threatening to contact the manager and demand that she be fired if it wasn't provided. Scowling ferociously, she led me to the kitchen and arranged for a tray I could take to my room—two sandwiches, a limp salad, and a glass of wine poured from an unlabeled bottle. The chef apologized in person for the fare.

I went upstairs with my "dinner" and found the telephone registering four calls—the Girards, the Doignes, Martin le Blanc, and the Fourniers, all of whom had been questioned as suspects in the attack on my wife. All were confused and angry. All demanded that I call back.

I dropped my head into my hands, no longer hungry, just wanting to sleep, but I called. Bertrand Fornier seemed to think that he had been accused because he recommended that Carolyn order the gratin potatoes with the fish in butter sauce. "I realize," he said, "that both dishes contain milk or butter, but when she said she had not yet sampled our wonderful Gratin Lyonnais—well, what could I do but be sure she did not miss it? And I was not, I assure you, in Old Lyon this afternoon. I took the afternoon off so that Nicole and I could choose the best restaurants to visit in Avignon." I calmed Bertrand by saying that my wife, having suffered a concussion, probably had no idea what she was saying to the inspector.

Then I called Catherine's student, who thought Carolyn had reported him to the police for objecting to her remark about William Rufus. "I admit that I am inclined to seek the company of men rather than women," he said, sounding anxious, "and that I do not want that discussed in the department. There are prejudices. Such gossip could ruin my chances of a faculty position after I leave Lyon. Still, I would not push your wife down Professor de Firenze's stairs to protect my . . . private life." I sighed and assured Le Blanc that neither Carolyn nor I had anything against homosexuals, and that my wife had been astonished, not angry, to find that she had offended him because of her interest in medieval history.

Charles Doigne was very grumpy. He couldn't understand what Carolyn might have against them, unless it was that they were Catholics. "Why would we push your wife down a flight of stairs? Especially Catherine's stairs. We don't even know where Catherine lives. She no longer socializes, and hasn't since her husband's death, after which she moved from their home to an apartment." I apologized for the inconvenience they had suffered and began to wonder if any of these people would speak to us when we got to the meeting. *If* we got there. Obviously I couldn't leave Carolyn in a French hospital by herself.

Last I called the Girards. Sylvie answered, close to hysterics. "She thinks I poisoned the pâté?" she demanded in a high, trembling voice. "My pâté was delicious. I am not sick. Gabrielle is not sick. Even Winston Churchill is not sick. I gave him the slice with the fly stuck in it. Why would Carolyn think such a thing?

"I have been driving her through Lyon for three days, taking pictures, which I am developing to make up an album so that she can remember her visit with pleasure. Of course the album is a surprise. You are not to tell her. Maybe I will not give it to her. I thought we were friends. Winston Churchill thinks he is her friend. If she felt ill and stumbled down some steps, it was not because of my pâté."

Thank God Raymond took the phone away from his wife and said, "Sylvie is upset."

"So I gathered. And Carolyn is in the hospital with a concussion and bruises and scrapes all over her body. I am sorry that Sylvie was distressed by the visit from the inspector, but perhaps you will understand that my wife is not herself when I tell you that she would not allow *me* to stay in her hospital room."

"She thinks *you* pushed her down the steps?" Raymond asked, amazed. "But I can testify that you were in the department. Poor woman. What does her doctor say?"

"Nothing. He'd gone home before I left Carolyn's hospital room. The thing is, Raymond, Robert died from eating pâté meant for us, according to the police. Their whole scenario sounds peculiar to me, but then the next day I just escaped being run down, and today—well, you can see that Carolyn might be seriously stressed at this point, and of course, she has a terrible headache."

"This is all very strange," Raymond admitted, "but each happening could have been unrelated, not an incident pre-planned by someone who means you ill. Why would anyone? You didn't know anyone here except the Guillots, who were in Paris. Has your wife accused them to the inspector, as well?"

"God only knows," I said wearily. "She and Albertine had words tonight when they came to the hospital with me."

"My friend, you need a snifter of cognac and a good night's sleep. I do myself with my Sylvie in hysterics."

I'd have agreed, but I had no cognac, just the meal on the bed, whose salad looked even more pathetic than when the chef scraped it out of the bottom of a bowl. As I ate, it occurred to me that if Carolyn had been attacked, she might also have been robbed, in which case, there might be someone out there using our credit cards. I drained the last of my wine and called Inspector Roux, asleep after conducting an investigation that alienated everyone I knew in the city.

"Monsieur, I do not investigate the snatching of purses," he mumbled. "Call a local station if your wife—"

"This is Jason Blue. I'm calling about Carolyn's purse. The lady who sent you off to accuse everyone we know of attempted murder. Was her purse found at the scene of her fall? Or with her when she was brought to the hospital?"

"No," said the inspector. "Why are you worrying about her purse? The poor lady is suffering terribly, and without medication for her pain. Her handbag is hardly a matter for—"

"It is if some thief has her credit card. Perhaps you can catch the person who attacked her by seeing if charges have been made on her card this evening."

"Ah, an excellent idea. My apologies, Professor. I was asleep."

"I wish I were." I mumbled and gave him the information on the one card I let Carolyn carry when we are traveling. I carried our other card, and each of us had the numbers of the card we didn't personally use. More cards than two, in my opinion, are too many, although Carolyn disagrees. She reads those endless offers and passes them on to me for consideration because of low interest rates or airline miles or money back at the end of the year. There's usually something in the small print that makes them undesirable, even if I wanted another card.

Having made what I hoped would be my second-to-last call, I then dialed the 800 number to report the loss of Carolyn's card. Calling an 800 number from a foreign country is a problematic endeavor, but I did finally reach the Visa office and was able to cancel Carolyn's card, which, it occurred to me, was not a bad idea. Without a card, she wouldn't be able to make any shockingly expensive purchases when we got to Avignon—French shoes and clothing; expensive, heavy books on the history of the Avignon Papacy; shopping lunches in three-star Michelin restaurants she just had to visit for her column and which are, as she always points out, tax deductible.

26
Albertine, Bearing Flowers

Carolyn

Someone was in the room again. I kept my eyes closed, hoping they'd go away, trusting the guard would keep away nonhospital people. Not that I trusted the hospital. No wonder they kill so many patients. It's not just the antibiotic-resistant bacteria. It's the harassment. Here we are, ill and in pain, and they won't let us rest.

All night they'd been destroying what little relief I managed to find. Once they wheeled me out to x-ray my head, the results of which, beyond exposing me to painfully glaring overhead lights, I'd never know because no one thought to speak to *me* in *my* language. In the comforting darkness of my room, strangers would intrude to hold my eyes open and shine light at my pupils. No warning but the quiet voices, then the fingers on my face and the light that stabbed my brain and left colored circles behind my lids. Then came the blood-pressure takers, who strapped cuffs onto my scrapes and bruises and pumped in air until the tears leaked from eyes still afflicted with ghastly round and colored apparitions.

Against the latest attack, I squeezed my eyes closed and hid my arms beneath the covers for protection, but this intruder spoke English and had a new errand. "Does madam need to vomit?" she asked. I said *no*. "Is madam just a bit afflicted with nausea?" she asked. What did she want? To stick her finger down my throat in an attempt to bring it on?

"No? Then I have for you an omelet. Do you feel well enough to eat?"

Without thinking it through, I opened my eyes, and then trembled with fear at what they might do to me upon seeing that I was awake and up to more tortures. But I did her an injustice. She wore a kindly smile and behind her was not some frightening medical apparatus, but instead a cart from which wafted the odor of eggs, cheese, herbs, and perhaps mushrooms.

"Come, let us see if you can sit," she coaxed and slipped an arm behind my back. Sitting up was not so pleasant. My head whirled, and I did feel a bit queasy, but I wanted that omelet. I'd had nothing but sips of water since Sylvie's picnic lunch. "Do you feel well enough to eat?" I nodded, a mistake. "You can have the killers for the pain now, as well as the omelet."

Oh, thank God, I thought and opened my mouth when she raised a fork full of golden eggs. Having borne children, I have been in hospitals where the food was disgusting enough to make you want to go home immediately. This omelet was so delicious that I could even forgive the nurses for speaking French, shining lights in my eyes, and bruising the bruises on my arms. The nurse fed me two more bites, and then, eager for more omelet faster, I took the fork myself.

"*Très bien*," said the nurse. "Can you swallow pills, do you think?" If they would drive away the pain in my head, which interfered with my enjoyment of the omelet, I would have swallowed pills the size of robin's eggs. I accepted a pill, washed it down with water, and went back to breakfast. Ah the mushrooms, so earthy, and the cheese, which had melted in the most delightful way, flavorful and not stringy.

"Do you think your chef would give me the recipe?" I asked, feeling so much better that I remembered my professional responsibilities.

The nurse's eyes twinkled, and she said, "If for me you will swallow one more pill, I will ask. No one has ever requested a recipe here. She will be amazed."

"No one has ever enjoyed an omelet here more than I," I assured her and swallowed the pill so that I could continue eating while the dear, sweet nurse left to get me the recipe.

I was halfway through the meal when my door opened to reveal, not the lovely nurse, not my husband, whom I vaguely remembered visiting last night, not even the inspector, but the person I least wanted to see—Albertine Guillot, bearing flowers. She clicked over to my bed in her high heels and informed me that I looked much better. Then she offered me the bouquet, and I sneezed, my mouth full of half-chewed omelet, which sprayed out onto the flowers and Albertine's hand. I was so embarrassed that I forgot she was a primary suspect and handed her my napkin.

"I see that you are allergic to my flowers. There is no need to apologize." Splattered as the flowers were with omelet bits, she plopped them hastily into my water pitcher, then went into my bathroom, carrying my napkin, to wash her hands. Now I had no water and no napkin, for she did not return the latter when she pulled up a chair and sat beside my bed. "Please do go on with your *petit déjeuner*, dreadful as it must be. You no doubt need your strength."

I resented her saying that my breakfast was dreadful, but before I could protest, she said, "I must apologize for my harsh words last night. I had no idea how deranged you were from the fall."

Deranged? What was she talking about? I may have been a bit fuzzy on what had happened the night before, but I certainly was not deranged.

"I have had many calls this morning from people you have met, saying that you told a policeman they were trying to kill you. Also Jason explained that there have been unfortunate and frightening events, of which Adrien and I knew nothing. I cannot explain them, but I can assure you that no one in the department is trying to kill you. They have all said they thought you were enjoying your visit and their company. Have you not been received hospitably? Of course you have.

"And if you are resentful that Adrien and I were not here to welcome you, surely you can see that we had to visit my mother, who seemed to be seriously ill, and may, I am told, experience more pain in the future. Therefore, I cannot understand why you would say my mother has syphilis. She is an old and respectable woman."

"Look, Albertine," I broke into her lecture, "first thing, the inspector asked who knew I would be in Catherine's stairway, and I provided the names of those I could remember. I didn't say I thought they were trying to kill us, although who knows . . . Well, he'll investigate. And secondly, I am not deranged. I was certainly in pain, but—well, they've finally given me painkillers, and I feel much better."

"I am delighted to hear it," said Albertine, "which still does not explain why you would say—"

"Thirdly, Gabrielle told me about your mother. I'm sorry. It must be terrible for her to have suffered so many years from such an—ah—embarrassing affliction. I thought penicillin cured it."

"My mother does not suffer from an embarrassing affliction, and at the risk of offending you, I do not believe that Gabrielle said my mother had syphilis."

"Well, to be perfectly accurate, she said your mother had the *foul pox*. I know it has many names—the French pox, the English pox, the—"

"My mother does not have a foul pox," said Albertine indignantly. "She does not have a pox of any kind. She had a childhood disease when she was a girl, which evidently leaves a virus in the nerves that can reappear years later as a rash attended by burning and agonizing pain, but it is *not* syphilis."

A childhood disease? A foul pox? My mind was functioning better than it had last night, not surprising considering my pain and how irritating everyone had been. Could Gabrielle have meant a *fowl* pox? In other words, *chicken* pox? "Your mother has shingles!" I exclaimed.

"Are you insulting my mother again?" Albertine gave me the same mean look she had given me in Sorrento when her dog and I clashed. "Shingles are something on a roof, are they not? Is the word slang for—"

"No, no," I said hastily. "Shingles—it's the same virus as chicken pox. It was a misunderstanding. A language problem. No wonder Gabrielle and Sylvie seemed so casual about your mother's illness." I started to giggle. Then I apologized between giggles while she stared at me as if she thought I was—well, deranged. I did feel somewhat light-headed and lay back on my pillow. "I do apologize, Albertine."

"I would find your apology more convincing if you weren't laughing," she replied.

"I know. Maybe I am, as you said, a bit deranged. I'm certainly sleepy. Every time I managed to doze off, they came in and woke me up in some painful way."

"Ah." She nodded. "They did the same thing to my mother. Hospitals are terrible places the world over, and unfortunately, your doctor says you must stay another day, which means that you will not be able to accompany us to Avignon, but you'll find the train very comfortable when you are ready to make the trip, and Adrien has promised to change the schedule in whatever way is necessary to accommodate Jason if he wishes to stay here with you."

Where was Jason? I wondered. Had I said something to offend him? Surely he wouldn't leave me here in Lyon by myself, at the mercy of malicious medical people. "At least the food is good," I said, trying to be brave.

"Well, I hope you are still able to tolerate it when you are in good enough health to judge it reasonably," said Albertine.

27

Late to Bed, Late to Rise
Tends to Strain the Marital Ties

Jason

I never set an alarm clock, even in different time zones, because I awaken automatically. Of all days to break my pattern, that was not the one. I'd planned to be at the hospital by seven, but I could tell by the light that I'd overslept. I could only assume that yesterday's stress, the late-night phone calls to angry faculty members, and the credit card problem had exhausted me more than I knew.

Frustrated and still worn out, I dressed and bolted a quick breakfast, proving that kiwi fruit, eaten too rapidly, is not a good idea, especially accompanied by three cups of strong coffee. I even took a cab to the hospital, where a floor nurse connected me with Carolyn's doctor. He said she was feeling better, had eaten a hearty breakfast, and was responding well to pain medication. However, I shouldn't think of taking her from the hospital today. They wanted one more X-ray of her head and antibiotic treatment for her scrapes. "We can only guess what was growing in that lightless passage," he said seriously. "Perhaps even toxic mold."

"Thank you," I replied, thinking that I might well be absent from the presentation of my own paper. I could instruct Mercedes to give it for me, although I doubted that she'd be able to answer questions that might arise. And she had her own poster to present, although on a different day. Wondering if Carolyn was in a more welcoming mood, and what the private room was going to cost me, I knocked hesitantly at my wife's door. The doctor had mentioned how fortunate she was not to be in a ward, as any other unidentified patient would have been, except that the hospital had fewer patients just now, the flu season having not yet hit.

Since there was no answer, I opened to door and peered in. Carolyn's bed was empty. Rushing back to the nurse, I demanded to know the whereabouts of my wife. *Have our enemies kidnapped her?* I wondered in a burst of paranoia.

"Ah, the X-ray of the head," the nurse replied cheerfully. "You are the husband? Yes?"

"And where is the guard at her door?" I asked.

"With the patient gone, he goes for café. Yes?"

"What if she were attacked during the X-ray?"

"How would the attacker know where to find her? I have told no one of her departure."

I returned to the room, where there was still no guard, but I did find my wife. "Where have you been?" she asked reproachfully. "I was here all night being battered by mean people and now all morning, and you didn't even visit. I was beginning to wonder if you'd gone off to Avignon with the Guillots. Or maybe you're just here to say good-bye before you leave.

"I wouldn't do that to *you*, Jason," she added bitterly. "It's obvious what comes first with you. Chemistry. So fine. If you ever have to go to the hospital, I'll take a trip to write about food."

I sighed. "I was here last night. Don't you remember? You told me to leave," I reminded her.

"I did?" She looked puzzled.

"And I'll admit to oversleeping for the first time in my life. I was on the telephone half the night."

"Why?"

"Well, there was your credit card to cancel," I began, fearing how she'd take the calls from the Lyon faculty.

"What am I supposed to do without a credit card?"

"It was stolen, Carolyn. You don't want someone charging on your card, do you?"

"Actually, I remember thinking of that yesterday, but I'd forgotten. And the key. They must have taken our room key."

"I used the chain last night. Simone is calling a locksmith today. Thank God Yvette wasn't the one I had to tell about that."

"And Catherine's key. I hope no one burglarized her apartment. I didn't even get to see it."

"Perhaps the inspector knows about Catherine's apartment. How are you feeling?"

"Much better," she replied. "They finally gave me painkillers after torturing me all night. You can't imagine how horrible it feels to have a bruise squeezed by a blood pressure cuff, or a light shined in your eyes when your head is aching. Or to be dragged off for another X-ray when you're finally feeling better after a nice breakfast."

"I think they can't give painkillers or let you sleep much when you have a concussion," I remarked, as mildly as possible. I didn't want to get in another fight with her. "The doctor says you may be here another day or so."

"He did? Why didn't he tell me? Now they're giving me shots, but the shot people don't speak English so I don't know why."

"You're sure the doctor hasn't spoken to you?" I asked, suddenly anxious. Could she be having memory lapses? Dear God, was her condition worse than he'd admitted?

"I talked to him last night. Before you came, I think."

"Do you remember talking to the inspector?" I asked.

"Yes, and according to Albertine I accused a lot of people of trying to kill us. Probably one of them did, but he asked who knew I'd be climbing Catherine's stairway, so I told him."

"Yes, I had a great many angry calls on voice mail at the hotel."

"Well, I don't know why they'd be upset. Don't they know that it's every citizen's duty to cooperate in police investigations? Anyway, they'll get over it. Albertine's all right with the syphilis misunderstanding."

I remembered that with a wince. I couldn't believe my wife had accused Albertine's mother of having syphilis.

"How was I to know that Gabrielle was talking about shingles? Wouldn't you think *syphilis* if someone said *foul pox*? I think Albertine understands, although she did say we couldn't ride with them because they're leaving this afternoon for Avignon, which I don't mind at all, and you shouldn't. Take my word for it, you wouldn't want to ride in a car with her dog."

"She's bringing the dog?"

"I don't know. I don't remember everything she said this morning. After all, I was sleepy because I'd had no sleep last night."

She *was* having memory lapses. "Well, don't worry about any of it, sweetheart. I'll be here in Lyon until you're released, even if I miss my paper."

"I do remember her saying Adrien would shift the schedule to accommodate you, but Jason, I don't want to stay here too long, even if the food *is* good. There are so many things I want to see—the papal palace and the half bridge and everything in Avignon. In Villenueve Avignon, a pope's nephew built a castle because Avignon was so nasty during the stay of the popes. There's a monastery and a fort and . . . Well, we'll leave tomorrow at the latest. Goodness, I'm so sleepy. Maybe I should have a little nap. Is the guard outside?"

"You go to sleep. I'll be right here," I assured her.

"If the guard's not here, someone might get you, too. Can't you look?"

I agreed to look and found him asleep in the chair. Some guard. He hadn't even noticed that I was in her room when he returned. When I tapped him on the shoulder, he woke up and addressed me in French with his hand on his gun.

"Esposo," I said in Spanish, not knowing the French word for husband. He nodded and went back to sleep. I returned to my chair to find my wife asleep as well, so I retrieved a printout of a paper on mercury poisoning that I'd been wanting to read and settled down, but before doing so I saw the bruises on one of Carolyn's arms. They looked terrible, although not as bad as the angry scrapes. Was her whole body covered with those? Had she really been pushed? Or had she fallen? It was hard to imagine that someone was trying to murder us, but still, dangerous things had been happening.

28
Au Revoir, Lyon

Carolyn

After Albertine, no academics came to visit. I suppose they were on their way to Avignon or mad at me, or both. I, meanwhile, was preparing to be released, although I hadn't yet discussed it with the doctor. He hadn't stopped by. Perhaps he felt it was enough to speak to Jason, an attitude that my mother-in-law would have deplored. Every time the nurse was out of the room, I insisted that Jason take me for a walk—to the bathroom or the window. He protested and with some reason. Getting up made me dizzy, but I clutched his arm and managed to stay upright.

While he was having lunch downstairs, the inspector arrived with the news that none of the people he interviewed seemed likely suspects. Many had alibis. I asked if he'd checked their alibis and received evasive replies.

"Could you not have fallen, madam?" he asked. "On a dark, rough stair, falling would be easy."

"Backward?" I retorted.

"You landed facedown."

"Well, I was trying to break my fall. I may have twisted several times. Goodness knows, I have bruises and scrapes everywhere. Why do you question that I was pushed?"

He straightened his handsome silk tie and stared at the ceiling, perhaps preparing some lie to pacify me. "Professor de Firenze's door was unlocked, and according to an aunt we contacted, cherished items are missing."

That was terrible news. "Valuable items?" I asked, dreading Jason's reaction to this news. "Perhaps someone burglarized the apartment before I was pushed down the stairs. That's it. They were escaping with the loot and, finding me on the stairs, pushed me down to keep their identity secret."

"Possibly, but there are only three keys to the apartment, one with the neighbor, which you were given; one taken to Avignon by the professor; and one in the hands of the aunt, who has had it for years. There was no sign of forced entry, which would have been difficult given the sturdy construction of the door. I think we must assume that the thief got the key from your handbag along with everything else you carried. Surely you do not think members of the faculty or their wives pushed you in order to rob you of money and credit cards and a colleague of family heirlooms."

"Family heirlooms?" I echoed weakly. He handed me a list of the missing items as described by the aunt—a Renaissance cross, gold inset with lapis; a necklace and earring set with pearls and rubies; an illuminated, medieval prayer book; a set of six engraved gold forks from the period of Catherine de Médicis, and ornate silver candlesticks from the seventeenth century, things that could never be replaced, even if we had the money to do so. "You must find out who stole them," I said frantically. "What will I say to her when I arrive in Avignon?"

"You are leaving Lyon?" asked the inspector. "The professor already knows of the theft, but are you able to travel? Surely, your physician—"

"I don't care what he says," I snapped. "I'm not going to miss Avignon."

"It is a delightful town," he agreed. "And the food— well, the food of Provence! Not as good as the food of Lyon, perhaps, but—"

"But you *will* keep investigating, won't you? Although I suppose the attacker will follow us." I blinked back tears.

"Do not be afraid, madam. I will call a colleague in Avignon and advise him of the situation so that they can be at your service." As he was writing down the name of this colleague, I was thinking that Jason and I would be more at risk in Avignon than here, where at least I knew the inspector.

Advising that I'd be better off to stay in Lyon, although he could not keep a guard at my door for longer than today, he left, and I managed to fit in another nap before the doctor finally arrived to peer into my eyes and tell me that I was doing well, and that perhaps my scrapes were not infected since they looked better. I didn't think they looked better. They didn't *feel* better, but I kept that to myself.

"I'm so pleased to hear that you think I've recovered because I have to leave tomorrow for Avignon."

"Madam," cried the doctor, "I did not mean to imply that you are ready to leave the hospital. We must continue the antibiotics and observe the progress of your head injury. How can you leave when you cannot yet stand?"

I assured him that I had been to the bathroom and the window several times.

"But that is dangerous. Are you not dizzy? What if you fall and hurt your head again? One head injury on top of another is very bad, and Avignon is an old town. The streets are not always easy walking, as are most streets here in our more modern Lyon. I must insist—"

"I'll be with friends. I'll have arms to support me." Although I had no assurance of that. Perhaps no one would want to sightsee with me. Catherine certainly wouldn't, not that she seemed the sightseeing type. "I can even get a cane if you insist. Just give me antibiotic pills, painkillers, and the name of an English-speaking doctor in Avignon, and I'll be on my way tomorrow."

"You will leave at your own risk. I cannot be responsible—"

"That's fine. If I have to sign papers, I can do that." The doctor threw up his hands and left my room.

When Jason returned from lunch, I told him my plans. "The doctor agreed?" he asked. I smiled. "Well, that's good news. I won't have to miss my paper," said my husband. "I'd better call Adrien to let him know."

"Yes, and you'll have to buy train tickets and pack our bags. You can bring the luggage, and we'll leave from here. You'll need to pick out something for me to wear. I doubt that the clothes I had on when I was brought in are wearable. And cosmetics. I'll need cosmetics." I could see that Jason was worrying about packing and paying for cabs.

However, he said, "I'll have to see about paying the bill. I wonder if they take Blue Cross Blue Shield."

"Doesn't France have socialized medicine? Since I was injured by a French criminal, we probably won't have to pay anything." That thought cheered my husband considerably, and he went off to get ready for departure. I went back to sleep.

Getting dressed the next morning was much more difficult than I anticipated because I was still dizzy; however, I had the whole train trip to Avignon to rest and drink in the scenery of Provence. The doctor never came to see me again, sulking probably because I hadn't followed his advice. I was given pills, the name of a doctor in Avignon, an ugly metal cane, and a lecture by the nurse, which, fortunately, Jason didn't hear because he was reloading our bags into a cab while I was wheeled down to the entrance. Also I had to sign some papers in French, probably absolving them if I came to grief.

Jason helped me from the wheelchair into the car, quite unaware of how much I needed that help, and then we were treated to a wild ride from a friendly cab driver to the Gare Part Deux, which had a delightful clock in front—a large clear plastic circle with red hands and gold balls at each hour position. I took a picture through the window.

Then the difficulties began. Jason could not handle all the luggage by himself, so I had to pull my bag while I clung desperately to his arm and he pulled his bag and hung both carry-ons from his shoulders. One of the carry-ons kept bumping my bruises. Rather than worry him, I clenched my teeth and kept my eyes wide open to prevent any telltale tears and groans, but I was so glad to sit down and mind the luggage while he went off to get a copy of the *Herald-Tribune* and find out our track number.

Then matters worsened as we resumed the bag dragging, amid crowds of travelers. My head began to ache abominably. Since Jason had to get the bags up into our train car by himself, he sent me ahead to secure seats. Climbing the narrow, high steps with a reeling head was dreadful, but once I got into the car, I could grab the seat handles as I staggered to the nearest open seat, which I fell into ahead of a mother and her child.

"*Excusez-moi,*" I said politely. I'd learned a few phrases, although not how to pronounce them. She gave me a furious look and dragged her whimpering child in the other direction.

Jason arrived about five minutes later, his forehead bedewed with perspiration. He was carrying the two computer cases, which are easier to steal than the large bags. He dumped those onto the seat beside me, which I had guarded vigilantly from people who wanted to sit there, and went back for his suitcase, which he then hefted onto the overhead rack with a grunt.

"Mine hasn't disappeared, has it?" I asked anxiously. That would really be the last straw. Three attempts on our lives, a whole department of chemists angry with us, and no clean clothes.

"I seriously doubt it," said Jason. "I could hardly get it onto the train. What thief would try to get it off? If I hadn't packed your bag myself, I'd have thought it was full of bricks."

"Do we have any water?" I asked, looking pathetic. "I need to take a pain pill."

Somewhat abashed, Jason said he'd see if he could buy a bottle. While he was gone, I worried that the train would leave without him. He had the tickets. However, he returned with water but not my bag. When I asked where it was, he said, not very pleasantly, that it would have to stay between the cars because there was no way he could lift it onto a rack.

I'd have worried about the bag all the way to Avignon if I hadn't fallen asleep as soon as I took the pain pills. Needless to say, I missed the lovely countryside of Provence. On the upside, my bag was still on the train when we arrived.

Avignon

"The most magical of all the provinces of France is Provence. Here the Latin civilization which is today the basis of the national culture took root earliest . . . You cannot live there long without becoming conscious of the vigorous pulse of the south. In comparison, Paris seems jaded."

Waverly Root, *The Food of France*

29
Surprise at the Hotel de l'Horlage

Jason

Carolyn slept so soundly that I began to worry, although it occurred to me that her pain medication might be the cause. Still, I decided to suggest that she spend the afternoon resting at the hotel so she'd be able to attend the reception at the Palace of the Popes.

Getting off the train at the *gare* in Avignon was almost as difficult as getting on at Lyon. I had to handle all the bags and carry the computer cases while Carolyn clung to the seat handles in the aisle and edged down to the platform, hanging on to the stair rails for dear life. Obviously she should have stayed in the hospital, which made me wonder if the doctor had actually released her. Whistles were blowing, conductors were calling out in French, and my wife was in a panic when I transferred the last bag to the platform.

In the terminal, she asked that I buy her a tourist picture book of Avignon. I doubt she really needed it so soon because she fell onto a bench, looking pale. She called after me to get water as well, which meant she wanted to wash down more pain pills. Obviously, I couldn't suggest taking public transportation to the hotel. In the taxi I eyed the meter while Carolyn exclaimed over one sight after another on the Rue de la Republique, ending with, "Look at that carousel!" It was a colorful and pretty attraction at the end of the Place de l'Horlage, which was lined with plane trees and sidewalk cafés shaded by colorful umbrellas that flapped in a stiff breeze.

Our hotel, down a side street, was a white building with red awnings and a very pleasant lady at the registration desk. I put my wife in a chair, took her passport, and signed us in.

"Professor, finally you are here!" I turned to find my graduate student, Mercedes Lizarreta, rushing toward me with arms outstretched. "Bonjour, *mon professeur*," she cried and kissed me on both cheeks. "Isn't France wonderful? I was so sorry to hear you were delayed in Lyon by an injury to your wife. Is she still in the hospital?"

I managed to extract myself from Mercedes's embrace—what was the girl thinking?—but not before Carolyn arrived and said, "Actually, I'm here, too. I don't believe we've met."

"Ah, señora, I am Mercedes, your husband's graduate student."

"Really? And I am Carolyn, your professor's wife. I didn't realize you were attending the conference." She shot me *the look*.

"Nor I you," said Mercedes. "What a pleasure to meet."

Carolyn did not look pleased. I should have mentioned that the girl was coming—at her own expense, of course. "Well, I'd better register for the conference." Under the circumstances, suggesting that my wife stay here would be a bad idea. "Carolyn, do you want to come with me? There's a reception tonight in an interesting venue, and then we'll find a good restaurant for dinner. Of course, if you want to rest this afternoon—"

Carolyn looked mutinous, but then sensibly decided that she'd unpack, rest, and choose a restaurant.

As my wife was waving a bellhop over, Mercedes said, "I'll walk over with you, Professor. Registration's in the Salle des Gardes."

"I can, no doubt, find it without help."

"Not easily. Finding rooms at the conference requires a map, even though it's within easy walking distance of our hotel. I don't mind going with you."

Because the bellhop was disappearing with the luggage, Carolyn had to follow, but she took the time to send me another *look*.

Carolyn

He never even mentioned that *she'd* be here. And at our hotel, lying in wait. Now she was going off somewhere with him, and I didn't even feel up to unpacking. I just wanted to fall into bed and wait for the pills to take effect, which I did as soon as I'd tipped the bellman with some amount of euros that I didn't even count. He looked pleased, which meant Jason wouldn't be, had he known. Too bad!

And she was gorgeous. Short—Jason would like that, being short himself. Large breasted—all men liked *that*! Slim otherwise, and here I was, worried about my weight, with all the temptations of Provençal cuisine ahead. And she had a pretty face and shiny black hair that she had evidently curled into ringlets. It bounced everywhere, and looked quite silly. How much time did she have to spend on that hairstyle? Too much for a graduate student, who should have been devoting every moment to study and research.

I glanced at the room, which was rather austere—two beds were pushed together and covered in white with an

iron bedstead behind and a peculiar brown wicker love seat
and chair to one side. Doors led to a cement-wall-enclosed
area open to the sky. It contained two canvas lawn chairs,
a small table, and no view. I closed my eyes, without further scrutiny, and went to sleep.

Jason

The papal palace was indeed difficult to navigate, a warren
of stone, rib-vaulted rooms, the reception area, or Salle des
Gardes, cathedral-like but with modern furniture and five
entrances into a wing for "Grand Dignitaries." Carolyn
would have loved it, as well as deploring the removal of
whatever had been in there before the furniture. We
chemists were doubtless not the guests envisioned by
whatever French pope built the place.

I registered Carolyn and myself with only a short wait
while Mercedes pointed out chemists to whom she had evidently introduced herself. No shrinking violet, my student. I rather wished she'd go away, but she chattered
about Avignon, thanking me repeatedly for the opportunity
to take her first trip to France, telling me that she had studied French language tapes on the flight from El Paso, even
greeting French professors on the organizing committee in
French.

"Bonsoir, Professor de Firenze," she cried. "My research director is here at last."

Catherine looked surprised to see me. "You have found
your wife?" she asked. "I have been told of the robbery, but
not—"

"Yes, yes," I agreed, dreading this conversation. "Your
neighbor found her at the bottom of the stairs and called an
ambulance. Carolyn was released from the hospital this
morning."

"I hope she did not suffer serious injury. I did advise her

to take care in my neighborhood, which has a mixed population due to city financing."

"Carolyn is terribly upset to hear that family heirlooms were taken when the thief stole your key from her purse."

"Well, my things were unique. The thief will find them hard to dispose of," she replied grimly. "At least, your wife survived the incident."

"Yes, she was lucky."

"Perhaps I, too, will be lucky. Ah, I see Adrien. I must have a word with him."

Catherine left me feeling responsible for her belongings. Surely, she wouldn't expect us to—

"Goodness," cried Mercedes, "I didn't realize that your wife was at fault for the stealing from Professor de Firenze's family treasures, which are so *precioso*. Perhaps American ladies do not realize—"

"My wife was a victim, too."

"Yes, of course. Would you like to see the Grand Audience Hall? It's immense. I think the first session will be there."

"It's very good of you, Mercedes, but I need to speak to Professor Laurent. You should make an effort to meet fellow graduate students. They will be your colleagues when you are finished with your education."

"Ah, but I like the professors. They know so much more."

"Even so," I replied and headed rapidly across the room toward Laurent. This was going to be a touchy situation. A headachy, possibly jealous wife, a student who might be harboring improper ideas about me, through no fault of mine, and a group of French men and women who were angry with Carolyn. I sighed and approached Laurent.

"We have been contacted by the police," he said. "They seem to think that someone in our department is intent on causing you harm. Perhaps you should remember that we are the ones who lost a colleague. Poor Robert. He is dead, and his lecture spot must be filled."

Now there was a questionable expression of grief, I thought, and changed the subject to my own assignment.

30

Albertine and Dog to the Rescue

Carolyn

I **woke up** without the headache. Maybe I was improving—physically. The surprise appearance of Mercedes had been a blow. Why hadn't Jason told me she'd be coming? It was bad enough having someone trying to kill you; having someone else trying to steal your husband was really too much. Well, Jason and I would enjoy a romantic dinner for two after the reception. Without Mercedes. I called the desk for advice on a restaurant, and Bridget said one of her favorites was L'Epicerie, on the square of the Saint Pierre church. "Is it very expensive?" I asked, keeping in mind that Jason would not be happy with a huge bill, no matter how romantic the evening.

"It's quite reasonable," Bridget replied, "and be sure to order the hors d'oeuvres platter. It's more than enough for two and wonderful."

I thanked her and picked up my book on Avignon, which was full of fascinating historical facts and marvelous pictures, even a picture of Saint Pierre—the church, not the saint. Then my telephone rang, Bridget announcing that Albertine was downstairs and wanted to come up. I agreed, since she might be the only female I knew who wasn't angry with me, now that her mother's illness had been identified as chicken pox, not syphilis.

Since I hadn't taken off the clothes I'd traveled in, I only had to comb my hair and refresh my lipstick. Of course, she'd probably be wearing something black and chic. *Ah, well,* I consoled myself, *we can't all be French women, and a good thing, too.*

Prepared to be hospitable, I drew back in dismay. She'd brought Charles de Gaulle. "You need not be afraid, Carolyn. Charles has received canine etiquette lessons and is a much more gentlemanly dog. Charles, say hello to Carolyn." The dog cocked his head to one side and held up his paw. "He wants to shake your hand," she explained.

Actually, he looked sort of cute, so I gave his paw a brief shake. When he neither launched himself at me, leaving bruises, nor licked my hand, I invited them in.

Albertine looked the room over and said, "An interesting décor."

"Rather monastic, don't you think?" I agreed.

"Except for the love seat. One would not find a wicker love seat in a monastery, although the upholstery on the cushions has a Franciscan look."

"We call that burlap," I replied. "Won't you sit down?" Wicker was the option, unless we went outside to the canvas sling chairs. Charles de Gaulle sniffed around the room, as if looking for a bomb, and then came over to sit in front of us. Perhaps he was waiting for another handshake, but I felt that one was enough.

"I have been thinking over the dangerous happenings since you arrived in France, and although I am quite sure that no one on our faculty is responsible, I do agree that you are being stacked."

"Stalked?" It was the first mistake I'd heard her make in English, and what a relief to find someone who really believed we were in danger. I wasn't sure that Inspector Roux and my own husband were convinced.

"Therefore, I take it upon myself, with the help of Charles, and because of the feminine bond we formed as we delivered Bianca's baby in Sorrento, to insure your safety. I shall stay with you except when you are in your room with your husband.

"No one will hurt you when you are accompanied by a friend and a large dog. Charles de Gaulle can be quite protective of those he loves, and he is fond of you. This will be a good strategy; you were alone when attacked in Lyon, but you will not be here."

"We can't keep Jason with us all the time," I pointed out. I was quite touched by Albertine's willingness to endanger herself to keep me company, although I felt that I had played the more difficult role in the delivery of a baby, something I hoped never to do again.

"Well, your husband will be either here with you or with hundreds of chemists at the Palais des Papes. No one would kill him there."

"The Palais des Papes?" I asked, confused.

"Yes, where the convention is being held."

"Jason didn't mention that. Does that mean I won't be able to see it?" I probably wouldn't have come if that were the case.

"Of course, you will see it. The congresses are held only in two wings, and we are sponsoring a tour for participants and their wives, to be led by an excellent historian from the university here in Avignon. It will be both delightful and informative.

"Now, Carolyn, we must push our heads together for reasoning and think who could have followed you and Jason to France with violent intent."

I didn't correct *push our heads together* or even giggle.

"I can't imagine why anyone would want to hurt us. For the most part, we lead very sedate lives."

"You are not thinking, Carolyn. There is a man in Italy who would wish to do you harm if he were not in prison."

"But he is in prison."

"I was just providing an example. Have you not done anything that would make some other violent person angry enough to attack you?"

I started to say no, but then hesitated. The cruise. The hijackers. At least one had been a terrorist, and terrorists have terrorist friends who are always eager to avenge them. Could Jason and I be under a death sentence by vengeful terrorists just because I had thwarted a plot to—

"You have a thought!" cried Albertine triumphantly. Charles de Gaulle, who seemed to understand what she was saying, opened his eyes and bared his teeth, as if ready to attack any terrorist who showed up.

I explained about my Mother's Day cruise, and Albertine nodded gloomily. "In France we have an Arab population. Not only do they commit terrorist acts but also they riot in the outskirts of Paris, which upsets my mother. So we must be on the lookout for Arabs. Have you seen any since you arrived?"

I remembered the crime-scene technician. Inspector Roux had said he was a French citizen, but of North African origin. Had he been sent to see if the poisoned pâté had killed us? How disappointing for him to discover that the victim had been an innocent Canadian of no interest. I'd call Inspector Roux, and I mentioned Bahari to Albertine.

"Ha!" she said. "Perhaps we are solving the mystery already. How terrible to think that our police force has been infiltrated. We must be vigilant, Carolyn."

If Albertine hadn't forced me to think about who, other than academics we knew in France, might be after us, I'd never have realized that Jason and I might be the target of terrorists.

31
Reconciliations and Strange Art

Jason

Albertine and Carolyn were to meet us at the Avignon City Hall for the wine-canapé-and-welcoming-speech-from-the-mayor reception. I hoped, for Carolyn's sake, that she was feeling better, didn't drink the wine, and found the building of historic interest. While walking into the Place de l'Horlage, past the brightly lit carousel, I heard my wife calling and spotted her riding sidesaddle on a fantastical creature and waving. Albertine, looking much less happy, rode but did not wave. Mercedes, who had tagged along with us, cried, "Oh, there are your wives, professors. Aren't they having fun? Seeing them makes me less worrisome about growing old."

By then the carousel had come to a halt, the music had stopped, and my wife tumbled off into my arms, laughing and saying, "So you think Jason and I are old, Mercedes? But then you are so young. Whew! That was fun, but a mistake. I'm dizzy."

I held Carolyn upright while she blinked and pressed both palms to her temples, and Albertine said, "From now on, Carolyn, you should listen to me. I am the most sensible."

"More sensible," said Carolyn. "More for two, most for more."

"You haven't been drinking, have you?" I asked.

She wrinkled her nose and replied, "No matter what Albertine thinks, I am an *amazingly* sensible woman. When one has a concussion, a bit of dizziness is normal, and who wouldn't want to ride on such a beautiful carousel?"

A professor from the Avignon university bowed to her and replied, "We in Avignon thank you, madam. We all agree that our carousel is the most irresistible to be found anywhere. If it were not for your concussion, I would be happy to accompany you on another ride."

"Give me a few days, and we'll do it. Oh, and Jason, I must tell you, Albertine has a brilliant idea about who is trying to kill us."

"Someone is trying to kill you?" cried Pierre, the Avignonnais, whom I found very irritating.

Albertine had missed this interchange because she was walking her dog back on a leash, while the carousel operator, with whom the dog had been left, glared. Pierre—I couldn't remember his last name, but who wanted to ride the carousel with Carolyn—took my wife's other arm, and we all proceeded toward the city hall. "Look at that," Carolyn exclaimed, "nineteenth century. Very rectangular and—ah—symmetrical, isn't it? Twenty identical windows, five on each side on each floor. Sort of Palladian.

"Unfortunately, they tore down the livree d'Albano, the 1326 home of Cardinal Pierre Colonna, but they did leave the big square tower with the machicolations for defense." She was peering at the tower behind the city hall. "Obviously they replaced the defensive part with the campanile and that spire with pinnacles. Can you see the clock and the figures on the little balcony? That's all fifteenth century. The square is named for the clock."

I dutifully looked up at the tower behind the offending

town hall. Pierre, the modern professor, not the late cardinal, said, "Madam, I have fallen in love. You know the history of our beautiful city. Professor, you are a fortunate man to have a wife so lovely and so interested in things of importance."

He was in love with my wife? I tried not to take it too seriously. Albertine remarked that Carolyn could be counted on to provide not only the history of places, but also the history of food, and Mercedes, if I heard correctly, muttered something about how boring that sounded and then asked me a question about a research problem. At that point we entered between the double-columned portico and through the rounded doors of the hall.

Albertine's dog pranced forward to nuzzle my wife's hand. "No, Charles de Gaulle," ordered his mistress, and he stopped, very different behavior from his shenanigans in Italy.

"Just scratch his head or ears, Carolyn, so he knows that you like him." Carolyn did that, and the dog shook himself with delight. "After the reception, we are going to a restaurant named L'Epicerie that Carolyn has chosen."

"An excellent choice!" exclaimed Pierre. "May I invite myself along?" Before my wife could answer, a small pug dog with a violet ribbon around its neck, bounced toward us, dragging along Sylvie Girard, and attacked Charles de Gaulle. Albertine snarled, her dog backed up in shock taking the pug with him, and Sylvie said firmly, "*Non*, Winston Churchill." Both dogs froze at the "*non*," although Charles de Gaulle by then had his teeth fastened to Winston Churchill's lavender bow, while Winston Churchill had his teeth in the fur on the poodle's ankle and shook his head instead of letting go.

My wife, who knows nothing about canines and has never shown any desire to have one, separated the dogs. First, she shook her finger at the poodle and tugged the ribbon from his mouth, after which she said, "*Bon*—ah—what's the French for dog?" Then she knelt by Winston Churchill and separated him from the poodle's ankle by speaking to him gently. He immediately rolled over on his stomach and wiggled his legs. To Sylvie Carolyn said, "I'd give him a scratch, but I'm afraid Charles de Gaulle would take offense."

"My dear dog has already taken offense," snapped Albertine, glaring at Sylvie. "Charles was attacked."

Sylvie shrugged. "Winnie is also in love with Carolyn, and he took offense because she was petting the ears of another dog. Tell me, Carolyn, are you going to report my dog to the police, and after I spent three days showing you around Lyon?"

"Oh, for goodness sake," said Carolyn, who was trying to get up and couldn't without help. "I had a concussion, I was in pain, and the inspector asked who had known I would be at Catherine's, so I told him. I didn't say you, or anyone else I know, attacked me. At the time, I could hardly put two words together, and my whole body is covered with scrapes and bruises. And let me give you some advice, Sylvie. I have learned over the years that if one doesn't want to do something, one shouldn't volunteer. You did."

Sylvie thought that over. "True, and I wanted to go, so I apologize."

"And I apologize—to everyone I may have mentioned to the inspector."

"I am happy to see that we are all now reconciled," said Jacques Laurent in his pompous way, "but I think that the mayor is about to speak."

The mayor was and spoke at length in French while waiters passed around champagne and small snacks. At least twenty people sidled over to my wife and whispered in her ear. After each visit, she made a mark on a tablet she carries. Then she whispered to Albertine, who nodded and slipped out of the hall, upon which her husband looked worried and asked me if Carolyn needed a doctor. The chairman frowned thunderously at everyone whose eye he could catch, but at last the mayor finished, and general conversation resumed. "May I ask what is going on?" Laurent demanded.

"So many people wish to join us at L'Epicerie that Albertine called the restaurant to ask how many they can accommodate."

"Twenty-two," said Albertine, cell phone in hand, "but only if we are willing to sit at tables outside on the terrace."

"Well, I'd love to go," said Mercedes, "unless, of course you don't want me." There was a bit of challenge in her voice, and I gritted my teeth. How did I, a perfectly innocent party, get into these messes?

"There are three more places," said Carolyn, and she marked across four vertical lines. "Now two." Two people immediately spoke up and were warned by my wife that everyone had to pay his or her bill, for which I shall always be thankful.

"Catherine," said Carolyn, spotting her in the group, "how can you ever forgive me for the things that were stolen from your apartment. I'm so sorry. Whoever pushed me downstairs and stole my purse, although I wasn't conscious during the theft—"

"Do not worry. I am equally sad for your injuries. I should never have allowed you to go by yourself. To show you are forgiven, let me take you to Villenueve Avignon. I lived there as a child and know it well. The sights will pique your interest in history. Tomorrow, perhaps. I can get away in the morning."

"That is so kind," said my wife. "I'd love to see the town across the river."

"Very good. My apartment, which was left to me by an

aunt, is very close to your hotel. I will come for you at nine."

"Has anyone noticed that peculiar exhibit?" asked Victoire Laurent. "What in the world is it supposed to be? I have always considered myself a lover of art, but *that* is most strange."

We all turned to stare at the exhibit, where white figures, perhaps made of plastic, looked as if sheets had been thrown over their heads; some had round, black circles for eyes; at least one sported a bow tie and a top hat; and on many, long squidlike tentacles undulated from their robes. The guesses were octopus, nuns, snowmen, and, from my wife, Casper the Friendly Ghost. Evidently Casper was not a character known in France, but Carolyn had a point. They did look like the cartoon character. But why would many Caspers, some with long tentacles, be displayed in the Avignon City Hall?

Carolyn was giggling and whispered to me, "Who is that painter who does cartoon characters and exhibits in famous museums? I can't remember his name. And I've never seen a cartoon *sculpture*."

32
On the Terrace

Carolyn

Those of us who were going to L'Epicerie straggled out and met at the carousel. Pierre, my admirer, offered to lead us. "Of course, I know where is my church," he said. It was a good thing he did. I doubt I'd ever have found the entrance, given the instructions I'd received from Bridget.

Albertine and her dog stayed close, and she whispered several times that I should keep alert for terrorists, as if I'd forgotten, but it was dark once we left the Place de l'Horlage and entered crooked, narrow streets with rough surfaces. Had there been a terrorist, I couldn't have spotted him. I was lucky to get to the restaurant without falling.

At one point I found myself beside Catherine's student, Martin. He would have moved away from me if I hadn't caught his arm. Jason had told me about his call and his impression that I disliked homosexuals. "Martin," I whispered, "one of the nicest men I ever met was homosexual." I was holding on to Martin's arm and could feel the muscles tense. "He was a Stanford graduate, a funny and delightful man, and a private detective in San Francisco. I have no prejudices against gays, and I meant nothing when I mentioned William Rufus. I didn't know you were gay, and furthermore, I don't care, nor do I think other people should. First, it's none of their business, and second, it's obviously a perfectly natural thing, given that one tenth of the population—"

"But other people do care," he interrupted. "Even my own professor says unpleasant things about—"

"Does she know about you?"

"No."

"Then she won't hear anything from me," I assured him. "I'm surprised at her. She's a scientist. And she seems nice enough in most ways. She even offered to show me Villenueve Avignon. Still, you needn't worry that I'll—"

"You are very kind, madam," he replied. "I apologize for my reaction at the dinner party. Perhaps I am oversensitive."

Pierre interrupted the conversation by announcing our arrival. Albertine and I went to find the lady in charge, who had arranged two long tables on the terrace and put lamps out at intervals. We talked about the menu in the colorful, crowded interior, and then Albertine and I went outside, to find only two seats left at either end of one table, which seemed to hold all the younger people. At the other table, my husband was seated at the head with Mercedes to his right. Victoire, who might well be looking for another lover or at least a brief fling since Robert died, sat at Jason's left.

I bit my lip, raised my chin, and headed for the other table, where Pierre was calling, "Carolyn, you are our hostess. Sit here." Martin towered across from Pierre, and he was smiling at me, as if I were his best friend. Albertine and Charles de Gaulle took the other end, but she stopped to whisper in my ear that she would send the dog down at intervals if she saw any suspicious persons.

Having heard, Pierre asked what suspicious persons could be found here by such a fine church. I murmured,

"Later," then tapped my wineglass, which was not yet filled, and suggested that we first order enough of L'Epicerie's bountiful hors d'oeuvres platters, which I had seen inside, to feed us all. After that, if still hungry, we could order separately, but if we were happy with our meal, we could split the bill evenly and save our waitress the trouble of dividing the costs. The young people agreed, and the waitress, when my suggestion was translated, kissed me on the cheek. At the other table they discussed, argued, and ordered different things, so we were served with wine and six platters before they got a bite to eat.

As sad as I felt, we were very merry, pouring and drinking the house wine, which came in pretty jugs, and transferring from the large platters to our small plates so many delights. There was pâté on toast, which I ate, hoping no terrorist had gained access to the kitchen, and eggplant puree, cheese with a rosemary flavor, and sweet marinated artichokes and peppers, a tapenade so delicious I couldn't believe it, not to mention a salty, sun-dried tomato tart, and delicious goat cheese. I hadn't had a pain pill since noon and hadn't drunk the champagne at the reception, so I drank the red wine and didn't fall off my chair, and we all made gluttons of ourselves and found, in good time, another six plates delivered to our table.

Pierre asked again why I thought suspicious persons might be lurking in the Place Saint-Pierre, so I told him about the beautiful pâté that killed a professor who came to welcome us. "The police think it was poisoned with puffer-fish toxin, but I couldn't find a single restaurant in Lyon that serves fugu, so perhaps their medical examiner was wrong. Have you heard of fugu?" The question went around the table, but only one person had, and he hadn't seen it in Lyon.

"What was the toxin? I don't know fish toxins," said Pierre.

"In English it's called tetrodotoxin," I replied. "And it's found in other fish and even in frogs and newts; the California newt, for instance, killed someone, although why anyone would eat a newt I can't imagine."

"What is this newt?" asked a young man from Slovenia.

"Something nasty the witches in Shakespeare's *Macbeth* put in their pots."

"Ah, *Macbeth*. I know *Macbeth*," said the young man, who had a broad forehead, mussed hair, and an interesting accent.

Martin was staring at me and asked for the name of the toxin again, so I told him. "Do you know it?" I asked. "It's very—well—toxic," and I giggled as Pierre poured me a third glass of wine.

"And now you eat the pâté of Avignon? You are not only beautiful, but brave. I am doubly in love," said Pierre, so flirtatiously that I had to laugh.

"And then," I said dramatically, holding my goblet up to the lamplight to admire the dark red of my wine. "This is not Beaujolais!" I exclaimed, because I don't like Beaujolais, especially the new variety. "And then someone in a black car tried to run down my husband, and did hit a dog."

"That is so sad," said Albertine. "This must be a terrible person. Everyone keep eyes open for this terrible person, who runs down dogs and poisons the fine pâté of Lyon."

I think Albertine had had more wine than I, or perhaps less food. "And then, on the stairway to an apartment in Old Lyon, someone pushed me backward, and I awoke in a hospital."

"Charles," said Albertine, "go down the table to protect Carolyn."

"Charles is our watchdog," I explained, as he trotted over to me and laid his head in my lap. What a sweet dog. "Now we must order dessert." I could see that people at the other table were casting glances at us when my young friends cheered and suggested that I choose one. Being a lover of coffee and chocolate, I chose a dessert called Café Glace with Whiskey. It took the restaurant quite a while to make so many of the same dessert, but it was lovely, as everyone agreed—coffee ice cream with crunchy chocolate bits, mint leaves, and whiskey.

We entertained ourselves, while waiting, by telling jokes and choosing the best raconteurs to receive the remaining hors d'oeuvres. My joke didn't win a prize, but the Slovenian told a hilarious communist political joke and won the last marinated sweet pepper. Albertine won a bite of goat cheese for a very risqué joke, although I was surprised she knew one. I know some. I just don't tell them. The luckiest person, a young docent from Germany, won the sun-dried tomato tart, and a student from St. Petersburg won the last bit of pâté.

Then the desserts came with strong coffee, of which I took only a sip because I wanted to sleep well tonight and feel well tomorrow for my trip to Villenueve-les-Avignon. Martin said, considering the fact that I was recovering from a concussion, perhaps I shouldn't go, there being long falls from the area of the fort.

He was sweet to worry about me, but I refused to miss the excursion. "And Charles de Gaulle and I will be along to watch over Carolyn," called Albertine from her end of the table. When the dog heard his name, he lifted his head from my lap and trotted back to his mistress.

At the other table they were still eating their entrées, so my young people insisted that I should be home in bed, getting my rest after my dangerous experiences in Lyon. They offered to escort me home. *Fine*, I thought, still angry that Jason was sitting with two sexually aggressive women and hadn't even saved a seat for me. Our waitress brought the bill, which sounded terribly expensive, but not bad at all when we divided it by twelve. I told her that my husband, the man with the beard at the end of the other table, would have to pay my share because he had the only credit card. Everyone, including the waitress, thought it a shame I didn't have my own card.

I had ten euros in my handbag, which I had insisted that Jason give me, so I put five into the empty ashtray, and the others contributed the usual change to the pot. Then we all rose, and our happy waitress said, "Madam, you must come again." With some of the group beginning to sing, we left.

"Carolyn, where are you going?" Jason shouted after me.

"My friends are seeing me to the hotel," I called back. As there were only two females in the group, they walked Albertine to her hotel first—it was much fancier than ours—and then me to mine, where they serenaded me as I wobbled into the hotel on Pierre's arm. Bridget whipped my key out and took me to my room.

What lovely people the French are, although of course Bridget was from Ireland, but I remember thinking the Irish must be lovely, too. After all, they made whiskey, and there had been whiskey on my dessert. Tomorrow, I reminded myself, I'd return to skipping dessert.

"Good night, madam," said Bridget and left me to fall, within minutes, into a deep sleep. I never heard Jason come in, and I ignored him when he spoke to me. Why wake up for a man who hadn't even saved me a seat at dinner?

Olives and olive oil are staples of Provençal food and of all those lands that border the Mediterranean. Whiskey is not, but the locals do love coffee in all its incarnations. Who doesn't? To begin and end a meal, here are two delicious recipes.

Tapenade

- In a food processor, chop *2 cups pitted black olives, 3 tablespoons rinsed capers, 1 crushed clove garlic, and 6 anchovies.*

- Add *2 teaspoons Dijon mustard, 1 tablespoon lemon juice, 1 teaspoon chopped thyme, 1 tablespoon chopped parsley,* and process to a coarse paste.

- Can be kept in the refrigerator covered for three days.

- Serve with bread or toast or as a dip for raw vegetable pieces.

Café Glace with Whiskey

- Soften mocha almond fudge or other coffee ice cream, drizzle a sweet whiskey on each serving, and decorate with mint leaves.

Carolyn Blue,
"Have Fork, Will Travel,"
Raleigh Herald

33

A Morning *Chat*

Jason

Carolyn didn't wake up when I got in, but she certainly did in the morning. I'd barely gotten into my running clothes when she sat up and said, "Where are you going?"

"For a run," I replied, sitting down to lace my shoes.

"Then meet me downstairs for breakfast."

I wonder if I looked as shocked as I felt. "They charge twelve euros for breakfast here. I can pick up coffee and a roll for nothing at the meeting."

"Oh yes, the meeting. In the Palais des Papes," said my wife, flinging back the covers. "I find it hard to believe that you never mentioned the actual *meeting* was at the palace. I'd have been very excited to hear that. Were you afraid I'd tell you more than you wanted to know about the *palais*?"

"Carolyn, I gave you the brochure. It mentioned the venue, which, frankly, is rather strange. It's like attending a scientific conference in a cathedral. I keep expecting some cardinal to show up during a paper and excommunicate the speaker."

"Very funny, but I think you're safe, Jason. You're not Catholic. Now, Mercedes probably is. Maybe he'll excommunicate her. And why would you think I'd look at anything in that brochure but the social events? I saw that the banquet would be held in the Grand Tinel, but I never realized—"

"Well, we can talk about the papal palace at dinner. I'll describe whatever rooms I see in the conference wings, but right now I really—"

"—need to explain to me why you didn't save me a seat at dinner last night. When Albertine and I got to the terrace, there you were with the two most sexually rapacious women in Avignon, and all the rest of the seats at your table were filled."

"*Sexually rapacious?* The chairman's wife was beside me."

"Yes, she was the mistress of your friend Robert. Now she's probably looking for a new lover. And Mercedes, who can't seem to keep her hands off you."

"Carolyn, I'm old enough to be her father."

"Then act like one. Her behavior is embarrassing, and you're not doing a thing to stop it, which makes me think—"

"What am I supposed to do?" I demanded. "I've never encouraged Mercedes."

"For starters, you could have said, 'I'm saving this seat for my wife.' "

"But I was talking to Victoire when Mercedes sat down. I couldn't very well tell one of them to find another seat. Really, Carolyn, you're overreacting, and I resent the implication—"

"And I resent the way it looks when that girl is always hanging on your arm, and making snide remarks to me."

"Well, for goodness sake, you seemed to be having a grand time yourself last night. Were you drinking? Surely the doctor told you not to. And then you walked off with all those young men." By then I was quite irritated. "You might consider how *that* looked."

"I had three glasses of wine, Jason. I'd had no pain pills since morning. And I was tired by the time we finished eating; I wanted to go home. Was I supposed to walk back in the dark by myself while you were finishing your entrée and flirting with your Latin ladies?"

"Look, Carolyn, you're being—"

"—a normal wife, who doesn't like to see her husband chasing after a student. Furthermore, you never let me tell you what Albertine and I think all the these attacks are about, or do you still think I just fell down those stairs?"

"I give up. What's going on?"

"Terrorists. I was the person primarily responsible for taking that boat back. And one of those men who are now in jail was a terrorist. He probably sent a fellow conspirator after us."

"But that's crazy. You think there's a—"

"Haven't you been following the news? Islamic people are burning cars and buildings on the outskirts of Paris—near the Saint-Denis Cathedral. Saint Denis is the patron saint of Paris—or is it France?—in case you don't remember. It makes me wonder if that Moroccan crime-scene person isn't a conspirator. He probably got himself assigned to our case to be sure that one or both of us died from the pâté, and when we didn't, he tried to run you down, and when that failed, he lay in wait and pushed me down the stairs. I called the inspector last night to tell him."

"And what did he say?" I asked sarcastically, glancing at my watch and then wishing that I hadn't asked. I'd be lucky to have enough time for half a mile if my wife kept talking.

"He said the fellow had been on the force for seven years. But of course, terrorists take those courses in Pakistan and then stay undercover for years in western countries until they're given an assignment.

"So you just go off for your run, Jason. Don't worry

about me. If I'm shot at Fort Andre or pushed down a well when Catherine and I visit Villenueve-les-Avignon this morning, maybe I'll be lucky again and only end up in the hospital."

"Then don't go," I retorted. "And Carolyn, I am not interested in Mercedes in any way except scientifically. She's an excellent student."

"I'm so happy to hear it. Maybe you should tell her that you're only attracted to her mind. I have a feeling she wouldn't believe me if I told her."

"I'm going now, Carolyn. I'll call you later, and we can make plans." As I left the room, Carolyn said, "Plans for the three of us? Or the four of us? Maybe we should invite Jacques Laurent and *his* girlfriend, the delightful Mademoiselle Zoe Thomas."

I stopped and turned around. "I can't believe Laurent is having an affair with that well-rounded, iron-willed secretary? Where do you hear these things?"

"They're common knowledge. Now all we need is another young man for Victoire and one for me. Then we'll all be taken care of."

"There's always Pierre," I snapped. "He declared his love at the city hall and probably several times at your table last night." With that, I left and slammed the door. *Rioting in Paris? Could that be right?*

34

A Twenty-four Euro Breakfast

Carolyn

I was in tears when Jason slammed the door, indifferent to my concerns and angry that I'd held him up. Why couldn't he understand that Mercedes's obvious infatuation, whether or not he returned it, was embarrassing to me? And he just brushed off the idea that terrorists might be after us. What was so unbelievable about that? They always retaliate. Look what had gone on for decades in the Middle East.

Before I could have a good cry, the telephone rang—Albertine calling to ask when Catherine planned to pick me up, so she and Charles de Gaulle could to join us. At least, someone cared what happened to me. I wiped my eyes and invited her to breakfast. That would cost twenty-four euros, which I'd put on the room bill since Jason had left before I could ask for his credit card. What was I supposed to do if we went across the Rhône by bus or had lunch after our trip?

Albertine accepted, so I dressed and went downstairs. We walked around the corner to the breakfast area and the row of tables with large windows looking out on the street. Once we had our food, Albertine mentioned "that young woman who seems to adore your husband." I mumbled that she was just a graduate student. "Then you should make sure she stays away from him on social occasions. She should have been at the young ones' table, and you and I with the notable professors."

I agreed, feeling morose.

"Well, I must think what to do, Carolyn. Perhaps you are naïve about these things, but you should realize that your husband is reaching a dangerous age. He needs to be protected from himself. I watch Adrien closely and have defended him and myself for at least ten years."

"Tell me, Albertine, why do so many Frenchwomen wear black?" I asked to change the course of an embarrassing subject. Albertine had on a handsome black suit with white trim, not to mention shoes quite unsuited for sightseeing.

"Black is chic," she replied, "but different Frenchwomen wear it for different reasons. I favor it because I look good in black, which compliments my complexion and hair. Victoire wears black because she wishes to look as thin as possible, although she looks skeletal in any color, while Catherine wears black because she is a widow."

"She's still in mourning?"

"Her husband died years ago, so she should have given up mourning clothes by now, but he killed himself. He was much older, and she was wildly in love with him, a student of his before they married. Unfortunately, she failed to notice that he was given to fits of depression. Why would he kill himself when he had her? she thought, so she blamed his death on criticism of his research, but her husband had been falling into melancholy long before that.

"Adrien says it was not so terrible a matter, the paper. All scientists make a mistake or two, which is pointed out in the literature. The offender then writes a courteous letter to the critic, a retraction to the journal, and that's the end of it. But Catherine wouldn't be consoled. After his death, she sold their home and bought that apartment. Perhaps she wanted to die, too, but not to kill herself, being a Catholic. Since then she no longer socializes. She spends all her time doing research and driving her poor students to despair. A woman her age should have remarried, or at least taken a lover. Her conduct is unhealthy."

"But it's sad, isn't it?" I said. I'd have to be extra nice to her. No wonder she had seemed standoffish when we first met.

The waitress told us that a lady was waiting for us in the lobby, so we finished our coffee and left to meet Catherine, who seemed quite surprised to see Albertine, or maybe she was surprised to see the dog. "I didn't know you were coming, Albertine. We will be crowded in my car."

Oh good! She had a car. I wouldn't have to use any money for bus fare, and I could always claim that I wasn't hungry if we went out to lunch. Of course, I'd be sure to mention to Jason tonight that I'd gone hungry. Catherine decided I should sit in front with her so that she could tell me about Villeneuve before we got there.

The ride was quite unusual. For one thing, she took shortcuts through streets that had posts coming up out of the pavement to block cars. At the first one, she clicked a gadget, and the posts retreated into the roadway. "That's Catherine's apartment," said Albertine, pointing to a gate through which I could see banks of squares that were actually apartments with balconies. Then the complex was gone, and we approached another street with posts.

"You'll have to get out and push or jump on that post, Carolyn," said our driver. "They'll all go down when you push down the first." Reluctantly, I approached a post, but pushing didn't accomplish anything. I had to climb onto it before it retreated under my weight, and then I more or less fell off. What if I'd hit my head again? After that we left the posted streets and headed for the bridge.

Catherine told me that Villeneuve-les-Avignon, which was on the right bank of the Rhône facing the papal city, had been occupied since the fifth century when the hermit, Saint Casarie, lived there. "In the tenth century a Benedictine monastery was founded on his site and named the Abbey of St. Andre, around which quarrymen and stonemasons formed a small town. Avignon ruled the town across the river until Louis VIII—"

"He's the one who besieged Avignon for three months because of its heretics and finally starved them into giving up," I exclaimed. "I hadn't realized until yesterday that Avignon was one of the places attacked by the crusade against the Albigensian Heresy."

"Yes," said Catherine, obviously resenting my interruption. "St. Andre then made a treaty with the king and later with Philippe le Bel, who built the tower at the end of Pont St. Benezet. In the fourteenth century, the bridge ran all the way across the Rhône. Then in the fifteenth century, when the papacy was moved to Avignon, the new town grew bigger with the palaces of rich men and cardinals who wanted to escape the filth and crime of Avignon, brought on by all the people who came to profit from the papal court. The fort and defensive walls were built by the kings of France as a barrier against the power of the church across the river."

Catherine recited these facts without much interest, which surprised me because it was she who had suggested the trip. She finished by saying that we would drive up Mount Andaon to see Fort St. Andre, and then back down to visit the Church of Notre-Dame, the museum, and the Monastery La Chartreuse.

What a tour it was! We walked at a tremendous pace through the monastery church, around the huge crenellated

walls, in and out of a funny old chapel, and up and down
rough paths cut through deep grass. I could hardly keep up,
but then both women had longer legs than I, although I
don't think Albertine was in any better shape, and she was
older and wearing heels. Charles de Gaulle was in seventh
heaven. The weather had turned cold, overcast, and windy,
but I was perspiring by the time we got to a group of huge,
round towers that had once guarded the only entrance to
the fort.

"I've saved the best for last, as you Americans say,"
Catherine remarked. "The view from the top is exquisite."

"We're going to climb up there?" Albertine was not
happy.

"You and the dog can rest," said Catherine, "but Car-
olyn would never forgive herself if she missed this view.
What could I say? Breathless and tired, I started up after
Catherine, who climbed stairs like a mountain goat.

"I'm following," called Albertine. When I glanced back,
Charles de Gaulle seemed the most eager of us all. He
strained at his leash. Then I lost sight of them as I puffed
upward. By the time we reached the top, I was dizzy, but
Catherine took my arm and led me across the open space
toward a lower crenellation around the edge of the tower.
Looking down made me twice as dizzy.

"Look," said Catherine, nudging me forward. "Isn't it
wonderful?"

"Wonderful," I echoed, wishing her hand was still on
my arm. No matter how wonderful the view, I intended to
back up before I fell over, and I nearly did. I heard Charles
de Gaulle give a deep-throated woof, his toenails scrab-
bling across the stones, and then a thump and a shriek from
Catherine. When I turned, she was on the pavement, the
dog standing over her.

I hurried toward Catherine as Albertine came into view.
"He got away from me," she gasped. Catherine tried to

give the dog a shove, and he shoved back until his front paws were planted on her midriff. "Charles, what do you think you're doing?" Albertine called. "Off! *Non!*" She used the last of her strength to reach us. The dog didn't move until she arrived and dragged him away. Catherine, meanwhile, shouted, probably curses, into his face.

"I can't imagine what got into him," said Albertine. "He's supposed to be protecting Carolyn, not knocking down members of the faculty. "Shame on you, Charles! Can't you tell an academic from a terrorist?"

Catherine staggered upright, not appeased in the least. "Look at my outfit! I can't go to the conference in torn, dusty clothes. Since I'll have to go home and change, this will be the end of our tour." And she strode off toward the stairs.

Albertine and I took our time because we weren't up to anything else. "I don't like standing on top of towers," I said. "It's scary."

35
ATM Shopping

Jason

While I **was** eating with colleagues in the Galerie du Cloitre, a long, narrow area with arched windows, Albertine Guillot and my wife marched in. "Jason, you forgot to leave me money or a credit card," said Carolyn.

"I shared our euros yesterday," I replied and made introductions.

"Well, I don't even have enough for lunch, and we're going shopping."

Much to my chagrin, several of my colleagues repressed chuckles. "My credit card's in my name, Carolyn, but I have some cash."

Albertine eyed me as if I were an abusive husband. "I'll take your ATM card," said my wife. "We have the same PIN." Beaten but worried, I complied. "We're going to Hiely Lucullus tonight with the Guillots," she announced and left with my card.

Albertine smirked and added, "Hiely is somewhat expensive, but it has wonderful food. Adrien and I will come by at eight." Then she followed Carolyn, leaving me to worry about what the shopping expedition and the dinner were going to cost me. Because my lecture was scheduled for that afternoon in the Herses Notre Dame, which held 230 people, I needed to put financial matters out of my mind. Unfortunately, I was also troubled because Carolyn had noted Mercedes's presence at the table. The girl had plopped herself down uninvited, but I knew Carolyn was taking it amiss.

Carolyn

Albertine chose our lunch venue, Venaissin on Place de l'Horlage, and she wanted to sit outside. It hadn't warmed up at all, but they had heaters, the chairs were comfy and padded, and we could look out at the beautiful square. I had a lovely Provençal vegetable soup with *pistou*, and Albertine had Croque Monsieur, over which she outlined her plan to wean my husband away from his student.

"She was at his table again, which is not proper. Of course, she cannot join us tonight, but tomorrow is the tour of the palais and, in the evening, the banquet. No doubt she will attend both. Therefore, we are going shopping to buy clothes that will divert his attention from her to you."

"I really shouldn't spend too much," I murmured, breaking off a piece of French bread.

"Indeed you should. A beautiful dress and elegant shoes. A man who is tempted to stray must pay the price that will bring him to a proper appreciation of his wife."

"What do you mean by elegant shoes?" I asked suspiciously.

"High heels. Why do you favor such boring shoes? When we have chosen your outfit for the banquet, you will be the most beautiful woman in the hall. Your husband will not be able to look away from you."

That sounded good, but I did mention that high heels hurt my feet and made me taller than Jason, which he wouldn't like.

"Sometimes pain must be endured for the sake of fashion, and your husband will learn to tolerate your height. Jacques has adjusted to Victoire's."

"But they both have lovers," I protested. I didn't want to attract a lover. I wanted my husband back. However, Albertine was determined. She paid our bill, which was high, although we were only eating lunch. Then we found an ATM, and I reimbursed her while getting cash for myself. Flush for shopping, we went off to a street with no cars and many lovely shops.

Of course, she insisted that I take the black dress, which was beautiful but quite revealing. If the weather didn't warm up, I'd freeze at the banquet. How could they adequately heat a huge hall with high vaulted ceilings? The skirt was long and split in front, but not long enough to cover my ankles, which meant, according to Albertine, I had to have shoes that flattered said ankles. Soon I was wobbling around in spike-heeled, satin sandals. My ankles did look good, but the shoes hurt dreadfully.

I hadn't worn heels since college, much less heels this high. When I complained, Albertine said, "Get used to them. Practice in your room. I do hope you have something dashing to wear tonight. Something that will go with those shoes. They are *très chic*."

"If I wear them tonight, I'll be crippled by tomorrow," I groaned. "And what if I fall down?"

"One must take chances and make sacrifices for love," said Albertine, and told the saleslady to wrap up the purchases and include a pair of sheer black hose. When I saw the bill, I had to go back to the ATM for more money. At least Jason wouldn't realize what I'd spent until after we flew home.

On the other hand, if the terrorist came after me tonight or tomorrow night while I was wearing the heels, I'd have no chance to escape. My only comfort was the thought that a banquet involved a lot of sitting. And I'd be sitting at dinner tonight, but I certainly hoped Hiely Lucullus was close to the hotel. "Are you picking us up in your car tonight?" I asked hopefully.

"It's not that far," said Albertine, shocked that I'd even ask. Well, she wouldn't think so. She was the woman who'd trudged all over the fort and up into the tower wearing heels.

I was so glad to get into my nice, comfy flats and return to the hotel, where I lay down and put my feet up on Jason's pillow. Of course, I should have been out exploring Avignon, but I didn't even want to put on those miserable but flattering heels and start practicing. What I wanted to do was go to sleep, and I did. I'd practice later.

Pistou is the pesto of Southern France and used to flavor soup as well as other Provençal dishes. Its most powerful ingredient, garlic, provides a wealth of stories and comments. Horace thought it repulsed the ladies, but Henry IV of France was reputed to have been baptized with a clove of garlic, to have eaten it often, which made him not only a famous lover whose affairs confirmed its reputation as an aphrodisiac but also a man with very strong breath.

Alexandre Dumas claimed that the air of Provence was healthful because it smelled of garlic, and in Marseilles in the eighteenth century, garlic soaked in vinegar and then used to impregnate a pad through which one breathed was believed to fend off plague.

However the priestesses of Cybele in Rome allowed no one with garlic breath to enter their temple, and King Alfonso of Castile in the fourteenth century barred knights with garlic or onion breath from entering his court or talking to his courtiers for four weeks after the offense.

Provençal Vegetable Soup with Pistou

- Soak *1½ cups of dried navy beans (or cannelloni or flageolet beans)* in cold water overnight, drain, put in saucepan, cover with cold water, set to boiling, lower heat, and simmer 1 hour or until tender. Drain well. Set aside.

- Make *pistou* by putting *6 garlic cloves, 1⅓ cups basil leaves,* and *1 cup grated Parmesan* into food processor and running until finely mashed. Then add *¾ cup olive oil* slowly while running motor to mix thoroughly. Cover with plastic wrap and set aside.

- Heat *3 tablespoons olive oil.* Add the *white and tender green parts of 2 medium leeks cut into thin rings, 1 finely chopped onion,* and *5 fat, fresh cloves garlic, peeled and quartered lengthwise.* Cook over low heat until softened but not browned.

- Add *1 chopped celety stalk, 3 diced carrots,* and a *bouquet garni of several fresh bay leaves, sprigs of parsley and thyme tied with kitchen twine.* Cook, stirring occasionally, 10 minutes.

- Add *4 diced potatoes, ¼ pound small, chopped green beans, 2 cups chicken stock,* and *7 cups water,* and simmer 10 minutes.

- Peel and chop fine *3 tomatoes,* discarding core, dice *4 zucchini* and add with white beans, *1½ cups vermicelli* snapped into pieces, and *1 cup fresh peas.* If using frozen peas, add them at last minute. Cook 10 minutes. Season to taste.

- Serve with half *pistou* on top, divided between four soup dishes. In separate dishes serve the other half *pistou, ½ cup each freshly grated Parmigiano-Reggiano* and *imported Gruyère.* These can be stirred into soup as desired by diners.

Carolyn Blue,
"Have Fork, Will Travel,"
Fresno Clarion

36
Haute Cuisine Provençal

Jason

My talk went well—good attendance, interesting questions, and afterward, congratulations from colleagues, including Mercedes, who was overly enthusiastic. My argument with Carolyn that morning had made me uneasy around the girl, hardly an auspicious situation for research collaborators. Then when Adrien mentioned our evening at Hiely Lucullus, Mercedes invited herself along. Patting her on the shoulder in an avuncular way, Adrien said that this outing was for her elders, but he had a graduate student who longed to meet her. He actually led her over to a young man, who looked quite happy to receive the introduction. Maybe they'd fall in love and relieve me of a troublesome situation.

When Adrien returned, he expressed surprise, given the probability of parking problems, at Albertine's insistence on taking their car to Hiely Lucullus. It occurred to me that the idea might have been my wife's. She isn't an enthusiastic walker, even if there is some place of historical interest within walking distance. I'd boarded many a bus, tram, and train while traveling with Carolyn, when left to my own devices I'd have preferred to walk.

The talks ran late because we would be losing the afternoon to the palais tour the next day. Therefore, it was seven-thirty when I got home, just enough time to take a shower and dress for what I assumed would be a fancy and expensive evening. Carolyn didn't renew our argument, for which I was very thankful, and she looked quite lovely in a dress the color of the Mediterranean on a sunny day—why did French women always dress as if they were in mourning?

At any rate, we climbed into the Guillots' black car—good heavens, what if Carolyn noticed the color and again accused them of returning to Avignon to run me down? No one had mentioned that Hiely Lucullus was on the second floor of the building, and we hadn't thought to look upstairs, so we lost time driving around, after which locating a parking place took more time, and it was distant from the restaurant. Both Guillots were short-tempered by then, as was the maitre d' because we were late for our reservation.

After that, things went more smoothly, although the prices were, as I had feared, high. Still, the food was good, and Adrien and I had a stimulating conversation about a paper we'd heard later that afternoon.

Carolyn

Albertine had looked grim when she saw that I wasn't wearing the high heels, but my feet still hurt from the practice session. Then Adrien grumbled all the way to the restaurant, and she hissed, "If you were not going to take my advice, you might have told me before I offended my husband by insisting that we drive."

I did my best to settle that problem by saying to Adrien, while we were waiting to be shown to our table, "It was so kind of you to drive. I must admit that I'm still feeling wobbly after my concussion, and I do appreciate your thoughtfulness."

I gave him my sweetest smile—if Jason wanted to flirt with other people, why shouldn't I?—and Adrien responded that I wasn't to worry in the least; he was glad to save me from excessive walking, no matter how ridiculous the parking situation in Avignon. Evidently I had appeased him, because he suggested driving us to the banquet the next night. What a relief that was! I could please Albertine by wearing those shoes and not have to walk very far in them because her husband was so chivalrous.

And the restaurant was beautiful, simple, and elegant, all white and gold with drapes spanning windows that overlooked the Rue de l'Republique. I was enchanted with both the place and the food.

"I still don't know what to think about Charles knocking Catherine down this morning," said Albertine, studying the menu and deciding on hen with peaches, which she said was a Provençal favorite.

"*Mon dieu!*" exclaimed her husband. "The wretched dog must be in love again. That is just what he did to Carolyn the first time he saw her. I thought he was over falling in love with women. Maybe we should have him—what is the English?—deprived of manhood, or doghood."

"What a terrible idea! Have you any idea, Adrien, what fees Charles commands when he makes puppies? And a dog of his excellent lineage has a duty to reproduce."

"The money is welcome, but his behavior is deplorable when he's on a breeding mission." Adrien then recommended cod fish with berries.

Was it that nasty salt cod so popular in Southern France and Catalonia? I didn't take his suggestion, at which he frowned. Men always think you should do what they want. Having been reminded that the dog was supposed to protect me that morning, not irritate Catherine, I glanced around the restaurant, just in case there was a terrorist lurking at some secluded table, not that I imagined terrorists came to restaurants like this.

At least four busboys looked somewhat Arabic to me, so I leaned over to tell Albertine, and she muttered that she would have brought Charles, except that Adrien had objected. "Let us hope," she murmured back, "that all the terrorists are busy torching cars in St. Denis and attacking cruise ships off the coast of Somalia."

"I think the cruise ship incident was due to pirates," said Adrien. "May I suggest that we order Châteauneuf du Pape, 2002, Blanc de Blanc?" Everyone agreed.

"If you've been attacked by pirates," I said to Adrien, "you'd see very little difference between them and terrorists. And surely the French government will control the rioters before they move out of their own districts. I think I'll have *this* and *this*," I announced, pointing to items on the menu. They turned out to be a sort of ratatouille cake on red salad leaves, followed by a tender white fish in a citron sauce.

"Do you even know what you're ordering, Carolyn?" Albertine asked, laughing.

"I feel adventurous," I replied, and my choices *were* tasty. Jason picked out a salmon salad and veal liver in a balsamic reduction. His sauce was wonderful, but I had no desire to eat liver, even if it came bathed in gold that I could take home and put in the bank.

Adrien commended him on his choice and advised him to get a half bottle of red wine to go with the liver. He didn't commend my choices, but I later placated him by telling him that the wine was marvelous. Men always like to be thought wine connoisseurs. Maybe he was. I'm not, but it did taste good with my appetizer and entrée. Jason ordered the half bottle of red, and I had a bit of that with my dessert. But as soon as we'd ordered, the men started talking toxins, while Albertine and I kept watch on suspicious busboys. Happily, nothing untoward happened.

I ended my meal with a beautiful little dessert plate containing a honey-soaked doughnut, a cup-shaped fruit cake, a torte alternating thin cake layers with white chocolate and liqueur-flavored pastry creams, and a nice tart. So much for resolutions about skipping dessert. Jason ate most of my tart, which was probably the least high cal of the four offerings. Then we went home.

As we were getting ready for bed, I commented on how wonderful the dinner had been. Jason agreed, but he did mention what it had cost. "It was *Albertine's* choice," I pointed out, "and L'Epicerie was *mine*. *My* meal last night wasn't all that expensive. Tell me, Jason, how much did *yours* cost?" I had him there. His had been about twice as expensive because at his table they'd ordered three courses and wine from the wine list.

"I hope you didn't spend a lot today," he grumbled.

"I had soup for lunch, and everything I eat is tax deductible. You might remember that." I didn't mention the shopping trip. He'd see the results of that tomorrow night, and I hoped that he'd be impressed enough to pass up asking what my outfit had cost. At least we hadn't spent the evening with Mercedes in tow.

"I'm being difficult, aren't I?" asked Jason somewhat ruefully.

"Absolutely," I replied, "and I appreciate your admitting it." Then I climbed into my bed, separated from Jason's by tucked sheets and blankets. Not very romantic.

"Then maybe you'll admit," said Jason, climbing into his, "that you were difficult this morning. It's not much fun to get out of bed on the day of your paper and be accused of all sorts of things."

"I suppose so, but Jason, I'm not the only person who notices that Mercedes is always trailing after you."

"It's her first international conference. She's probably feeling shy and—"

"Shy?" I exclaimed and snapped off the light. "She's not shy." How could Jason be so dense? Or maybe he wasn't that dense. Maybe he enjoyed having a pretty young thing clinging to him in front of other men his age. She'd looked even better today because she'd abandoned the silly curls and let her hair go straight and long. Maybe Jason was—I'd never get to sleep if I kept thinking that way. I closed my eyes tight and listened to the wind. Was that a mistral blowing in from Africa? I imagined it picking up sand from the Sahara, fluttering the robes of Arabs in the markets, tugging at their turbans, exposing the hair of the veiled women in Tunisia, and swooping across the Mediterranean, kicking up waves that rocked the cruise ships, where passengers were worrying about pirates, and . . . I fell asleep.

More vegetables, fruit, and herbs are grown in Provence than anywhere else in France, also the most olives and the best olive oil, and ratatouille is the best of all the Provençal's many wonderful vegetable dishes, in my opinion. It's hard to believe that olive oil was once thought to be too important for its medical and religious uses to be wasted in cooking. Also Greeks and other early Mediterranean peoples used it to rub on their skin and to light their lamps. What a waste.

I learned just lately that once you've opened a bottle of olive oil, it should be refrigerated. Who knew? But it will last unopened in a dark, cool, dry place for two years.

Ratatouille

- In a casserole, brown *two sliced onions* in *olive oil.*

- Cube and shallow-fry separately *4 small eggplants* and *4 small zucchini.* Add to onions.

- Chop *2 peppers* and brown slightly. Add to casserole.

- Chop *4 ripe tomatoes.* Pound *8 cloves garlic.* Add those with *salt, pepper, a large bunch of basil,* and a dash of *olive oil* to casserole.

- Cover and cook 1 to 2 hours, stirring occasionally, until ratatouille is very thick. Serve hot as a stew or at room temperature, molded on *salad leaves.*

Carolyn Blue,
"Have Fork, Will Travel,"
Oklahoma City Times

37

Sightseeing with Boring Hair

Carolyn

After breakfast, I practiced wearing my heels. They were still uncomfortable, but I felt somewhat steadier, especially since the maid came in to make up the room and stayed to give me instructions, demonstrations actually, since she spoke no English. She looked as silly demonstrating in her tennis shoes as I looked walking in my heels.

At ten I went down to the lobby to meet Albertine and Charles, who sidled up for an ear rub. His mistress complimented me on having charmed Adrien so thoroughly that he offered to drive to the banquet. "If you can work such a miracle with my husband," she said, "surely you can do the same with your own."

"I shouldn't have to with Jason," I said stubbornly, and she rolled her eyes at my naïveté.

"Every woman has to manipulate her husband. Otherwise, there would be no marriages left. Lucky for you, I have plans."

"What?" I asked suspiciously, afraid that she would next insist that I wear a corset or a padded bra.

Albertine just shrugged mysteriously, and we set off for

Pont St. Benezet, built by a shepherd of that name and finished at the end of the twelfth century, torn down, rebuilt, and then washed away repeatedly by the Rhône until the people of Avignon gave up in the seventeenth century. The four remaining fourteenth-century arches are rather plain, but still interesting. I enjoyed walking out onto the bridge and visiting the chapel of St. Nicholas. Albertine said the people of Avignon go out to dance on an island under an arch of the bridge, which spawned a popular song I'd never heard of. She sang a bit for me, and I could only hope it sounded better when sung by someone who could carry a tune.

Charles de Gaulle, taking his guard duties seriously, barked at a few people who got too close, but acted with discretion in the chapel. Perhaps his lessons had included proper behavior in churches. He became quite frisky when we went to Saint Pierre, which I wanted to see in the daylight. The front was marvelously ornate, flamboyant Gothic with a hint of Renaissance symmetry in the double-pointed towers and matching windows. The *doors* were gorgeous, carved walnut depicting St. Jerome, St. Michael with *very* impressive wings, and the Annunciation.

We went around to see the belfry on another side and then inside, where the décor was less elaborate. There were pictures by French painters I'd never heard of, but Albertine seemed to like them, or at least know things about them. The dog examined them carefully as well, and then sniffed his way by the pews that faced the organ loft and looked for a minute as if he were considering leaping up onto a sixteenth-century throne. Albertine discouraged that by tugging his leash.

Then we dashed over to L'Epicerie for an early lunch. I had a *taramasalata,* a tomato salad with basil dressing that tasted a bit like tapenade. The carp roe that accompanied it wasn't bad, either. Since Charles de Gaulle didn't eat my salad, as he had in Naples, we had a pleasant, noncon-frontational lunch, after which we went on to the palais. The tour for the meeting had been moved up so that a poster session could be fitted in between the tour and the banquet. "Now, be nice to your husband," Albertine whispered to me as we assembled in front.

A good thought, but I didn't get to because Mercedes talked to him from the Court of Honor, where the tour started, to the very end. I don't know what was so important that he couldn't pay attention to a magnificent palace and a hundred years of church history, but I gave up trying to attract his attention and stuck with the historian. He was terribly learned and interesting, although he had bad breath. Poor man. Someone ought to drop him a hint.

The outside of the Palais des Papes is a veritable fortress. The inside, which includes the old palace built by Benedict XII and the "new" palace by Clement VI, is as amazing as the outside. We saw the frescoed chapel of Saint Jean, and the Consistory, where the pontiff and his cardinals met, with its portraits of all the Avignon popes. The Grand Tinel, where we would banquet tonight, had a paneled vault and the most gorgeous Gobelin tapestries, one scene of which was Attila halted at the gates of Rome by a persuasive pope. The St. Martial Chapel, again full of frescoes, led off eastward from the Grand Tinel. What a lovely banquet it would be. I could hardly wait.

Charles had to be dragged from the banqueting hall to visit the pope's dressing room and bedroom, both huge, both be-tapestried and be-muraled. Benedict probably never had a moment alone if he had to dress and sleep in rooms so large.

Then we entered the palace of Clement VI, where we looked at sacristies, the very large Grand Chapel and the Grand Audience, a hall of justice with vaults and pillars, and wonderful stairways that made for hard climbing—not to mention more frescoes and statues. One was of Emperor Charles IV, who evidently lived there for a time. I think he was the Bohemian Holy Roman Emperor, and Charles de Gaulle evidently thought he was dangerous because the dog barked at the statue.

I had to scratch his ears to shut him up before a guard arrived to throw us all out, but then Sylvie and her dog arrived, and Winston Churchill again tried to attack Charles de Gaulle. What a fuss. I had thought we would go on to the Cathedral of Notre-Dame des Doms with its huge gold statue of the Virgin, but that evidently wasn't on the agenda. Maybe they'd dropped it to make room for the poster session.

So the wives and their dogs emerged from the palais, and the professors and their students went off for more chemistry. Jason barely waved good-bye to me, which Albertine noticed. "Now I know that I have made the correct decision," she said when her husband, who *had* accompanied us, left. "I have reserved an appointment for you with the best hairdresser in Avignon."

"Oh, Albertine, I hate beauty shops. And what's wrong with my hair?"

"The hair itself is quite nice, but the styling is so very boring. You will do as I say, and tonight your husband won't even see that Mexican girl when he catches the first glimpse of his remodeled wife."

I didn't much care for her insistence that I be remodeled, and what would the best hairdresser in Avignon cost? Not that I was given any choice. I had to hold the leash while Albertine studied the directions she had written down. Then, although I was tired after climbing up and down long staircases and walking on marble and stone floors, we walked to the salon. A man almost as bossy as Albertine sat me down in a chair that was *not* facing one of the gilded mirrors and began to discuss my hair with Albertine. Obviously they both disapproved. When he combed my side and top hair forward, I cried, "I don't want my hair cut off."

"Only the front," Albertine assured me. "You may have a chignon in back, but the front must be more flattering." She translated this for Jean-Marc, who agreed and gave me a command, after which he chopped off a hunk of my hair. By then it was too late, so I concentrated on not bursting into tears.

I think, after the shampoo, which was administered by a lady, and some glop rubbed in and heated, that the man cut every separate hair a different length while I pictured myself as a scarecrow with straw sticking out of my head in all directions. The traumatic cutting over, Jean-Marc combed and brushed and blow-dried and sprayed and pinned until I was numb and half asleep.

"Voila!" he cried, waking me up and whirling my chair round to face the mirror.

Was that me? With those wispy bangs and pretty waves falling down over my ears to curl around to the chignon, which looked almost fluffy when he handed me a mirror so that I could see it. In a daze I paid the awful bill with the last of my euros.

"You must bathe, not shower, so that you do not ruin the effect," said Albertine, as we walked back to the hotel, "and I expect to see you wearing the dress *and* the shoes *and* the hose, not to mention suitable jewelry. I hope you have some. And I hope you realize how truly beautiful you look. I shall not let you near my husband for fear that you will enchant him."

"I'll be lucky to enchant my own husband, and if you hear that I'm dead, you'll know that he killed me because of all the money I've spent, but I do thank you, Albertine. I'll probably feel like a princess."

"Every woman is a princess, my dear, if she only takes the trouble. We'll see you at seven-thirty."

I was still bemused when I got to my room. Instead of falling onto the bed, I got out the shoes and practiced. Then I went to sleep in the wicker chair lest sleeping on the bed ruin my hair. What a wonderful time I was going to have tonight, banqueting in a papal palace with an astonished, adoring husband at my side. I felt like Cinderella.

38

Banquet Blues

Jason

I **had to** stay for the whole poster session because Mercedes had been so nervous she talked to me throughout the tour. What should she say if they asked her this? Or that? What if no one stopped to look at her poster? I'd never known her to be so insecure. Of course she did beautifully, as I knew she would, but I returned to the hotel with very little time to dress for the banquet. Carolyn was asleep in one of those chairs, and her hair! When she opened her eyes and smiled at me, I said, "What in God's name did you do to your hair?" Her smile disappeared.

"Albertine talked me into having it styled. Don't you like it?"

"I like it long," I mumbled, sorry to have spoiled what she'd evidently meant to be a nice surprise.

"I've got a chignon in back."

"That's good, I guess, but it's still fussy up front. Anyway, I've got to shower and dress." I rushed into the bathroom to escape Carolyn's disappointment. I couldn't seem to do anything right lately.

When I came out wearing the toweling robe provided

by the hotel, Carolyn had discarded her robe and was now wearing—good lord! The most ridiculous shoes I'd ever seen. "Did Albertine talk you into those shoes, too? You'll be limping before we reach the banquet."

She burst into tears, ran into the bathroom, and didn't come out until the telephone rang announcing the arrival of the Guillots. I had to tie my aggravating bow tie without a mirror and put in my own cuff links. However, she had calmed down. Both Albertine and Adrien told her how beautiful she looked, which made me feel like a lout as we walked to the car. The two of us sat stiffly in the backseat, perfectly silent, all the way to the palace, where Adrien dropped us off and drove away to park.

Carolyn's new hairstyle was caught in the wind, which was blowing out of an ominous sky, so she and Albertine rushed off to make repairs, leaving me to find my way to the Grand Tinel. There I was caught by my exuberant graduate student, who was bubbling over about what a success we had been, me yesterday, her today.

Carolyn

I looked into the mirror in despair. "I'll never be able to resurrect Jean-Marc's creation."

"Nonsense," Albertine replied, as she began to fix her own windblown hair. "So, how did he like the new Carolyn? Was he absolutely delighted and overwhelmed?"

"He thought I'd cut the back and said the front was fussy. And when he saw the shoes, he said they'd cripple me."

"But the dress—surely he loved—"

"He didn't even mention it," I replied dolefully and burst into tears.

"The man is a fool. And don't cry. You'll ruin your makeup." Albertine ran a tissue under my eyes to make

sure my mascara hadn't run and then went to work on my
hair. In no time, she had me looking presentable. "I think
plan two is in order. I'll introduce you to every handsome
bachelor in the hall. We'll table hop. He'll be so jealous by
dessert that he'll have to drag you away from all your new
admirers."

· I tried to believe her, and also to get to the Grand Tinel
without breaking an ankle. The hall was so beautiful when
we arrived—three rows of tables with white clothes, red
seats, flickering lamps on each table, waiters straightening
place settings, conferees in tuxes and ladies in evening
gowns, beautiful tapestries glowing on the walls. It had
been the pope's banqueting hall. Again I felt excited and
full of anticipation—until I spotted my husband, further
down the hall, several men in his group, and Mercedes
with her arms thrown around his neck, his hand on her
waist.

Catherine stopped beside us and said, "There's that
Mexican girl who's been clinging to your husband, Carolyn. No woman should put up with a man who can't carry
on an affair with discretion, who actually throws his sexual
forays into her face. It's quite shocking. Don't you agree,
Albertine?"

Tears of humiliation welled in my eyes. I couldn't stay
here a minute longer. Albertine was rebuking Catherine
for her insensitivity, so I grasped the chance to slip away.
By the time I got out the door, my cheeks were wet, so I
turned away from the incoming people, thus getting
hopelessly lost. I'm not sure how long I wandered, man-
aging only to get to the first floor, when a man in a uniform asked me something in French. "Anglaise," I
mumbled.

"Can I assist?"

"I'm trying to find the street."

"Which street, madam?"

"Any street." I didn't care. I just wanted to get away, back to the hotel. Once I escaped from the palais, I'd know the way, although walking so far in these shoes would cripple me, as Jason had said. But it would be his fault.

The guard took my arm and led me through a courtyard, a corridor, and finally outside. "Voila! A street, madam."

It was, but I didn't recognize it. Somehow I'd thought all the entrances were in front. This was a roughly paved alley with stray blocks of stone standing near walls that towered over me, straggly greenery sprouting here and there from the stones, a steep slope, and hardly any light. I had no idea where to go and saw no one to ask, so I chose to walk down, perhaps not the best decision, because walking downhill in high heels is worse than walking up.

I stayed close to the walls for balance and inched along, but the slope made my toes slip forward in the sandals until they scraped on the pavement and tore my stockings. More tears blinded me, making it necessary to feel my way along the wall, and then one of the stiletto heels caught in a crack I couldn't even see, and my foot twisted. A terrible pain flashed through my ankle as I fell. Almost immediately it climbed my leg to the knee like a fire. Crumpled awkwardly on the stones, I stayed as still as I could, hoping the pain would ease. It didn't. I couldn't move at all without causing more agony.

What if I lay here all night? It was cold. The wind swooped down the alley, making me shiver. A mistral, as I had thought last night, but not from Africa, according to Albertine. At least I had pain pills in my purse. I managed to free the arm trapped beneath me and fumble the pills from the purse in my other hand. After trying to dry swallow two, I gagged, coughed them up, and started to chew. They tasted terrible, and I was a miserable fool. For wearing these shoes, which my husband hated. For leaving him in the clutches of Mercedes, when I should have dragged him away. And my poor head now hurt as much as my ankle, bringing on hiccupping sobs that didn't make me feel better in the least.

39
A Gunshot in the Grand Tinel

Having failed so *miserably before, this might be my last chance. She had left, and he was perfectly positioned. I worked my way through the champagne drinkers awaiting the call to be seated and slipped in the door of the Chapelle de Saint-Martial, a gloomy place covered with ugly frescoes depicting the saint's life. After checking the load in my gun, for I'd have only one shot, I opened the door a crack. Yes, there he was with his paramour. Taking aim carefully, I pulled the trigger, withdrew the barrel, closed the door, and exited through another door that always went unnoticed.*

Then I made my way around until I could reenter the Grand Tinel with the last of the banqueters. Imagine my disgust when I saw that I'd hit the wrong person. Still, my mistake might have a happy ending. The wife, probably eaten up with jealousy, had not returned. It might be thought that she had shot the Mexican girl. What grief that would cause.

Jason

I was standing with my back to our table, Mercedes embarrassing me by clinging to my arm. While I made a point about my research to a chemist from Rouen, I scanned the hall for Carolyn, who had been at the back with Catherine and Albertine.

Then, in a move that was even more embarrassing, Mercedes whirled in front of me, grasped both my arms, and exclaimed, "Oh, Professor, that is so brilliant." I had just said something quite ordinary about aflatoxins. "No one but you could have realized that." Whatever else she had to say was cut off by a bang, after which she fell, forcing me to catch her. Her behavior was highly improper, so I grasped her arms, preparing to push her away, only to realize she was bleeding on me. A hullabaloo in foreign tongues ensued, and the professor from Rouen said, "I believe your student has been shot."

"Shot?" How had she managed to get shot in the Grand Tinel? "Could someone call nine-one-one?" The people surrounding us looked blank. "An ambulance," I added, and several people pulled out cell phones while more people crowded around us. "Perhaps we'd better—" Actually, I had no idea what to do, but a professor from Paris had taken a medical degree before his doctorate in chemistry. He directed the placing of Mercedes on a banquet table after the hasty removal of place settings. Then he packed the wound. She was still conscious, moaning and insisting that I hold her hand, which I didn't want to do. The professor said that he did not think the wound life threatening, that it seemed to have missed the vital organs.

Others were theorizing about where the shot came from. "The Chapelle de Saint-Martial," said someone. "Unless the shooter stood here in the banquet hall and fired." Nobody thought that possible. The gunman would have been seen here in the hall. Therefore, several men approached the door of the chapel, opened it, and peered in, which seemed foolish to me. What if the armed man was

still in there? The academic investigators would be shot as
well.

Could Carolyn have been right about a terrorist stalking
us? And where was she? Admittedly, with such a crowd
around me, I couldn't scan the reaches of the hall, but
surely if she were here, she'd come over to see if I'd been
hurt. Since I'd no doubt been the target, I'd have been
wounded if Mercedes hadn't stepped in front of me. It was
this thought that convinced me I must go to the hospital
with her when the ambulance attendants arrived, carrying
a stretcher. A gurney wouldn't have worked on the long
flight of stairs to the lower floor.

When Mercedes begged me to stay with her and hold
her hand, I agreed. "Adrien, can you find Carolyn and tell
her what's happened? She was right. Someone is trying to
kill us. I'd be grateful if you and Albertine could see that
she takes no chances." Then, after retrieving a slip of paper
that Carolyn had provided, I asked the ambulance attendants if we could go to the Centre Hospitalier d'Avignon,
where Blue Cross Blue Shield was accepted. "You do have
university insurance, don't you, Mercedes?"

They moved her from table to stretcher, having taken
her vital signs and inspected the rough-and-ready bandag-
ing made up of cummerbunds and handkerchiefs. As soon
as we were out of the hall, Mercedes looked up at me with
tear-filled eyes and said, "Your wife has done this. She is
jealous of the feeling that has grown between us."

"What's that supposed to mean? My wife has no reason
to be jealous, nor would she shoot someone if she were.
Furthermore, my feelings, Mercedes, are strictly professional."

She wept more copiously, splotching her mascara.
"Well, of course you would say that. Oh, my wound hurts
so much!"

"Can't you give her something for pain?" I demanded irritably.

Evidently the ambulance attendants understood some English because they replied haltingly that no pain medication could be administered until we arrived at the hospital. Because they understood my request, I had to assume that they might have understood Mercedes's accusation. "Why do these things happen to me?" I muttered aloud.

Mercedes squeezed my hand and said comfortingly that she was going to survive, no matter what my wife intended. I pulled my hand away, and of course she cried some more.

"Monsieur, it is best to keep the lady calm. If your hand comforts her—" The attendant shrugged expressively. When we got out of the palace, the pavilion in front was full of people, many standing around the ambulance and conversing with the driver; the air had turned cold, and the sky, heavy with dark clouds, showed only the occasional star and no moon.

Mercedes shivered and asked for my jacket, but the attendants covered her with a blanket. Then she begged me again to come to the hospital, and the attendants insisted that I agree because she had told them I was her only friend in Avignon. Accordingly, we roared off, sirens shrieking, crowds scrambling aside.

I tried calling Carolyn at our hotel while Mercedes was being examined, but got no answer. I called the Guillots' hotel in case the banquet had been cancelled and they had returned, taking my distraught wife with them. They weren't in. By then I was sent back to Mercedes, who told me sadly that she needed an operation to remove the bullet. "It will leave a scar. I will never be able to wear a bikini again, or a low-necked dress."

The dress she had worn to the banquet was certainly

low-necked. Had I been her father, I might have considered the predicted scar a blessing.

"I know your wife meant to kill me, but—"

"She did no such thing," I snapped.

"Do not speak cruelly to me when I love you with all my heart, dear Jason."

"You are my student and not allowed to call me Jason, or to love me." Thoroughly tired of being pursued by this foolish girl, I decided never to take another female student. However, such a policy would be noticed and cause me trouble, maybe even lawsuits supported by the Equal Employment Opportunity people, who always have their eyes on us and love to receive complaints against professors from female students.

Nurses came in to transfer Mercedes to the operating room, and the English speaker assured me that my daughter would soon be in recovery. Mercedes protested that she was not my daughter, but my lover, and that I must be here when the anesthetic wore off. Of course, I denied that we were lovers while the nurses raised their eyebrows, but I realized that I'd have to stay, if only to stop her from telling people that Carolyn shot her.

Where *was* my wife? I wanted to know that she hadn't—no, I couldn't even think that. Carolyn wouldn't shoot anyone.

I soon found that I couldn't have left the hospital if I wanted to. The police arrived and, unable to interview Mercedes, settled for me. What happened? She got shot. What was our relationship? Student and professor. Who was present? Around four hundred people. Did I see anyone fire the shot? No. Had there been arguments prior to the shooting? No. Did I know anyone who would want to hurt her? No. What about my wife?

I gave the inspector an angry look. "My wife has no reason to hurt Mercedes."

"She likes the young lady?"

I compromised by saying, "They've only met a few times. And my wife would not shoot anyone. I doubt that she's ever held a gun."

"Then why does mademoiselle think your wife shot her?"

It was obviously too late to silence Mercedes on that subject, but by God, she'd have to find another research professor. How had they found out? From the ambulance attendants, no doubt. "Mercedes Lizarreta has foolishly decided that she is infatuated with me, although I have given her no encouragement and do not return her feelings. Perhaps she said that, hoping that it was true, or to cause trouble in my marriage. Whatever her reasons, my wife did *not* shoot her."

"Where is your wife?"

"I don't know. At the palais or our hotel. I had to come here with my student before I could find my wife."

"No one can find your wife, Professor. She evidently disappeared before the shooting, distressed over what she saw between you and the young lady. We must assume that she went to the Chapelle de Saint-Martial, fired the shot, and then escaped through a little-known exit."

"That's absolute nonsense. Someone said the chapel was empty and there was not way out but the door into the Grand Tinel."

"They were wrong. If you hear from Madam Blue, we must insist that you call us immediately."

"Look," I said desperately, "that shot was meant for me. If Mercedes hadn't stepped in front of me, *I'd* have been here in the hospital."

"And still we would be looking for your wife. We are aware that American ladies are less tolerant of husbands with mistresses than are French ladies."

"I don't have a mistress, and it's not the first time someone has tried to hurt me. A car almost ran me down in Lyon."

"Well, those things happen, monsieur. Especially in Lyon, where the drivers are arrogant and reckless. Soon I expect to see the riots from Paris spreading to Lyon."

"Ah, here you are," said a doctor, walking into the waiting room. "Your daughter is out of surgery. You can go in to see her, monsieur."

"She's not my daughter," I protested wearily.

"And I am Inspector Villon. I must interview the victim. Perhaps this gentleman should be kept away from her since the shooting seems to be an affair of the heart. Not his it seems, but still I must ask you to . . ."

At least I wouldn't have to put up with any more romantic nonsense from Mercedes; I was barred from her presence. I shook the detective's hand, which seemed to surprise him, and was about to leave when the doctor insisted that I stay to provide information about Mercedes's family.

Oh God, could I never get free to find my wife?

40
Rescue

Carolyn

It was so cold my teeth chattered, so cold the wind numbed my pain, although it might have been the nasty-tasting pills I chewed. Through the narrow opening between the stone walls, no light shone, not a star, not a golden ray from the moon. I couldn't tell how long I had been lying there, but only one person had passed. He couldn't see me because I wasn't close enough to the dim lantern farther down, so I called "S'il vous plaît" when I heard his heavy steps. "Do you have a cell phone? Call a hospital, s'il vous plaît." He jerked, peered in my direction, and hurried away, although I shouted after him. Perhaps he thought I was a decoy, that he would be attacked and robbed by someone coming out of the shadows if he came to my assistance.

Once I heard a siren and took heart. Perhaps he had called for help, even if he wouldn't approach me. I waited and waited, but no one came. Then the siren resumed and went away, and I cried. *Well, crying will do no good,* I told myself. *Maybe I can scoot downhill.* I tried. The first push with my hands and my good foot caused a bolt of pain, so I stopped. I'd be here all night, possibly catch pneumonia, or die of hypothermia. How cold did it get here in the fall when the winds rose and the temperatures dropped?

I cushioned my head on my hand to keep the concussion bump from resting on stone and wished myself asleep. I was even feeling a bit drowsy when I heard a door open above me and then thud closed, the same thud I'd heard when the guard ushered me out and left me. Footsteps rang on stone. "Help," I called.

"Madam Blue, are you there?"

The voice was familiar. Not Jason's. He was probably eating a wonderful dinner with Mercedes at his side. Then a giant towered over me, frightening me half to death since I immediately thought that he might be a giant terrorist.

"Is it you, madam? I have been looking for you." He knelt beside me and flicked a cigarette lighter so that he could see my face. And I could see the red hair on the giant's head. "I saw you leave the banquet, looking so sad. You have been very kind to me, so I came to see if I could help. It is me, Martin. Are you hurt?"

"Yes," I sniffled, weak with relief and gratitude.

"I searched the palais but couldn't find you until a guard said he had guided you out here and that you were crying. Did my professor say something to cause you such pain?"

That surprised me, but his professor was Catherine, who had indeed spoken cruelly about Jason's behavior. "I think my ankle is broken, Martin. Do you have a cell phone? Can you call for help?"

"She is a cruel woman," he muttered and pulled something from his pocket. I heard the clicks, then the pause, then a flood of French. "They can not get an ambulance into this alley. I have said that I will carry you to the square. Do you think you can bear that?"

As long as I got to a doctor, I didn't care how Martin rescued me, but what if he couldn't carry me that far, or dropped me? I needn't have worried. When I agreed to his plan, he swooped me up as if I were a small child and strode off. When we reached the square, he would not put me down, although people gathered around us. He shouted at them, perhaps telling them to back away and mind my ankle. When the ambulance arrived, he told them who I was, "Madam Carolyn Blue."

"Can I go to the Centre Hospitalier d'Avignon?" I asked, remembering the name of the institution here that took Blue Cross. I'd had a hospital for Lyon as well, but being unconscious, hadn't been able to request it of whoever took me away from the traboule.

"Certainly, madam," said the English speaker. "We have already made one trip there tonight."

Probably the siren that didn't come for me, I thought, shivering.

"She is cold," said Martin. He helped them settle me on the cot and spread a blanket himself, but they wouldn't let him accompany me.

"Don't worry, Martin. You've saved my life, and I shall be forever grateful. Go back to the banquet and enjoy the evening." He looked reluctant, but he stood aside when they closed the doors.

The attendants padded my injury, which made the trip less agonizing. By the time I was taken into the emergency room, I wasn't feeling so shaky and frightened. "My name is Carolyn Blue," I said to the doctor who approached me. "This is my insurance card. Blue Cross." Thank goodness I hadn't lost that in Lyon.

"Really? Blue?" He took my card and walked away. To give the card to whoever registered patients, I supposed. Then my ankle was X-rayed and pronounced broken, but not badly. Not badly? It certainly felt bad. "We will give you a—what would be the word?—shoe? For your ankle. Much nicer than a cast. And pills for the pain, but madam, you must start to walk on the leg, wearing the shoe, of course, as soon as you can. Soon walking, soon healing, *oui*?"

He expected me to walk on it? It hurt when he was washing it off with alcohol. It hurt when he was wrapping it in gauze, explaining that when I got home, I could and should wear a sock. And it really hurt when he fitted me for the shoe, which was actually a boot, and strapped it onto me. The thing, a sickly green, with which I'd have nothing to wear, covered my foot except for the toes and rose all the way up my shin. "Now madam, I will give you some pills for pain. You have pain?" I agreed that I did, and I didn't mention that I'd already taken several concussion pills. I wanted relief! "Once you are more comfortable, you can go home."

"*Walk* home?" I asked, horrified. These people were sadists.

"*Non, non,* madam. We will call a family member."

"My only family member is at a banquet and doesn't have a cell phone."

"At a banquet. Amazing. We will call for you a cab."

What was amazing about my husband being incommunicado at a banquet? I was the only one who had reason to consider that cause for dismay. A nurse approached with water and pills in a little cup, and I swallowed them eagerly. "Maybe I need crutches," I suggested. Otherwise, how would I get to my room? I was *not* going to walk on the ankle tonight. I'd consider it tomorrow, but tonight I was going to bed, knocked out by four pain pills.

"We have crutches," said the doctor soothingly, "but remember to walk. Walking is healing."

I wanted to tell him to shut up; instead he told me to rest, and I obediently closed my eyes. I was truly in less pain. With luck it would abate even further.

"Madam Carolyn Blue?" asked a commanding voice. I

jerked out of my doze and stared, confused, at a man I hadn't seen before.

"Yes. Has the cab come?"

"You will not be leaving immediately. I have questions to ask."

"For the bill, I suppose. Will Blue Cross pay most of it, do you think? Jason took care of the bill in Lyon." I felt very fuzzy. Perhaps the added pain pills hadn't been a good idea. "My ankle does feel better," I murmured to myself.

"I'm pleased to hear that, but it is not your hospital bill I wish to discuss. You are the wife of Professor Jason Blue, *non*?"

Of course, I was. Hadn't I just mentioned my husband?

"Where did you leave the gun?"

"What?"

"Do not dissemble. We know you shot the student from the Chapelle de Saint-Martial and then left with the help of a palais guard, after which a fall and a broken ankle foiled your escape. But we did not find the gun in your handbag, so you must have hidden it. In the palais? In the ambulance?" He bellowed to someone leaning against the wall in the corner, and that person scurried out.

"I don't have a gun. What are you talking about?" Who *was* this person with his square, pitted face and tiny eyes?

"Even the victim says you shot her, Madam Blue, and of course we understand these spousal quarrels that end in violence. Our courts will understand, as well, but you must confess. Failure to express remorse will make your punishment more severe."

I closed my eyes, sure I was having a bizarre dream, but when I opened them again, he was still there. "Perhaps you have the wrong person," I suggested wearily, wishing that he'd go away and let me rest. "I don't know of anyone who's been shot, and I certainly don't have a gun. I'm a tourist. Guns aren't allowed on planes, you know. Are you a policeman?"

"I am an inspector of the Avignon—"

"Then you must know Inspector Theodore Roux in Lyon. Perhaps you're even the inspector whose name he gave me. Maybe you should call him. He'll tell you that I'm the victim, my husband and I, not a criminal."

"A Mademoiselle Mercedes Lizarreta was shot this evening in the papal palace while in your husband's arms," he said very slowly.

"She was?" I took that in and then added, "Well, I didn't shoot her."

"You will admit that you had cause?" he persisted.

"Certainly not. There is never cause to shoot anyone, and I have never done so—well, in New Orleans," I amended, remembering that incident. "I guess you could say I shot the priest, in a manner of speaking." The inspector's mouth dropped open. Perhaps mentioning the priest hadn't been a good idea. "He wasn't a *real* priest, and it was *his* gun. I thought it was a toy, so I tried to knock it out of his hand. It fired and hit his ear, but even the New Orleans police agreed that having one's fingerprints on the barrel is not evidence that one has shot someone. He was a known criminal."

"Madam obviously has an interesting history," said the inspector dryly, "but I am interested in the location of the gun you shot from the Chapelle—"

"I didn't do that. I wasn't in any chapelle tonight, and all you have to do is check my hands for—what's it called?—gunshot residue. It's something you get on your hands if you shoot a gun. I've seen it on TV." When I held out my hands, he scowled.

"Since you offer, no doubt you washed it off."

"Where?" I asked. "In the palais? I only know one ladies' room there and couldn't find it. If I had, I'd have ducked in and washed my face. Or maybe you think I washed my hands in the alley. Maybe I rubbed the residue off against the stones after I fell, or cried it off because my ankle hurt so much, or they washed it off in the ambulance or here in the hospital. Ask the medical people. The only thing on me that's been washed is my leg, and that hurt. So just do whatever you do to look for gunpowder residue." He did.

Then my cab and crutches came, and I said if he wasn't going to arrest me, I was going home to sleep. Because the inspector evidently didn't have enough evidence for an arrest, I was wheeled to the cab, helped in and later out by the driver, and escorted upstairs by Bridget with the help of the crutches, which I couldn't handle well. Maybe starting to walk tomorrow was the right thing to do. With that thought, I fell onto my bed and into sleep.

41

"Where Have You *Been*?"

Jason

Having escaped from the hospital and failed to contact Carolyn at the hotel, I headed toward the palais. Lately Carolyn's complaints had involved Mercedes, and she'd been right. The girl did have designs on me, but that didn't mean I was guilty of anything.

It seemed to me that Carolyn might have returned to the banquet from, say, the ladies' room, heard that I'd left for the hospital with Mercedes, and taken her place at our table, leaving me to the mess for which she blamed me. It just wasn't possible that she'd actually shot Mercedes. Was it? No. I felt better by the time I arrived at the Grand Tinel.

Dessert was being served; Jacques Laurent was on the podium at the far end of the hall speaking in French, while a translator gave a shortened version in English; and people were looking at me strangely. Only then did I remember that Mercedes had bled all over me. No wonder they were staring. The apparition at the feast had just walked in.

Closer to the table, I saw the Guillots, but not Carolyn. So much for optimistic logic. I'd rather my wife had been there and angry than missing and unaccounted for. Albertine glared and refused to answer when I asked if she'd seen Carolyn. Several people asked how the "Mexican girl" was, and I replied that the bullet had been removed, and she was recovering at the Centre Hospitalier d'Avignon.

"And why would someone have shot her?" Adrien asked curiously. "It seems a strange thing."

"I imagine the gunman was targeting me," I replied. "This is, after all, attempt number four." I needed to say that to absolve my wife, but just saying it gave me chills. Was attempt number five being planned? Or had the person—perhaps, as Carolyn thought, a terrorist—caught and killed her, after failing with me? I left. In the square, where the musicians were still playing, the strollers were leaving because of the chill and the threatening sky. From there I ran to the hotel and finally burst into our room. The door was unlocked, a very bad sign.

But after all my anxiety, my wife lay fast asleep in bed. I could see her by the light coming through the window from the street below. She had simply left the banquet without telling me, come back, and—I couldn't believe it. Without even turning on a light, I growled, "Where have you *been,* Carolyn?"

She sat straight up, groggily, and stared at me. "Where have *I* been? Well, I went to the banquet, all dressed up to please you, although you didn't say one single nice thing to me." Her voice was slurred. Was she drunk?

"And there you were with Mercedes, her arms around your neck, your hands on her waist, right there in the banquet hall in front of everyone. How do you think I felt? Catherine saw it and said if it were her, she wouldn't put up with a husband who couldn't even carry on an affair with discretion, who threw his sexual forays in her face— her exact words. I was so humiliated. I was so *hurt*, and on the verge of weeping and embarrassing myself even more. So I left."

She swung her legs out of bed and groaned when she tried unsuccessfully to stand.

"What's that on your leg?" I asked, distracted from the tongue-lashing I'd just received.

"My ankle is broken. I fell in an alley while I was trying to get away from all those people who felt sorry for me. I'd still have been on that hill, in agony and freezing to death, if Martin hadn't come along, called an ambulance, and carried me down to the square. *He* came looking for me. Tell me, Jason, when did you realize I was gone? When the banquet was over?"

By now Carolyn was back in bed, crying, still wearing the black dress. And I felt terrible. "You—you don't know what happened after—I guess after you left. Someone shot Mercedes."

"I can see her blood," Carolyn said bitterly. "Was she in your arms when it happened?"

"Well, not exactly. She—stepped in front of me, and the bullet hit her."

"Weren't you lucky, and shouldn't you be comforting her? She may have saved your life." My wife didn't sound as if she cared.

"I was at the hospital, and sweetheart—"

"Don't call me that."

"You have to let me tell you the rest. There was an inspector there who seemed to think that you shot her. I told him that was ridiculous. Of course you didn't." Then I couldn't help asking, "Did you?"

"No, Jason, I didn't." She went, in just a second, from sarcastic to furious. "Even if you don't love me anymore, you ought to know that I wouldn't shoot anyone, even Mercedes."

"But, Carolyn, I do love you. I was never interested in her. She's a student, for Pete's sake. I can't help it if she—

she had a thing for me, which she evidently did, but I told her to forget it."

"When was this? After I warned you about her? After I begged you to—"

"Well, it was before she went into surgery."

"That must have done her a world of good."

"She's fine. She's probably given up on me. God knows, I hope so. What we have to do is figure out how to convince the police that you didn't—"

"I doubt that you're the person to do that, Jason. You aren't convinced yourself. As for me, I was grilled by some square-faced inspector while I was drugged with more painkillers. I told him to take a sample from my hands for gunshot residue and then leave me alone. Since I haven't held a gun since New Orleans, he'll have to give up the stupid idea that I shot her. Let me guess? Did *she* tell him that?" Before I could stammer out an answer, Carolyn said, "I'm going back to bed. Sitting up makes my ankle hurt. I need to get some sleep so I can start walking tomorrow."

"You can't be serious. You said your ankle was broken."

"Don't tell me what to do, Jason, and I'll never forgive you for not thinking I looked pretty in my new dress, and shoes—well, the shoes were a mistake, and don't you dare say 'I told you so,' but the hairstyle was pretty. You're really mean and stodgy."

With that she flopped down on the pillow and ordered me to put the sheet and blanket over her. I had to wonder if I'd ever be forgiven. How had our comfortable marriage come to this? We'd been so happy. I sighed and went into the bathroom. When I returned, my wife was deeply asleep, and she didn't move so much as a finger or change the rhythm of her breathing when I climbed into the other bed. At least, she *was* breathing. The stalker hadn't killed her.

42
The Morning After

Carolyn

I had the hazy impression that it stormed all night, but if so, I hadn't awakened, probably because I was both tired and drugged. My ankle hurt, mostly when I moved, which made the doctor's advice to walk as much as possible, as soon as possible, very hard to take seriously. On the other hand, I was awake because I needed to use the bathroom, something I couldn't put off forever. I viewed the partially open door with a rueful eye. Jason wasn't here to help me. I then turned to the clock on the nightstand. Nine-thirty. He was at either the conference or the hospital. Much he cared about me!

I sat up and edged the booted leg over and then to the floor, using my hands to hold it at the knee so that it wouldn't thud down. Actually the boot didn't weigh that much, which was a good thing. With my second foot on the floor, I looked for the wretched crutches and spotted them and the Lyon cane leaning within reach against the night-stand. At least my husband had given my condition *some* thought before he left.

I chose the cane, grasped it with my left hand, and stood up on my right foot. Rising revealed that I was now lopsided because the boot had a thick sole. I tried shifting my weight from the cane to the right foot and back, dragging the boot. That hurt so much I felt faint. Obviously I had to walk on both boot and foot, which would cause me to limp and look ridiculous, as well as hurt.

And it was becoming crucial that I get to the bathroom, so I did, groaning all the way and reaching the facilities without a moment to spare. The doctor had said I could bathe or shower without the boot as long as I didn't put un-supported weight on my ankle, fall down, or knock it into anything. Three impossible conditions to meet.

I got off as many clothes as I could without rising—my beautiful, dust-covered, torn black dress, my slip, and the bra that I'd worn. The expensive hose and the shoes had been bagged at the hospital. I pulled up my panties; then, using the cane for leverage, I rose and wheeled to the sink and mirror for a much needed sponge bath. And what did I find when I faced the mirror? A Post-it note from Jason. "I love you. Take care. Will call at ten." He was thinking of me!

The bath that followed was more exhausting than trying to keep up with Catherine at Fort Andre. Drying could be managed only with much precarious twisting about while standing on one foot. After that I was too tired to favor the broken ankle. I just put my full weight on it and—sur-prise!—it didn't hurt as much. I got to the bed in time to pick up the ringing phone without causing myself horren-dous pain.

It was Bridget, asking if she could send up breakfast? Of course, she could, I answered. It was only after I'd hung up that I realized I couldn't open the door wearing only my panties and boot. I dropped my head into my hands, van-quished, until I remembered the robe and spotted it lying across Jason's bed. Had he been thoughtful? Or just neat?

Anyway, I could and did put on the robe. *Now* I could go
to the door.

The phone rang again, and this time it was my husband.
"I hope I didn't wake you." He hadn't. "How are you feeling?" I said I'd managed to walk to and from the bathroom
without causing further damage.

When I asked him if he'd been to see Mercedes, he
replied, "I have not, but the wretched girl called me out of
a lecture to ask when I'd be there. I told her never, that her
conduct had been so improper I wanted her to find another
research director. In fact, I suggested one at another university. Then, of course, we had a nasty argument. Nasty
on her part. I was moderately calm and polite, but the up-
shot is that she's threatening to sue me because she's in the
hospital with a bullet wound. Carolyn, I'm at my wit's end.
What am I supposed to do?"

"Tell her that you're going to countersue for sexual harassment," I replied flippantly.

There was a silence. Then Jason started to laugh, after
which he said, "Embarrassing as that sounds, I'm putting a
call through to Human Resources at home as soon as I
can."

"You aren't?" I retorted, starting to laugh myself.

"Damn right I am. You're a very smart woman, my love.
I'll call you around noon."

I hung up, all smiles. Probably I should have stayed
angry longer, but the idea that Mercedes was about to be
charged with sexually harassing my husband was just too
delightful to ignore. Of course, I'd be peeved if he didn't
do it. In a much better mood, I limped over to admit the
bellman with my breakfast, which I enjoyed immensely.

Only after the last bite did I realize that I'd be stuck here
all day, and maybe for as long as the meeting lasted. How
much walking was I allowed to do? Another knock on my

door produced Albertine, arriving with candy and flowers, and shocked when I opened the door myself.

"My dear Carolyn, you are walking! Do sit down." She scolded me for leaving the banquet and not standing up to Mercedes, although I felt that there was some justice in Mercedes taking the bullet for Jason. Albertine complained because he had gone to the hospital with the "awful girl." I passed on the good news that he had told his troublesome student to find a new professor, and that he planned to file a sexual harassment complaint against her.

"You Americans!" Albertine exclaimed. "Always going to court. These things can be settled less publicly." Then she commiserated with me for being stuck inside on such a nice day, when the conference had announced a tour of the cathedral, the gardens, and a portion of the walls. The organizers wanted to make up for yesterday's truncated outing. The very thought that I would miss the new tour sent me into despondency. It wasn't fair. "I'm walking pretty well," I said hopefully.

"Don't even think of it," Albertine replied. "I'd rather stay here with you than have you take any more chances with—" I interrupted to ask what time the tour began. "Two, but you can't go. You have a broken ankle. You probably shouldn't be walking on it now."

"The doctor said I should. And I'm going to. Of course, it would be nice if you drove me over there. You do drive, don't you?"

"Of course I do, but I can't drive you through the cathedral or the gardens."

"If I can get up to the gardens, I can walk along the walls, can't I? How much climbing is there?" I thought about climbing. "What I need is a pair of shoes with a heel that brings my other foot to the level of the boot. Could I find such a thing?"

"One can find anything if one knows where to look, and

the shoe is a very sensible idea. Hobbling at two heights could damage your hip. Very well, I'll pick you up at one, but I won't promise to take you to the cathedral. First, we must see how the new shoe works. That saleslady where we bought the first pair will be able to suggest something. How are your pretty sandals, by the way?"

"The heel broke when I broke my ankle. If I'd been in flats—"

"I take no responsibility for your fall, Carolyn. If you hadn't left the banquet hall, you'd be fine. Did your beautiful dress survive? I see that your hair has held up well in front, although the back is not good. Shall I comb it for you?"

"The dress is dusty and torn, and I'd appreciate your help with my hair. In fact, I've been worrying about how I'm going to get dressed. I'll have to wear a skirt."

"Ah! I shall chose clothing for you and help you dress. Then we will do your hair."

"Thank you so much, Albertine. You're such a good friend." I had no intention of being talked out of the cathedral, and possibly I'd insist on the rest. I did have pills.

"Of course I'm a good friend. I told you that in Sorrento, but obviously you did not believe me. Even Charles de Gaulle is your good friend. Poor dear, I left him in the room, lest his presence make you anxious, but I think we must bring him this afternoon for safety. The shooter might try again." She stopped rustling through my closet and looked thoughtful. "Perhaps you should not—"

"At least don't leave me wearing nothing but a robe, panties, and messy hair," I pleaded. Once I was dressed and groomed, I'd address the visit to the shop and the tour. She'd never be able to resist shopping.

She did think Jason might be upset if I purchased more shoes, but I answered, "I don't intend to worry about his concerns until I'm sure that he's filed that complaint against Mercedes."

"Hmmm," said Albertine, and brought over a gathered skirt and blouse made from one of those travel fabrics that you can wad up in your suitcase and put right on once you've unpacked. It wasn't exactly what I'd have chosen for a casual occasion, but what else was there? I wondered if I could pull on slacks without the boot and then Velcro the boot over the trouser leg. I'd probably better consult the doctor about that.

43
Phone Calls and Gifts

Carolyn

Once Albertine left, I called the hospital to ask about putting the leg of my slacks inside the orthopedic boot. The doctor thought the bunched material around my broken ankle would make the boot less efficient. He was, however, pleased that I had been walking and intended to shop for a shoe with a heel the same height as the boot.

"But perhaps you do not know that in France is not possible to buy only one shoe. You must buy a pair. Also I must warn you not to fall, which can happen while shopping in such a city as Avignon with pavements of ancient unevenness. You could wear tights instead of slacks, but you must keep the foot in the proper position while putting them on, the position in which your foot is held by the boot."

While he talked on and on, I decided I could wear those shin-length pants, if they were sold in France. And did he really think that I could buy one shoe in the United States? What strange perceptions people had of our country. If I couldn't find capris, I'd try for tights. That shopping decision made, I sat back on the bed, my ankle resting on a pillow to prevent swelling, and clicked on the TV, which showed one picture after another of cars and buildings burning in Paris, as well as youths running around at night and policemen chasing them. Watching the policemen reminded me of Inspector Roux and the horrid Inspector Villon. I was glad that I hadn't heard from Villon. No doubt the gunshot residue had cleared me and embarrassed him, which meant he owed me an apology.

I also felt that my police friend in Lyon would want to hear about the new attempt on our lives, this time with a gun, not to mention the theory that the attacker might be a terrorist. That hadn't even occurred to me when we were in Lyon.

Jason called first and admitted that Mercedes had apologized for threatening him. When he said that he had accepted her apology, I was ready to hang up, but he added that he still insisted on her finding a new research director, after which she threatened him again. Dreadful girl! I wondered if there was any way to have her calls to him switched over here to me. I'd *love* to talk to her.

Before I could explore that possibility, Jason detailed the rest of their conversation: the imminent arrival of her parents, who would punish him for the way he had treated her; Jason's retort that she must be an embarrassment to her family; Mercedes hanging up on him; and his request that no more of her calls be put through. He was sure the whole conference would have heard and be laughing at his expense.

"You poor dear," I replied. "I'm so proud of you. If her father tries anything, I'll be happy to tell him off. In fact, I'll be happy to tell her off. In fact, I could stop by the hospital on my way to shop with Albertine." Poor Jason. He was horrified at my plans to visit Mercedes and go shopping.

"But, Jason, I intend to get a refund on the heels that broke and the dress that got torn because the heels broke."

"Good luck with that," said my husband dryly.

"Then, when I have my money back, I hope to find a shoe of the proper height, some capri pants to wear with my boot, and if not those, tights. The doctor wasn't very happy with the idea of strapping the boot on over slacks."

"Well, for heaven's sake, Carolyn, do what he tells you, and you shouldn't be out shopping."

"He told me to walk, and I'm walking. It's not too bad, but I need a shoe so I don't limp and dislocate my hip."

"Good lord. Is that a possibility?"

"I hope not, but Albertine mentioned it. And then if the shoe works, I'm going to the impromptu cathedral tour."

"Carolyn!"

"Albertine's driving." I didn't tell him about the papal gardens and the city walls. "And Bridget's sending up food, so I'm not starving."

"Sweetheart, will you please be careful, and don't try to do too much?" I promised and hung up. If my ankle hurt much, obviously I'd stop walking.

I then called Lyon and asked for Inspector Roux. He was interested to hear about the bullet that had, happily, missed us, but saddened to hear about my broken ankle. "So you are back in the hospital? You are having many un-lucky events, but you must not think that France is a—"

"Goodness, Inspector. Don't tell me how safe France is. Look what's happening in Paris. They're torching cars and nursery schools. I'd say that France is exceptionally dangerous. I hope you aren't having problems in Lyon."

"No, no. Our minority youths are well treated and hap-pier than those in Paris, and we keep our eyes open, as we do for whoever stalks you, although that person must now be in Avignon, so perhaps there is no need—"

"That reminds me, Inspector. Another suspect has come to mind." And I told him the story of the *Bountiful Feast*, the hijacking, and the hijacker who might be a terrorist and have sent his friends after us. The inspector was astonished at my ill luck and promised to consult with colleagues who tracked terrorists.

Satisfied with his response, but not with the fact that the Avignon police had never contacted him, I watched a few more burning cars and buildings on TV and answered my door to receive a lunch of soup and a tuna-salad-filled croissant. Then I lay down and was awakened at one by the telephone. Bridget's replacement informed me that a huge man named Monsieur Le Blanc was in the lobby asking to talk to me. What should she do with him?

Martin was sweet to come by, but I couldn't invite him to my room. I offered to come downstairs. After all, the French were given to thinking that everyone had affairs. No doubt, they thought that about my husband and Mercedes. I certainly didn't want to give cause for gossip about Martin and me.

When I stepped off the elevator, he was standing in the lobby holding a small bouquet of flowers and a large manila envelope. "I did not mean for you to meet me, madam. I would have been happy to talk on the telephone and leave these for you." He was shifting from foot to foot and holding out the two gifts. "I just wanted to know that you were better and to give you my wishes for a speedy recovery. I should have gone with you to the hospital, and then to find—you will have heard—that a student of your husband had been shot and that I could not tell your husband of your accident so that he could be with you. Did he find you there, I hope?"

"Please sit down, Martin. Aren't you missing lunch at the palais?" He pulled a package out to show that he was not. "My husband did find me, but here at the hotel, and thank you for the flowers. They're very pretty."

"I took them from a yard," he confessed, and then blushed. A blush on a redheaded man his size was a sight to see, but I *didn't* giggle. "The envelope, that is the important thing," Martin added.

"Oh?" I opened it and found a photocopy of a scientific paper not yet prepared for publication. The drawings of compounds had obviously been done by hand. "How lovely," I said, wondering what he expected me to do with it. "Your research? I wish I could say that I'll understand it, but at least I'll cherish it for your thoughtfulness."

"*Non.* Your husband must read it. It is *her* research. He will understand when he sees it."

"I'm sure he will," I replied, all the more puzzled. A bouquet for me and a photocopy for Jason? "Your professor's research? How kind of her to send it."

Poor Martin now looked miserable. "She did not send it, but your husband will be—interested."

"I understand." Of course, I didn't. "I'll give it to him tonight."

"That is good," said Martin. "Do not forget."

I assured him that I wouldn't.

"You are walking. That is surely a miracle. Is it safe?"

"The doctor advised it," I replied. "I'm going shopping this afternoon and to the tour of the cathedral." Martin looked so stunned at my plans that I couldn't resist adding, "And then I hope to visit the gardens and the walls, which I so much want to see. I hear that the views of the river and the countryside are spectacular."

"You really must see these things?" he asked disapprovingly. "Then I must walk with you."

Obviously I'd gone too far. "You needn't worry, Martin. I'm going with Albertine Guillot."

"I must go with you," he insisted. "How would you climb the stairs? There are stairs. I will carry you, and you will not miss this important sightseeing."

"Well, Martin, what are *you* doing here?" Albertine asked, striding up to us.

"I am going on your excursion, Madam Guillot. When Madam Blue cannot manage, I will carry her."

Albertine didn't argue. She just said, "Well, it looks like we'll be doing the whole tour." She didn't sound particularly happy about it. I had no plans to be carried about like a cripple, but accepted so she couldn't back out. When I asked Martin to take the envelope and flowers to the desk for safekeeping until I returned, Albertine whispered, "I do believe that young Norman is in love."

"Not with me," I replied without explaining my answer. Martin's secrets were safe with me. I owed him, as my son would say.

44
A Perfect Afternoon

Carolyn

While Martin wandered around blinking at dresses and lingerie, I told the saleslady I wished to return the shoes and dress I had bought earlier. She examined them and pointed out the damage, which made them nonreturnable.

"Ha!" cried Albertine. "You told her the heels would withstand stone streets, but look at them! The left one broke, causing Madam Blue's ankle to break and her dress to be damaged when she fell." Albertine then pulled the salesclerk aside for a conversation in French. Meanwhile Martin stopped inspecting ladies' wear and towered over the combatants, scowling. At length the saleslady agreed to let me choose merchandise to replace the value of the shoes and to put their seamstress to work repairing the dress.

I was both pleased and puzzled until Albertine told me she had warned the woman about Americans, who loved lawsuits. She predicted that I would sue the establishment for the money I had paid, for my pain and suffering, and for my medical expenses, which were not covered by French health care.

I'm not sure whether Martin's immense, glowering

presence or Albertine's argument did the trick, but I was soon trying on shoes with heels of the proper height. I found one pair made of leather so soft they felt like bedroom slippers. And they were pretty. I wouldn't mind wearing both when I had two free feet again. I also looked at cropped pants and had to settle for a pair with side lacings up over the knee. I'd probably never wear them at home, but at least I could pull them over my boot to try them on. And they had a matching top.

My two-piece dress, at which the salesperson looked askance, my slip, one new shoe, and one old shoe were bundled into a shopping bag and deposited in Albertine's trunk, the torn evening dress was left for remodeling, and we started toward another shop Albertine wished to visit. However, Martin objected and made me sit down to rest.

It was there that Sylvie and Winston Churchill found us. While the dog sniffed my gauze-wrapped toes, Sylvie sat down to tell me about a restaurant, La Compagnie des Comptoirs. "I know how much you've been craving Japanese food, Carolyn, and they have sushi."

I couldn't very well say that it wasn't Japanese food I yearned for, but I was saved from disappointing her when Albertine arrived, listened to the description of the restaurant, and decided that the six of us should meet for dinner the next night. "Oh, very well," said Sylvie. "But neither of us can bring our dogs, Albertine. They'll squabble over Carolyn. I'll make reservations. Rue Joseph Vernet, number eighty-three. We'll see you at eight." Then she took a picture of me sitting on the bench with Martin, who was being sniffed suspiciously by Winston Churchill.

We stopped at a bistro so that Albertine could have lunch. I had a tasty dish of glacé and two pain pills, after which we walked to Albertine's car and headed for the cathedral. Unfortunately, having a car didn't help much because there were many stairs to climb in order to reach

Notre-Dame des Doms. The other wives stared when Martin carried me into the church at the head of our group. It was horribly embarrassing. I should probably have stayed home, but the church was interesting.

It was built in the Romanesque style in three different periods during the twelfth century, and then changed inside in the seventeenth century. Still, for all the fiddling with the old Romanesque architecture, there were lovely things to see, two fine chapels, one with frescoed arches dedicated to the Holy Sacrament and another to St. Roch with statues and lush ornamentation, not to mention a bishop's chair with red velvet drapes and a pretty baroque organ above. I was, however, disappointed to hear that the huge statue of the Virgin on top of the bell tower was actually gilded lead, not gold. Of course if it had been gold, some conqueror would have made off with it.

From the cathedral we went into the gardens, with their shady trees, flowers, lakes with swans, and naked statues, also benches, on which Martin insisted that I rest, although he had been carrying me every time there was even one step to climb.

I thought maybe he'd become discouraged when Winston Churchill, who joined the tour with Sylvie, tried to bite his ankle, but Martin simply lifted his leg with the dog attached and flung it gently away. After that, Sylvie carried the dog, and Martin continued to carry me. Albertine was snickering, and the other ladies still staring, while the guide seemed distressed over the interruptions to her talk.

And, oh, the views of the Rhône, wide and gray-blue, and of Avignon and the town and fort across the river. The ramparts were built of thick stone with out-thrust ribs rising to the walkways and crenellated towers. No wonder the French king could only take the city by siege and starvation. We could have walked down the long flight of stairs where the walls descended from the Dom to the bridge of

St. Benezet, but I decided against that. The stairs were narrow and steep, and large as my Norman knight was, I did not want to put him and myself at risk.

After all, Albertine and I had already seen the bridge, and Martin, although willing, did not insist. Given all the whispering among the ladies when he picked me up, his fear of having his sexual orientation discovered was now no longer a problem. No doubt they thought he was having a fling with me. Was that why he was so insistent on *not* letting me attempt any stairs?

45
The Telltale Research

Jason

"What's this I hear about my wife being repeatedly swept into the arms of Martin the Norman?" I asked. "Now the conferees think we're both having affairs with graduate students."

"Martin was preventing me from going up and down stairs." She'd been lying on the bed reading. "Actually, I wanted to try stairs to see if I could."

"Then I owe the young man my thanks. Why did you think you could climb stairs wearing that boot?"

"I could have if there'd been railings, and what's your excuse for Mercedes?"

"She was trying to keep me from being shot. You should be grateful, too. What's this?" Carolyn had just handed me a manila envelope.

She rolled off the bed and walked over to the door that led to our cement-walled patio. "Look at the sky, Jason. More clouds are gathering. I got a wonderful picture of the cathedral with that same sky behind it. Positively menacing."

"That reminds me, Bertrand and Nicole Fournier want us to meet them at La Fourchette. They say a member of the Hiely-Lucullus family runs it, but it's less expensive and close by. They have reservations, but the way the weather's looking, maybe we should stay here."

"L'Horlage doesn't serve dinner, and we have umbrellas." She pulled the drapes across the door as if hiding the sky would change my mind.

I mentioned the danger of falling on wet pavement, damage to the orthopedic boot, which was undoubtedly going to cost us something excessive, and damage to her new shoe. Arguing with Carolyn didn't work; she had plastic boots to cover her shoe, called downstairs to get a plastic garbage bag to tie over the orthopedic boot—evidently they liked her, because they sent one up—and then she promised to cling to my arm so that she wouldn't fall.

While I was picturing both of us falling in a heavy rainstorm, I examined the manila envelope, which contained a chemistry paper in its early stages. The drawing of the compound on the second page was so interesting that I immediately sat down to read.

When the garbage bag arrived, my wife gathered clothes for the evening and went into the bathroom to tie the bag around her knee, thus protecting the boot while she took a shower. The paper described the synthesis of the molecule pictured, plus notes on possible medical applications for a dilute solution of the stuff. It had a French name with which I was unfamiliar.

When Carolyn limped out of the bathroom a half hour later, looking very pretty except for the boot under her skirt, she announced that the garbage bag had been a great success, and she felt much better for having had a shower. "Sponge baths are *very* unsatisfactory."

My wife is given to frequent bathing, changing of clothes, and washing said clothes. "This is a fascinating piece of work," I told her. "A compound I've never seen before with excellent medical applications when dilute enough to be nontoxic."

"Toxic?"

"Of course. Why would anyone send me a paper that wasn't about toxins? Who did the work, by the way? There's no name."

"Martin brought it over, but it's Catherine's experiment." Instead of sitting down, or putting on the shoe that balanced her boot, she stared at me anxiously.

"Catherine's? Then I look forward to discussing it with her."

"Jason, you can't do that. I don't think Catherine knows he copied it and brought it to you. You'd get him in trouble. What's the name of the compound?"

"It's something in French. I don't recognize the word, but it's very strange that her graduate student would bring you a stolen copy of her research. Maybe you misunderstood."

"Maybe," said my wife, and reminded me that I should take my shower if we were to arrive on time at the restaurant. She was right, and I went in, only to find the floor as covered with water as the floor of that bathroom in Lyon had been. However, this one had never flooded before. Still, I made no complaint, imagining the difficulties of showering while wearing a garbage-bag-wrapped orthopedic boot.

When I'd finished, I returned to the room to see Carolyn staring at the screen of her computer with the research papers in her hand. "Jason," she said, looking up, "this compound is tetrodotoxin."

I laughed and began to dress.

"No, really," she continued, sounding peeved. "I compared the drawing I downloaded to my computer to the one in the paper. They match atom for atom."

"Well, the positioning and bonds could make it an entirely different—"

"Will you look? She's the person who tried to kill us. She didn't have to find fugu. She made the toxin herself."

I looked, and the molecules did match, but the idea that Catherine put fish toxin in our pâté—well, I didn't believe that for a minute. "Two points, my love," I said. "Well, three. First, you've decided that it was a terrorist. Second, Catherine wasn't in Avignon when you were pushed down those stairs, and third, that research is medical in nature. The compound in dilute solution holds promise to relieve all kinds of pain—that of recovering heroin addicts, and intractable arthritis pain, for instance."

"Fine, Jason. Just promise me that first, you'll keep away from her; and second, you won't get Martin in trouble by telling her that he stole the research—he was trying to help us—and third, I'll never forgive you if you talk to her about this research no matter how wonderful you think it is. I—well, I need to check some things out."

Carolyn wouldn't put her knee-highs or her new shoe or her jewelry on until I gave her my word. Since we hadn't cancelled on the Fourniers, the weather had cleared, and they'd be waiting for us, I gave in and promised to stay away from Catherine. What else could I do?

46

Good Food, Good Gossip

Carolyn

La Fourchette was crowded, bustling, and noisy, with
half-paneling below and white walls above covered with
pictures and cooking implements, white tablecloths, and
hard chairs. The Fourniers were seated, studying menus
and wine lists. After the usual expressions of sympathy
about my ankle and questions about why I had been out in
an alley instead of attending the delicious banquet—which
they described in detail, relieving me of an explanation for
my absence—they began to tell us what we should order.

We let them choose the wine, which had worked well
before, and then Jason ordered a sardine appetizer in a
bright green sauce and carpaccio in white coriander sauce,
while I had twelve snails, each tucked into its own com-
partment and bathed in a butter and green herb sauce, and
as my entrée, La Daube de Boeuf a la Avignonnaise, which
was stew of tender, tasty beef chunks in dark red wine. The
Cote de Luberon Maison that Bertrand ordered went wonderfully with my choices, but I only took a sip or two.

That, of course, raised objections. The Fourniers
couldn't seem to understand that I shouldn't be drinking at
all while taking pain pills. Jason pacified Bertrand by en-

gaging him in a serious discussion of chemistry, while I pursued my suspicions of Catherine by asking Nicole questions about the dead husband.

"My dear," said Nicole, settling down for a good gossip, "that was fifteen years ago at least and quite a scandal. Because he killed himself, the priest, called while he was dying, refused to give him the last rites. Catherine was furious and had him buried in a Protestant cemetery rather than risk having him refused burial in sacred ground."

"How did he kill himself?"

"With a gun, of course. Probably a target pistol. They both owned guns and enjoyed shooting. I don't believe they hunted, but they belonged to a club for shooting at targets and clay birds."

I wondered whether a target pistol had been the weapon used to shoot Mercedes. "What was his name? I don't believe anyone has ever mentioned it."

"Maurice Bellamee. She kept her own name when they married. Very modern, but then she was quite a young woman. She'd been his student, but she had to change professors when they fell in love, and they couldn't marry until she took her degree. Then Maurice insisted that the university hire her. That caused scandal, too, but Maurice was well thought of, a dear man really, except for his mental illness.

"Some people say it was simple melancholy, but I think the priest was wrong to deny him the last rights. Poor Maurice couldn't help it when his condition became so serious he killed himself. He wasn't in his right mind, you know. I've always felt that God will forgive him, after a suitable time in purgatory, because the poor man wasn't responsible."

"I'm sure you're right, Nicole. I hope you told Catherine that. It must have been a comfort to her."

"Oh, no. Catherine would not be comforted. She's still

in mourning. In fact, I did tell her, and she screamed at me. Catherine never accepted that Maurice had psychiatric problems. And they came and went. He was quite normal and cheerful while they were falling in love and during the first year of their marriage. I've often wondered if it wasn't the strain of being married to a woman so much younger that set off the depression again, but of course, I couldn't say that to Catherine. She'd probably have pushed me down the stairs. Bad enough that she screamed at me."

"Pushed you down the stairs?" I echoed weakly, remembering my fall into space before I lost consciousness in her stairway.

"Well, that's just a figure of speech, my dear, and an unfortunate one, considering your fall in Lyon, but surely you didn't think that Bertrand or I would have pushed you, anymore than I think Catherine would have pushed me."

"No, of course not," I replied. "I was in pain and very groggy when the inspector asked who knew where I'd be. It never occurred to me that he'd rush off and question everyone I named. I was very embarrassed by the whole misunderstanding."

"Well, don't give it another thought. We've forgiven you, haven't we, Bertrand?"

He didn't answer because he and Jason were eating and drawing molecules on pieces of paper that Jason carried in his pockets because I'd gotten tired of him irritating restaurant employees by drawing on their napkins and tablecloths.

"The fact is that Catherine blamed a stranger for his death. Someone said, in print, mind you, that a paper Maurice published was all wrong, and Maurice was upset about the criticism, but one doesn't kill oneself over chemical data. The poor man probably *was* wrong. He was already depressed before that letter about his paper was published.

I remember saying hello to him in the hall outside his office when I was meeting Bertrand.

"In fact, we were going to the very restaurant where we took you and your husband in Lyon. We had—what was it?—ah, a lovely capon with truffles under the skin. I'll never forget that dish. But as I was saying, I greeted Maurice, and he didn't even look up. He just continued down the hall with his head hanging. So sad.

"I don't suppose the medications for such problems were as good then, or perhaps he didn't want to take them because of what Catherine would think. She never, never accepted that he had a problem. Blaming his death on a professional conflict was just Catherine's way of rationalizing his suicide. She probably thought that if he had really been in love with her, he wouldn't have been depressed."

At that point the profiteroles ordered by Bertrand arrived, and they were marvelous, with an exceptional dark chocolate sauce, crispy pastries, and inside a rich vanilla and chocolate ice cream. I ate all three of mine and had a sip of wine with each.

"Ah, I see you cannot resist the wine, after all," said Bertrand, sounding pleased, "and you can be sure that the chocolate used to make the sauce is Lyonnais. Note how fine and smooth it is, how rich. Only chocolate made with the very best varieties of cocoa tastes like this."

La Daube de Boeuf a l'Avignonnaise

- Make a marinade: Push *2 cloves* into an *onion cut in 4 pieces*. Put the onion into a mixture of *2 cups red wine, 3 strips orange zest, 3 cloves garlic, ½ stalk celery, 2 bay leaves,* and *several parsley stalks*.

- Cut *3 pounds beef rump* into large chunks, *salt* and *pepper,* and leave overnight in marinade.

- Heat *2 tablespoons oil* in saucepan. Take beef from marinade and pat dry. Brown in batches and put on plate. If necessary use small amounts of marinade to deglaze pan between batches to prevent bits from sticking and burning to bottom.

- Strain marinade through sieve and put contents of sieve into saucepan to brown. Remove. Add marinade liquid to saucepan and boil, stirring 30 seconds to deglaze.

- Put *2 ounces pork fat* in a large casserole with a *7-ounce piece of bacon,* beef, and marinade ingredients. Pour in marinade liquid from saucepan and *2½ cups beef stock,* bring to boil, cover, reduce heat, and simmer gently 2 to 2½ hours or until meat is tender.

- Remove meat to serving dish, and keep warm by covering. Throw away garlic, onion, pork fat, and bacon. Pour liquid through a fine sieve and skim off fat, return to casserole, boil, and reduce by half until syrupy. Pour gravy over meat and serve.

Carolyn Blue,
"Have Fork, Will Travel,"
Dover (Maryland) News-Ledger

I could have pushed her over the walls or down the stairs to the bridge if that Norman lout hadn't been there carrying her around. I could have slipped a knife between her ribs in that crowd of sightseers, and who would have noticed had it not been for him? So many opportunities missed. I must be the least successful assassin who ever plotted a death. Will I find another chance at one or both of them? If so, I must succeed.

47
Facing the Angry Parents

Jason

I **was talking** with colleagues between sessions when a young woman from the registration desk tapped my arm. "Professor Blue, perhaps I could speak to you privately," she whispered. Of course that caught the interest of the others.

"If it's about that student of mine," I said brusquely, "just tell me what the problem is."

She hesitated. "It is her father. He and the mother are at the hospital and they *demand*—that was his word—that you and your wife meet them there. I am so sorry to bring this message, but he threatened to call the police if you do not come immediately."

I thanked her as calmly as I could and excused myself. Once I was safely away from spectators, I said a few choice words and went in search of a telephone. It wasn't that I wanted Carolyn to go with me, but I did need to warn her in case they, or the police, showed up at the hotel. I was hoping that my wife would already be out sightseeing, but she picked up, so I outlined the problem.

"Albertine should be here any moment," said Carolyn. I was relieved until Carolyn insisted that I stay at the palais until she arrived to talk to me. "Mercedes and her father can wait a bit."

"What if he follows through and calls the police?"

"Let him. He'll be more embarrassed than we could ever be when he discovers what his daughter's been up to. Did you get hold of Human Resources at home?"

"Yes, and I've faxed them the complaint."

"Oh, good. I hope you kept a copy. Do show it to the Lizarretas."

I did wait for her but wished I hadn't when I discovered what she intended. At Carolyn's insistence, Albertine drove us to the hospital to meet the parents, both tall, thin, and dark-haired, both hovering over my former student, who, according to the floor nurse, refused to leave the hospital although she could have been discharged. The three glared at us when we were shown into Mercedes's hospital room. She was wearing a frilly bed jacket of the type seen in old black-and-white movies and looked as if a hairdresser and makeup artist had come in to make her glamorous.

"You're looking well, Mercedes," said Carolyn. "Why is it you won't leave the hospital?"

"I am safe from being shot while I'm here," said Mercedes crisply.

Her father, face reddening, turned to me and shouted, "You are the professor of my daughter. And you let your mad wife shoot her? You were the father in absentia. It was your duty—"

"Mercedes wasn't treating my husband like a father," said Carolyn sweetly. "If she treats you the way she treated Jason here in Lyon, your friends must be gossiping behind your back. All the conferees are certainly talking about her behavior. She's been acting like a trollop."

"What did you call *mi hija*?" cried the mother.

"If she hadn't draped herself all over Jason, she

wouldn't have been shot," Carolyn continued. "Of course, I'm grateful that Jason wasn't hurt, but I doubt that Mercedes had anything in mind other than trying to get close to him."

"Then you confess to the shooting!" said the father triumphantly. "The police will wish to hear this. They are looking for the weapon and tell me that you have no alibi for the time when—"

"My wife meant no such thing," I protested. "In fact, at that time, she was incapacitated with a broken ankle outside the palais. As you can see, she's wearing an orthopedic boot."

"Yes," Carolyn agreed. "I even heard the ambulance that came for your daughter; I really wished they were coming for me. Furthermore, Jason was the target of the gunman, not Mercedes. If she hadn't thrown herself at him, the bullet wouldn't have hit her."

"So you are saying that not you, señora, but perhaps another angry father was trying to shoot your husband?" asked Señor Lizarreta.

"She's lying," cried Mercedes. "She shot me because she knew that Jason and I are in love."

"I am not in love with you, Mercedes. I never was in love with you, and I've never given you any reason to think I was. In fact, I've found your conduct at the conference extremely embarrassing."

"What is this?" growled Señor Lizarreta, turning toward his daughter. "You are in love with a married man?"

"Yes," she snapped. "And he loves me."

"Really," said Carolyn. "If he's so much in love, why has Jason insisted that you find another research director, preferably at another university?"

"He just told *you* that. He doesn't want me to leave him," said Mercedes.

Tired of the whole argument, I opened my briefcase on

the nightstand and pulled out the copy of the harassment complaint, which I handed to her father. While he read it, Mercedes demanded to be told what it was, and I told her. She screamed at me in Spanish, which was probably a good thing. I didn't really want to know what she had to say, but I did notice that her mother turned white and spoke sharply to her.

"No *hombre Mexicano* would be so unmanly as to accuse a pretty girl of harassing him," said the father. "Have you no pride, señor?"

"We take sexual harassment seriously in our country," I replied. "Evidently that is not the case in Mexico." Carolyn clapped her hand over her mouth, to stifle a giggle would be my guess.

"As for you, Mercedes," said her father, "you will accompany us to Mexico City immediately. Raquel," he addressed his wife, "see that she dresses while I pay the hospital bill."

"Her university Blue Cross Blue Shield will cover part of it," my wife said helpfully. "I found that out when I had a concussion in Lyon and the broken ankle here."

The father gave Carolyn a contemptuous look, as if using health insurance was a lower-class tactic.

"Out of the room," ordered the mother. "My daughter wishes to dress."

"I do not," said Mercedes.

Carolyn and I left quietly and found Albertine in the hall, eavesdropping. *"Mon Dieu,"* she said. "What an unpleasant threesome, although I must agree with the father. Filing a complaint against the girl is not dignified, Jason. Adrien agrees with me."

I shrugged. "If she really disappears into Mexico, I'll withdraw it." That would have been my preference, but I'd wait until I was sure no lawsuits against me were impending. And the next time I accepted a female graduate stu-

dent, she'd be homely and devoted to science. I doubted
that discrimination could be charged if I showed a preference for ugly, chemistry-obsessed girls.

Carolyn slipped her hand through my arm and whispered, "Wasn't that fun? Aren't you glad I came along?"

My wife has a somewhat twisted idea about what's
"fun." I just hoped that the police no longer considered her
a suspect. Perhaps if the victim left town, the investigation
would die a natural death, not that I wouldn't be relieved if
the French police actually caught whoever seemed to be
targeting us, even though the attacker had been mercifully
unsuccessful.

48

A Word to the Gallant Pierre

Carolyn

Albertine drove Jason back to the palais and went in to tell Adrien, belatedly, about the dinner date with the Girards, so I took the opportunity to have a word with my admirer, Pierre. In fact, I had to drag him into a chapel to make my request without being overheard. "Pierre, could you find out who wrote a letter to a journal fifteen or sixteen years ago criticizing the work of Maurice Bellamee, a chemist from Lyon."

"You have a new beau!" Pierre looked crestfallen. "Here am I, madly in love, and you want me to provide information so you can defend the work of this Maurice. Why, may I ask? Is Maurice—"

"Dead," I replied, "and keep your voice down. You mustn't tell anyone I asked. Can you do it? Or is it too long ago?"

"But of course I can. The Internet holds all information if you know how to use it and have access to the necessary websites. You are pining for this dead person? I am hurt. Bad enough to compete with a live husband for your affections, but what man can compete with the memory of one who is dead? I am devastated."

"You're an outrageous flirt, Pierre, and this has nothing to do with my affections. However, if you can find the information, I shall hold you in affection forever."

With that Pierre beamed at me, kissed me on both cheeks, and promised to call once he got to his computer. "Well, well!" said my husband from the door. "Albertine said you'd ducked in here with Lamont. It seems I can't let you out of my sight, Carolyn."

"Do not be worried, *mon professeur*," said Pierre gaily. "Much as I adore your wife, she has yet to express any return of my affections."

Jason shook his head as Pierre left the chapel and then turned to me. "I'll return to the hotel before the Guillots pick us up at seven-forty-five. Does that suit you?"

"Absolutely. Sylvie says they even have Japanese food at this place."

"Carolyn, this isn't another tetrodotoxin thing, is it?"

"No, Jason," I replied meekly. "This is a column about the variety of cuisines to be found in Southern France."

"And why was Pierre kissing you?"

"The French are cheek kissers. Charles de Gaulle used to do that, and to men."

"The dog?" asked my husband.

"The general, silly. If you like, I can ask Pierre to kiss you."

"Oh, thanks." Jason turned to leave as Albertine arrived to ask where I wanted to have lunch. Since I hadn't chosen a place, she suggested La Salicorne, where we ate in a dining room that resembled a cave with yellow and green decorative touches and many salads and fondues on the lunch menu. Always mindful of her figure, Albertine ordered a salad. Always tempted by high-calorie treats, I had a wonderful cheese fondue, followed by an equally wonderful chocolate fondue.

Even Albertine was tempted by my dessert and shared

it while berating me for being a bad influence. I explained that I had subjected myself and my family all summer to salads and felt that I deserved a reward for now being able to fit into my size-10 clothes after a gluttonous spring cruise. Albertine said that sensible eating at all times was the key to keeping one's figure. I didn't pay her much mind since she ate as much chocolate fondue as I did. Charles de Gaulle sat on the floor looking hopeful, but we saved his life by refusing him chocolate.

After lunch we drove by the Church of St. Martial, part of what had once been a Benedictine monastery. I particularly liked the ruins of the cloister, which housed worn statues in the arches and looked ready to tumble down— very scenic. I took a picture. Then we viewed Gallo-Roman foundations, part of a monument in Avignon's Roman Forum, and finally we visited two museums, the Musée Lapidaire and the Musée Calvet, to see finds from local archeological digs.

My favorites were a third-millennium stela in the Calvet, rather human, with a rough nose and long hair, two holes for eyes, a hole above the nose for goodness knows what, and eight chiseled lines radiating from another hole in the lower right section. There was no mouth.

In the Lapidaire were a bust of Jupiter with frizzy hair and beard, as if someone had taken a curling iron to him and, best of all, a stone carving of a boat with a man and two large barrels being towed down the Durance river by two very gnomish peasants. Peasants are always depicted as short and stocky. I wonder if they were that short in real life, perhaps as a result of poor diet, or if they were depicted that way as a class distinction. At any rate, I'd enjoyed the lunch and the afternoon. I do love to sightsee, although doing it with my foot in an orthopedic boot destroyed some of the joy. Then from the museum to the hotel, Charles de Gaulle pushed his head over the front seat and rested it on my shoulder—shades of Sorrento, but this time he didn't drool on my blouse. I was glad to be dropped off at the hotel, where I could prop up my leg and rest before dressing for dinner.

Inspector Roux interrupted my nap by calling to tell me their antiterrorism unit knew of a suspect in Lyon with ties to a violent Indonesian organization, but that the man seemed to have left the city. I sighed. That certainly fit with the chief steward on the cruise, now incarcerated. He'd claimed to be Indian, but he was from Indonesia. His designated assassin was probably in Avignon, looking for another chance to kill us.

"I've faxed a picture to your hotel. It's blurry, but it will give you something to look out for. And I called Inspector Villon with the news, but unfortunately, he still thinks you shot the young woman at the palais."

"But haven't they finished the gunpowder test."

"He says you probably washed the residue off. They're still looking for the gun, which was a target pistol. He imagines you bought it as a souvenir and then had it fixed by a gunsmith so that it would shoot."

"Who'd want a souvenir pistol?" I asked irritably. "I have another suspect who actually is known to have used target pistols. But I haven't any evidence against her beyond that and a bit of scientific information that can, according to my husband, be interpreted in a wholly unincriminating way."

"You think a woman is the culprit?" The inspector obviously, chauvinist that he was, considered a female assassin a peculiar idea, goodness knows why. Women have even gone into the suicide bombing profession in the Middle East. "Villon will never believe you unless there is jealousy involved," said Inspector Roux. "Is she, too, in love with your husband?"

"I don't know why you'd say that, as if three women

could not possibly be in love with my husband. Jason is very attractive. But no, she isn't in love with him."

"Well, keep the eyes open for the man whose picture I send."

I agreed and called Albertine to tell her. "In that case, I must bring Charles de Gaulle tonight," she replied. "You're crippled, I certainly can't overpower a terrorist by myself if we should see him in the restaurant, and the men will never listen to us."

I had to agree with that and with bringing the dog, although Sylvie would be furious. They'd had an agreement. I went downstairs for the fax, a dim likeness of a small man with a beard and a large nose.

When Jason got home, I showed him the picture. He was pleased, thinking that the new lead meant Catherine was no longer suspect and he could talk to her about her fascinating research. I had to remind him that he couldn't for Martin's sake.

"Well, he shouldn't be passing around his professor's work," said my husband. "If I were the sort, I could publish it myself."

"Anyone would know, Jason, that you'd never steal a colleague's research," I said soothingly. "Martin was just worried about us. Give the paper back to me, and I'll see that he returns it discreetly. Then she won't know, and he won't get in trouble." Of course, that wasn't what I had in mind. That paper might well be evidence if I could discover any other clues to implicate Catherine. I was finding it extremely hard to protect the two of us when Jason pooh-poohed my hypotheses.

49

A Terrorist at Large?

Jason

Why the Guillots brought their huge dog I couldn't imagine, but the poodle sat between us in the backseat and stared wistfully at Carolyn. Bad enough to have Pierre and Martin mooning over her, but the dog was the last straw. And *she* complained about Mercedes! If I was lucky, Mercedes was already on her way to Mexico City, that is if she and her parents hadn't been held up by rioting in Lyon and Paris. This wasn't the most felicitous time to hold a meeting in France, but then my colleagues couldn't have predicted a sudden onset of car and school burnings. The scenes on TV before we left the hotel were upsetting, especially since we, too, had to pass through Lyon and Paris to get home.

The restaurant was a stone building with an interior courtyard furnished with a pool, palms, tables, chairs, and brightly colored lanterns, none of which we could enjoy because the weather was cold and blustery. On one side of the courtyard was a green plastic bar with white leather chairs and low tables, under which one obviously couldn't fit one's knees. I fervently hoped no one wanted a drink before dinner.

Happily, we were shown to a long room on the other side. It looked out through Roman arched windows on the courtyard. Inside it was rather dark, but not so dark that Sylvie didn't immediately spot the dog and complain that Albertine had broken some agreement.

"Charles de Gaulle is here to protect Carolyn and Jason against a terrorist from Lyon," Albertine retorted.

"Who followed them to *this* restaurant?" demanded Sylvie, who obviously didn't believe a word of it. Adrien and Raymond both chuckled.

Carolyn's explanation was delayed when a tall waitress, who looked and dressed like a gypsy, accosted us at our table, and we had to try to read our lengthy menus in the dark.

My wife ordered something called Cocotte des Legumes, which irritated Sylvie. "I found this place so that you could have Japanese food. Aren't you going to order any?" she demanded. Then when Carolyn looked mutinous and insisted on her legumes, Sylvie added that Madam Blue would also have sushi. The gypsy asked what kind, and Sylvie said, "How should I know? I don't eat Japanese food. Just bring her some." Carolyn went on to order lamb chops, which brought more grumbles from Sylvie. I assumed that Raymond's wife was still angry at being fingered by mine as the staircase mugger.

The rest of us ordered without disagreement until Carolyn realized that I'd chosen a steak from a "fighting bull." "You're going to eat some poor creature that was stabbed in a bull ring?" she exclaimed.

"In southern France we don't kill the bulls in the ring," said Raymond. "They're sent in with a white cockade fastened between the horns and thoroughly irritated by men trying to steal the cockade with hooks."

"If you can get beans in black truffle sauce," I retorted, "I don't see why I can't try bull with truffle slices."

As soon as she heard that the bull came with truffles, she relented and informed me that Provence produced more and better truffles than any place in the world. "Did you know that the Romans ate them like sweets at theater performances, and opera goers in the eighteenth century ate them between acts?" I hadn't, and I must say that her legumes looked and tasted wonderful. She gave me a bite. During the first course, Raymond bemoaned the fact that he could have become an aeronautical engineer in Toulouse and made big money.

"You don't like chemistry?" Carolyn asked, as she lifted a truffle-bedewed snow pea to her mouth.

"I love chemistry. However, I have a wife who loves expensive, dagger-toed, high-heeled shoes and boots. No young chemistry professor can afford a wardrobe of such high-priced footwear."

"And high heels are dangerous," Carolyn agreed. "Were you named after one of the famous Raymonds in the history of Toulouse?"

"I certainly hope not. One of them gave up Toulouse to the French king without a fight. I once asked my father if he'd been named after the man who let Paris take us over, but he wouldn't talk about it."

Everyone had to sample the plate of sushi because Carolyn ate only one piece. She was too delighted with her truffled beans and vegetables to be diverted by something she could get in El Paso. The sushi did look like some I'd had at a place not far from our house.

A busboy arrived and snatched up our plates, while our gypsy swished over to serve the entrees. The meat of a fighting bull, in case you've never had it, is very different from ordinary beef. I can't quite describe it and am not sure to this day that I really liked it, but it was certainly unusual, and the truffles and vegetable flan were excellent. In fact, the menu and our table were full of vegetables and fruits.

We were all eating healthfully when I spotted a new diner being led to a table. He was by himself and looked familiar in the dusk of the dining room. I squinted, and just then, as he picked up his menu, he turned his head and looked back at me. Good lord! I dropped my eyes and asked my wife in a whisper if she'd brought the fax. Speechless and wide-eyed, she fumbled in her purse, and we studied the bleary picture while I told her to glance discreetly toward the man at the next table.

Carolyn's eyes went back and forth between diner and picture, after which she exclaimed, "It's him." Then in a whisper, "Albertine, look. It's him." She passed the fax to Albertine, who studied it, turned to study the diner, and then passed it to Adrien with a whisper.

"Perhaps," said Adrien.

"I think it is," said his wife.

"So do I," said Carolyn. "Look at the beard and the nose."

"What are you talking about?" Sylvie demanded. Just then the man looked over at our table again and scowled. Albertine narrowed her eyes and snapped her fingers; Charles de Gaulle popped up from his resting place half under the table; then Albertine whispered in French and pointed straight at the man. The only word I understood was "Carolyn," but the dog launched himself at the man, knocked him off his chair, and, growling, planted two paws on his chest.

Bedlam ensued.

50

The Terrorist, the Police,
and Martin

Carolyn

Charles de Gaulle let out a deep, hoarse growl and bared his teeth, while I watched the little man anxiously to see if he was going to pull a gun. Instead he shouted for help, restaurant employees converged on the scene, and the maitre d' demanded that the "wretched" dog be removed from both Monsieur Dubois and the restaurant. Albertine thrust her face into the maitre d's and declared that her dog was not wretched, and that he had just captured an Indonesian terrorist who was here to assassinate two members of her party.

"Monsieur Dubois is a wealthy industrialist from Toulouse who dines here frequently," said the gypsy.

"Show them the picture, Carolyn." I obeyed, but without taking my eyes off our captive. He was still pinned down by Charles de Gaulle and shouting in French— something that evidently upset the restaurant staff. "He says he will never come here again. He will sue the restaurant and all of us. He is a man of great importance in France and unused to being treated like a criminal," Albertine translated. Then she turned to the maitre d' and demanded that he call the police.

Having studied the fax and the valued customer, the maitre d' shrugged. He didn't see a resemblance. The little man, still flat on his back, insisted that the police be summoned to arrest *us*. That call was made, and Charles de Gaulle removed from the chest of the furious diner. I was beginning to think we might have made a mistake.

Then, worse luck, Inspector Villon arrived. He actually knew the industrialist and scoffed at the idea that Monsieur Dubois could also be a terrorist with Indonesian connections. "If there is a criminal here, it is you, madam, my chief suspect," the inspector said to me. "Gunshot residue can be washed off. I have applied for permission to search your hotel room and your luggage. You are under surveillance so that you cannot dispose of the pistol, and you may not leave Avignon until the case is solved."

"I have been subjected to this indignity at the word of a criminal?" cried Monsieur Dubois, trying to brush black dog hair off his gray suit.

I passed him the fax. "Don't you think this looks like you? It's the picture of a terrorist sent to me by an inspector in Lyon."

"We can't stay in Avignon indefinitely," protested my husband. "We have tickets home in a few days."

"*You* may leave, sir," said the inspector. "Your *wife* may not."

Monsieur Dubois was staring at the fax. "How can this be? I am not a terrorist. What is the name of the inspector in Avignon? I insist that he does not spread my picture about under the guise of combating violence."

"At least you understand why we thought you were—"

"I do not understand. I am an innocent industrialist with high political connections, and that lady—" He pointed accusingly at Albertine. "—instructed her dog to attack me."

"Ah ha!" snarled Inspector Villon. "We must confiscate the dog."

I thought Albertine was going to attack the inspector, but finally the multifaceted argument was settled, if not amicably, at least without anyone going to jail, including Charles de Gaulle, who, once removed from the industrialist's chest, stood guard at my side while people shouted at one another. He evidently did consider himself my knight in shining—well, if not armor, then fur.

Jason explained at length our trials here in France. Albertine explained that the dog loved me and wished to protect me. The inspector doubted that a dog could love more than one woman and wondered why that woman wasn't his mistress. Sylvie said that I enthralled dogs by feeding them sausage under tables. I apologized to the industrialist and gave him Inspector Roux's telephone number, although I explained that the inspector was busy with riots in Lyon.

The industrialist muttered that rioting had come to Toulouse as well, which was why he was trying to have a peaceful dinner here in Avignon. Jason remarked that he thought Mercedes, for whose shooting the inspector blamed me, had already left the city. The industrialist left the restaurant in search of some quieter place, and the rest of us sat down, under the glowering eyes of the management, to finish our entrées and order dessert. My lamb chops were lovely, and I skimped on calories by ordering sorbet and fruit for dessert.

This is a very tasty dish, and thyme is an interesting herb. It's said to be good for the stomach, the digestion, and the lungs, to heal wounds and kill germs, not to mention its romantic effect. If a bunch of thyme is left on your doorstep, it means someone loves you, or so the girls in Provence believe. Ladies, you might mention that to your significant others to see if a thyme bouquet shows up at the door.

Lemon-Thyme Lamb Chops

• Put *8 single-rib ½-inch lamb chops* into a shallow dish with *3 tablespoons fresh lemon juice, 1½ teaspoons fresh chopped thyme leaves,* and *¼ cup extra-virgin olive oil.* Cover and marinate for 30 minutes at room temperature; turn over several times.

• Preheat a heavy cast-iron skillet for 5 minutes, lower heat to moderate, add lamb chops and cook until browned, about 2 minutes on each side. Season each side with *salt* and *pepper* after cooking.

• Pour remaining marinade over chops and serve.

Carolyn Blue,
"Have Fork, Will Travel,"
Boston Telegraph

In the hotel lobby, I was told I had a message, so I stayed to retrieve and read it while Jason went upstairs, completely exhausted by our traumatic dinner and worrying that we wouldn't be able to leave France on time. The message, from Pierre, informed me that my own husband in 1990 had written a letter to the editor of *JACS* pointing out errors in the work of the French scientist Maurice Bellamee.

Dropping onto one of the couches with the note in my hand, I considered the undeniable implication. Catherine, still in mourning for her husband and blaming his death on a critical American chemist, my husband, had reason to kill us. But there was so little hard evidence, at least evidence that the blockheaded Inspector Villon would accept: a research outline that didn't have her name on it, recollections of her reaction to her husband's death fifteen years ago, and the long time she'd held a grudge against someone she'd never met. Even Jason wouldn't be convinced. He didn't think chemists killed one another.

I used the telephone in the lounge to call Martin at his hostel, which had only one phone. Once they found him, I told him about Jason's letter to the editor and asked if he really thought his research director would have tried to poison us with her synthesized toxin. He did, but understood that there was not enough evidence to denounce her. "I have the key to her apartment," he said. "We could search for clues while she is at the meeting."

"Don't you have to be there yourself?" I asked. "I don't want to get you in trouble."

"I will not be her student after this semester. I have made arrangements with another university. Why should I work for a woman who would hate me if she knew . . . about me?"

Was he leading me into an accusation against Catherine because *he* hated her? I wondered. "How did you get her key?"

"Every day she sends me for something she forgets. I am her errand boy," he replied bitterly. "When I found the fish paper in her desk, I know something is wrong, so I copy that and her key at a key store in case of need. Now I never eat or drink near her. You and your husband should not, either."

"Can you be at my hotel tomorrow at nine with the key?" I asked.

"*Oui*, madam. I will come. But I will go to the apartment with you. What if she comes back? You would be at her mercy."

"Yes," I agreed, deciding to invite Albertine, just in case

I needed protection against Martin. Poor fellow. I'd become paranoid. If Jason and I survived this trip, it would be due to Martin's loyalty. And I wouldn't mention our breaking-and-entering foray to my husband, since he didn't take the idea of Catherine as a murderess seriously. Albertine, however, was delighted when I called her. She promised to join us, with her dog. And to think that I had once disliked her intensely.

51
Illegal Entry

Carolyn

Albertine parked her car at the gate to the complex, where each apartment for seven or more floors was a concrete square, open in front above the balcony edge, as if someone had piled the apartments on top of each other and side by side on three sides enclosing the courtyard, with its zigzag pattern in red and brown. The crowning touch was a red metal clock in the shape of a lobster. At least it looked like a lobster with the usual legs and claws, not to mention black metal gears sticking out. Presumably the gears ran the black clock hands, one of which appeared to be topped by a pair of spectacles. The sign in front said the gates were locked at night, and I imagined with a shudder being locked in there, with Catherine hunting me through the corridors and stairways.

We had to cross the courtyard, wondering who might be watching as we prepared to enter Catherine's fourth-floor apartment illegally. What a sight we must have made—two middle-aged women, a towering, redheaded youth, and a large black poodle, pulling excitedly at his leash. It was a relief when Martin used his copied key to open the door and we slipped inside.

"Well, this is a surprise," said Albertine, looking at the starkly modern décor. "Catherine and Maurice loved antiques, or maybe it was just Maurice."

There were four rooms and a bath, a combination living and dining room decorated in burnished steel, glass, and black canvas, a kitchen with stainless steel appliances and gray granite counters, a bedroom all white with unfinished wood furniture, and a study lined with glass-doored bookcases and a black desk under a window with gray blinds. The impression was cold, grim, and industrial. I'd have hated to live here. Martin showed us the drawer where he'd found the paper on tetrodotoxin. The original was still there. I took a photo with my digital camera.

He continued to search in the office and found a photocopy of Jason's letter to the editor about Maurice's mistakes. I came in from the bedroom to photograph that. Meanwhile Albertine was poking around the living area and remarking on the paucity of decorative interest and drawers in which to search. She gave up there and went into the kitchen.

Having opted for the bedroom, I found nothing in the nightstand or in the top dresser drawer. However, in the second drawer, beneath some plain underwear and two nightgowns, I discovered a fragile, illuminated prayer book swaddled in gauze and nested in a wooden box. The language, I thought, was Latin, which meant it dated from the Middle Ages, before religious books were translated into the vernacular. There had been a prayer book on the list of items stolen from Catherine's Lyon apartment the day I was pushed down the stairs. I carried the box to the bed and photographed it, then returned it to its drawer and placed it carefully under the nightgowns. The chest yielded nothing else.

I was studying the closet shelves, which contained several stacked boxes, when Albertine arrived with a handgun wrapped in a dishtowel. "I found this under a silverware tray," she announced. Martin looked in, but none of us knew whether it was a target pistol. I snapped a picture of the gun and began to hand down boxes to Albertine. One contained a hat, black of course. Another housed a locked jewelry box, and the third, bundles wrapped in soft gray cloth—a set of silver candlesticks and six engraved gold forks.

"She pushed me down the stairs, then left her apartment door ajar, and took the items with her that were reported stolen by her aunt," I concluded. "And I felt so terrible about the loss of her heirlooms! Martin, can you get that jewelry box open? There were several pieces of jewelry on the list."

Martin tried, but his fingers were too large to fiddle with the tiny lock. Albertine pushed him aside, retrieved a hairpin from her chignon, and had the lock open in seconds. Among other things in the box were a gold cross with inlaid blue stones and a pearl and ruby necklace and earring set. I thought those had been on the list, but I'd have to ask Inspector Roux to fax it to me. In the meantime, I took more photographs. Then we carefully put everything back where we'd found it, including the gun in its dishtowel, and prepared to visit Inspector Villon to report our discoveries.

He'd have to get a warrant and come back. I did hope the gun was the one that had been used to shoot Mercedes. Perhaps it was also the gun with which Maurice killed himself. Catherine would probably find killing one of us with Maurice's gun a fine symbolic revenge.

"Oh, and Martin, would you look at some little vials I found in the pantry?" Albertine asked. Martin wanted to leave, but there was no denying Albertine. We went to the kitchen, where we found Charles de Gaulle with his nose in the refrigerator, eating a sausage. On the floor were two rounds of partially eaten cheese.

"Naughty dog," said Albertine. "He is so clever. We had to have special handles put on our refrigerator. He simply clamps his teeth on an ordinary handle and pulls the door open."

While Albertine showed Martin two tiny vials of colorless liquid she'd found behind a box of rice in a pantry, I cleaned up the dog's mess. He hid under the kitchen table, looking out at me sadly because I'd taken the sausage away from him.

"These could be samples of the toxin," said Martin.

Just in case, I took pictures of those, although they were barely visible between Martin's very large fingers. I just hoped that we could convince Inspector Villon to seize the evidence before Catherine got home from the meeting and noticed that her refrigerator had been raided, or that something was out of place in her obsessively tidy and austere apartment.

52
Convincing the Police

Carolyn

Inspector Villon was too busy to see us—no surprise there. Albertine tried to make an appointment, but I was tired of being a suspect, so I took Charles de Gaulle, just in case there were criminals lurking in the hallways, and marched off in search of the inspector's office with two policemen chasing me, shouting in French, and Albertine behind them. The five of us piled into Villon's office in a noisy clump. Evidently Martin, now worried about his possession and use of Catherine's key, had stayed behind, or perhaps decamped entirely.

Over the babble of the pursuing officers, who were now trying to explain why they hadn't been able to keep me out, I said loudly, "Inspector Villon, Madam Guillot and I have discovered who shot Mercedes Lizarreta."

"That is no longer of interest to me," he snarled, "since, as your husband warned, the young woman has left the city without filing charges. I shall, however, determine whether you frightened her away. That, too, is a crime."

I plopped myself down on a chair, so clearly angry that the dog pushed his head onto the desk and growled on my behalf. Villon gave an order to his subordinates, but they

backed away. When the order was repeated in booming
tones, they drew guns, upon which Albertine placed herself in the line of fire and railed at them in French. She
took no time to translate, so I turned back to Inspector
Villon.

"You don't care that a murderer is at large? She's killed
one man in Lyon, a professor who ate poisoned pâté she
meant for us. This morning we found what may be vials of
it in her pantry. She tried to run my husband down with her
car. On another day she lured me to her apartment and
pushed me down the stairs, then took away some possessions of hers so that it would look like a robbery. We found
those items in her apartment here in Avignon.

"Once we arrived in Avignon, she made me feel so bad
that I left the banquet, and then she attempted to shoot
Jason and hit Mercedes instead, making it look as if I'd
done it when I wasn't even there. We found what may be
the gun in her apartment; and in fact—this hadn't occurred to me before—Albertine, do you remember when
Charles de Gaulle knocked her down at Fort Andre?
Maybe he realized that she planned to push me off the
tower."

"Of course," Albertine agreed. "That explains his behavior."

"Madam Guillot, you give your dog too much credit.
You think he can read minds?" asked the inspector.

"Why not?" I said. "He can open refrigerators."

"Well," said Villon, "I can believe that a woman would
fail in so many attempts on the lives of you and your husband, but you have given me no motive. Is this a ménage a
trois that has—"

"Of course not," I snapped. "She blames my husband
for the suicide of hers fifteen years ago. We can show you
the paper Jason wrote calling Maurice Bellamee's work

in question. It's a matter of science, and all in her head anyway."

Villon snorted with laughter. "Attempted murder over science? Sex, I could believe. Money, I could believe. Did the suicidal husband lose money because of your husband's criticism?"

"No one makes money on scientific papers," I retorted. The inspector obviously knew nothing about academia. "In fact, the author or his university pay to have papers published. I insist that you search her apartment. I can show you pictures of the evidence, but it is all in place for you to find and document properly."

"And how did you, madam, get into this lady's apartment? Did she invite you in to find evidence against her?"

"She's at the conference. A student of hers had a key and let us in." This was the tricky part. What we'd done was probably against the law, especially since Martin had had the key copied without permission. Maybe it was a good thing that he'd left.

"Your theory of the crime is ridiculous, and how do I know that all these other things happened? Please leave my office and take the canine with you. He has drooled on official documents."

"All you have to do is get hold of Inspector Roux in Lyon. He can outline the whole case for you."

Sneering, Inspector Villon picked up his phone and told someone to contact Lyon. Obviously be expected to learn nothing. However, Roux came on the line and, when he heard what Villon had to say, asked to speak to me. I told him about the evidence, and he congratulated me on my persistence, then told Villon that he would have someone fax the case file, which he hadn't time to go over in person because Lyon was under attack by midnight rioters, who were being rounded up, when possible, the next day. Then he asked to speak to me again and complained that a famous Toulouse industrialist had dragged him away from a burning school the night before, furious about being attacked by a dog and identified as a terrorist.

"He looked just like your fax," I said. Evidently Monsieur Dubois had also called several of Roux's superiors. Then Roux asked to speak to Villon again and told him, loudly enough that Albertine could overhear and translate, that if the mad female professor from Lyon killed either of the American tourists, our deaths would be on Villon's head.

Thoroughly outraged, Inspector Villon ordered me to leave my camera with him and wait for a call in case the faxed files made it necessary for him to search the apartment of Professor de Firenze. Albertine gave him her cell phone number because I didn't have one, and Villon expressed his disdain for Americans who felt it perfectly proper to attack Iraq on the basis of false information and to travel around Europe without cell phones, which all civilized persons carried. I provided my hotel and room number, scowling all the while, and then we headed for the door, with the two officers, who were afraid of the dog, trailing behind to make sure that we actually left the premises.

Before we could enter the hall, another officer appeared carrying a large Styrofoam box. Charles de Gaulle leapt forward and snatched it between his teeth, after which he dashed into the hall, dropped the box, and tore into it. Before he could be stopped, he had wolfed down a sausage and started on the inspector's French fries.

There was, needless to say, another heated argument between Albertine and the inspector, who resented the poaching of his lunch. "We have just solved the case," she said. "If you attempt to imprison my dog, you may be sure I shall tell the newspapers that your case was solved by two ladies, a graduate student from Normandy, and a dog." The inspector, face dark red with fury, decided not to punish the dog, and we were allowed to leave.

Martin was lurking outside, looking abashed, so we took him to lunch and plied him with delicious food and wine until he was much less stressed about the possibility of being arrested for letting us into Catherine's apartment.

53

Evidence of Intruders

I **couldn't find** *my tame Norman anywhere and had to skip a lecture to pick up papers I'd left at home. The stress of recent days had made me forgetful, but that was no excuse for him. I knew as soon as I opened the door that something was wrong, even the smell, although I couldn't identify the odor. And the four books on the coffee table were piled in the wrong order. The top one should have been the one I was reading.*

With the hair on my arms prickling in alarm, I hurried to the kitchen and fished the gun from beneath the flatware container in the drawer. At least it was in its place. Holding it in my right hand, I moved silently from room to room, but found no one. What did I have here that I wouldn't want an intruder to see? I'd brought things from Lyon but found it hard to remember what—ah, the items supposedly stolen from my apartment. I had to put the pistol down, which made me uneasy under the circumstances, in order to pull the boxes from the closet shelf.

The spoons and candlesticks were in the proper box, wrapped in silverware cloths. I couldn't be sure that they hadn't been disturbed, but they looked as they had when I arrived and put them away. The jewelry box was still locked and showed no signs of having been pried open.

Nonetheless, I checked for the cross and the jewelry set that had belonged to the first Catherine of Avignon, the one who had married a wealthy moneylender of the papal city and moved here from her family home in Lyon.

After putting the boxes back on the shelf, I checked the drawers of my plain wooden dresser. How the aunt who left me this place would have hated the décor, but I found it soothing. It did not remind me of happier times. My medieval prayer book was swaddled carefully in its carved walnut box, much to my relief—until I remembered that it should have been beneath the nunlike underwear, which had replaced the silken lingerie I once wore to please my love. Now the box lay beneath heavy cotton nightgowns. In the wrong place!

Why would a thief enter my apartment and steal nothing? If the intruder were a pervert, ransacking my underwear drawer, why not take a sample with him? I hurried to the laundry container in the bathroom but found everything that I had worn and discarded since coming to Avignon piled within, perhaps not in a particular order, but I could be responsible for that. Not even I fold unwashed laundry and put it away in any order, although Maurice used to laugh about my compulsive neatness.

The desk. My books! I had first editions of early scientific treatises that had belonged to—I ran into the other bedroom, heart pounding, but they too were in their places in the glass-fronted cabinets that protected them. Nor could I find anything amiss in my desk, yet I knew that someone had been here. Could Martin have been nosing through my things? I'd have his head if he'd done anything here but what he was sent to do—fetch papers for me from specified files.

The intruder had come today. If someone, Martin, for instance, had visited my apartment while I was at the palais, Marie-Solange might have seen him. Our concierge *is a nosy woman, always looking out her window. I had had to bring my treasures in by the back stairs to avoid questions. Whipping my cell phone from my handbag, I called her. She had indeed seen strangers entering the compound a bit after nine, two women, a large black dog, and a tall, redheaded man, whom she had seen here before.*

I might have been unsure about the women had it not been for the dog and Martin. Had I failed to retrieve my key from him yesterday? The women must have been Carolyn and Albertine, searching for something in my apartment. What did they know? What did they suspect? And what had they found? The prayer book, but if Albertine or Martin found it, it would have meant nothing to them. The inspector in Lyon, however, might have told Carolyn what was reported stolen from my apartment. Or had I told her? I was losing track of my actions—due to the stress of my failures.

"My goodness," said Marie-Solange. "A police car just pulled into the courtyard. Fools! It's not for cars. I must go and send them away."

She hung up, and I rushed to the window, where I saw four men pile out of the car and Marie-Solange, waving her arms and berating them. Mon Dieu. *Were they here for me? I had things yet to accomplish. Perhaps I could still kill the woman if she was at her hotel. The man no, he was at the palais. I could not embarrass my colleagues by killing him in front of everyone. And there were things I would need to take with me. No time for everything, even things that might incriminate me if the police came here, but things I'd need. Even as I thought this, I began to collect, in my haste to escape down the back stairs, the things that would suit my purposes.*

54

Found: The Evidence,
but Not the Suspect

Carolyn

After lunch, Albertine, Charles de Gaulle, Martin, and I set out to entertain ourselves while we waited for word from Villon. Martin was astounded at the idea of driving around to visit more sites, but he was equally nervous about running into his research director at the conference, so he accompanied us.

We visited the eighteenth-century Comedy Theater, a square two-story building with a nice balustrade on top and ugly windows that had been added later. In fact, according to Albertine, both inside and outside had been ruined when it closed and was purchased by soulless business interests. Later the city bought it back and began refurbishing. The Place Crillon, where it sat, had paving of squares within squares within squares. I do love the many configurations of paving in Europe. I even saw one such display of intersecting brick half circles outside a store at home, but that area was very small. I'd have taken a picture of Place Crillon, but Inspector Villon had my camera.

We also drove by some nice city gates inset in the walls.

Martin was more interested in those and thought the walls so fine that Normans must have built them. At the church of Saint Didier, we stopped and went inside to see a famous marble altarpiece called Le Portement de la Croix or Notre Dame du Spasme. The background buildings didn't look at all like Jerusalem in the early Christian era, nor did the clothing. I'd have guessed Assisi and the Middle Ages, but the altarpiece was said to be one of the oldest works of the French Renaissance, so what did I know?

While we were looking at a large Annunciation fresco, Albertine's cell phone rang. It was the inspector, and whatever he said caused her to drop into a pew and shake her head. "What?" I asked. "He decided not to search her apartment?"

"No, he checked the faxes from Lyon against our pictures and information, and they made the concierge open the apartment. The woman insisted that Catherine was there, but she wasn't."

"Well, of course not. She's at the conference."

"She hasn't been seen at the palais since lunchtime and isn't there now."

My heart sank. If Catherine had come home and detected our visit, she might have fled, or be out looking for us. "We've got to call Jason and warn him."

Albertine nodded. "The concierge was talking to Catherine on the telephone, telling her about the strangers she'd seen, which is to say us, when the woman saw the police drive into the courtyard."

"I didn't see any cars in the courtyard."

"They're not supposed to be. Anyway, she mentioned that to Catherine and then left to insist that they park on the street."

"And Catherine got out the back way. Is there a back way?"

"Yes," said Martin. "Stairs."

"So she's escaped. She's probably halfway to the border of Spain by now," said Albertine. "How could she tell we'd been there? We didn't take anything. We didn't move anything."

"Maybe she noticed the sausage and cheese missing from her refrigerator," Martin suggested.

For safety's sake, Albertine called her husband so that mine would be warned while I fretted that we'd left the gun behind where Catherine could get it. Then we all went over to the palais, seeking safety in numbers, while the police searched Avignon for Catherine.

From inside their room, the lock of which I'd opened with an ice pick, I found that I could hear the elevator doors. I'd entered the hotel without being seen by using the door on the side street that led into the deserted breakfast area. From there I located stairs and climbed to their floor. Now all I had to do was wait. Carolyn would arrive first, after an afternoon of sightseeing or whatever she chose to do after searching my apartment. I planned to shoot her with Maurice's pistol and hope the shot went unheard. I had prepared a surprise for the bereaved husband by pouring one of the two vials of tetrodotoxin into an open bottle of wine in their bar. Neither of them would expect to find me in their own room after they'd denounced me to the police. They'd expect me to flee the country.

I thought of leaving a note by Carolyn's body, but that would warn the husband. Instead, I tucked copies of Maurice's paper and Jason Blue's response into the pocket of his suitcase. When he discovered it, if he lived, he'd understand that his wife's death was the price he paid for killing my husband. And if he died, so much the better. I might even get away, although going back for my car would be dangerous.

A cab! That was the thing. I'd have a bullet left after

*killing Carolyn. The gun might persuade the driver to take
me to the nearest border, where being a citizen of the European Union, I could cross with my driver's license. And
if the driver tried to refuse, I'd shoot him. I felt quite cheerful at my prospects. I had money; I had a Swiss bank account. Yes, the cab could take me to Switzerland. And I had
a gun. At last, I would prevail and make Maurice proud of
me. And if I were taken between Avignon and Switzerland,
there was always the second vial.*

*I would not spend the rest of my life in jail for doing
what was only right. The French are so cold; they don't understand the Italian concept of family honor and vendetta,
but I was still, after all these centuries, an Italian at heart.
I would have my revenge.*

*Time passed slowly, but I was patient and calm. When I
heard the elevator doors opening, I stood and checked my
pistol. Mother of God! What had I done? The two chambers were empty. I had not reloaded after shooting the
Mexican girl. And in my panic at the arrival of the police,
I hadn't thought of anything but the gun itself and the
toxin. Maurice had always loaded the weapons.*

*I heard two voices coming down the hall. A man and a
woman. With no bullets, I couldn't overcome them both.
Carolyn alone I might have managed, but both of them? It
would not be possible. I would be caught and imprisoned.
Panic-stricken, I ran into the bathroom and locked the
door. They were in the room now, only feet from me. I
dragged the second vial from my handbag and poured the
liquid down my throat, thinking that the result would be
immediate, but I felt nothing. Too slow. Too slow.*

*I watched the doorknob turning futilely. She said, "I
can't get into the bathroom, Jason," and she rattled the
knob.*

*Looking desperately around the little room, from which
I could not escape, I saw the hair dryer hanging beside the*

sink, its long cord dangling against the wall. My eyes swept from the dryer to the tub with its white-on-white flowered curtain and saw my last hope. Sweeping the dryer from its cradle, I stepped into the tub and turned the water on full force with my free hand, then pushed in the lever that would divert the flow to the showerhead. `

"Jason, did you leave the water running?" she called.

I stood under the heavy spray until I was soaked, which took only seconds, and then I pressed the switch on the hair dryer and let the current sear through my body like the burning flash of lightning. "Maurice," I thought in the last moment of consciousness. "I tried."

55
French Fried

Carolyn

Jason flipped the light switch, dropped his briefcase on the bed, and took off his coat while I tried to get into the bathroom, only to discover that the door was locked. "I can't get into the bathroom, Jason," I said over my shoulder and rattled the knob. What in the world was wrong with it? And I could hear water running inside. I tried the knob again and asked Jason if he'd left the shower on. He hadn't. Then the lights went out while I was banging on the door. I thought I'd heard something inside, but I couldn't be sure what it was.

"Jason, we'd better call the desk. I don't understand this at all. Could we have caught one of the maids taking a shower in our bath, and now she's afraid to come out?"

"That doesn't explain the power outage." He called downstairs and was told that he could expect the return of electricity shortly. Having reported that to me, he came over and put his ear to the door, where he could hear only the sound of the water bursting from the showerhead. "Considering how slowly the tub drains, we'd better get someone up here to open the door and turn the water off," he decided.

He called downstairs again and explained the situation to Bridget. In the time it must have taken to climb the stairs, because the elevators were no longer working, a breathless young woman in a maid's uniform arrived with a key, opened the door, reached behind the shower curtain to turn off the water—and screamed.

"Floor's probably flooded," Jason guessed from his wicker chair. The girl stumbled out of the bathroom, stammering in French. "Do you speak English?" he asked calmly. "Perhaps you should get a mop." To our amazement, she ran out of the room with no indication that she'd be back.

Frowning, Jason went to investigate and remarked that the floor was dry, but she'd forgotten to turn off the water. I had come to the doorway in time to see him reach in. "What the hell?" he said, and he too backed away.

"What's wrong?"

"There's someone in there," he answered, and after that he did turn off the water.

In the dim light from the frosted window, I pulled back the other side of the curtain to see for myself, and caught sight of a woman, doubled over, face down, her clothes and hair soaking, and, of all things, a hair dryer in her hand. I looked back to see that it was attached to the wall unit from which it had hung.

"Don't touch her," said Jason. "If the hair dryer was going when she stepped into the water, she's been electrocuted. You could be, too."

"There's no electricity," I pointed out, reaching down to touch her neck in search of a pulse.

"Don't touch her!" Jason pulled me roughly away. "The current could come back any minute. Don't even touch the curtain."

"Jason." My voice trembled. "I think it might be Catherine."

"What the hell would Catherine be doing in our shower with a hair dryer in her hand?" he snapped. "She's supposed to be on the run."

"Maybe she came back to kill us. What if she's only unconscious?"

"Well, she can't kill us with the hair dryer, and I don't see any other weapons around."

"Let's lock her in and call Inspector Villon." I was so frightened my teeth were chattering. When Jason noticed, he led me out of the bathroom and locked the door. "Maybe she was trying to kill herself," I speculated. "Why else would she carry a hair dryer into the shower?"

"Hell of a way to do it," he muttered. "You're saying she French fried herself?"

He led me to the rattan love seat and sat me down. My mouth had dropped open at his question. *French fried?* That was an insensitive way to describe Catherine's death. If she *was* dead. I kept expecting her to burst out of the bathroom. And I don't suppose she deserved any sensitivity from us.

Jason was on the phone again telling Bridget that we had a woman, possibly dead, in our shower. "Call Inspector François Villon of the local police," he ordered. "Tell him to get over here. My wife thinks it's the woman he's looking for." He put the phone down and rubbed his forehead. "What I need is a stiff drink," he muttered and went to the bar, where he found the half bottle of wine we'd shared before dinner last night. "Want some?" He poured wine into one glass and was lifting it to his lips when I dove across the room. The wine spattered on both of us, the glass fell to the floor, and Jason looked at me askance.

"What if she poisoned it?"

"Well, we'll never know now." He didn't sound as if he believed I might have saved his life. Before he could pick up the bottle again, I grabbed it, ran over to the balcony, and poured the remaining wine over the cement wall. "That was a very good red," he complained, "and I paid a lot for it."

"Look in the waste basket," I retorted. I'd just spotted a small vial. "That's one of the vials we found behind the rice in her pantry. Why would she bring it here if she didn't mean to poison us?"

My husband swore and called downstairs again, asking them to send up two bottles of wine that had not been opened, two clean wineglasses, and a corkscrew. *What a good idea*, I thought while we were waiting for the wine. There were two small bottles of whiskey in the bar, but they had screw tops, and we didn't dare try those. However, once the sealed wine arrived, I was certainly happy to join Jason in a drink. In fact, we'd finished off the first bottle by the time the inspector arrived, and I was feeling much more relaxed. Nothing had been heard from the bathroom.

We explained to the inspector what had happened, and he actually kicked the door open. I thought that only happened on television. Then he pushed back the shower curtain and pulled on the cord of the hair dryer until it appeared over the side of the tub, a hand still clutching it. "So this is the woman who tried to kill you?" Inspector Villon asked.

"I don't know," I replied. "I can't see her face, and people look different from any perspective when they're all wet."

"Did you electrocute her?" he asked, as unpleasant as ever.

"That does it," said my husband angrily, as he opened the second bottle. "You've harassed my wife one too many times. We're the victims here, not the woman in the tub. If she's dead—"

"She's dead," the inspector assured us. "*Looks* like she was electrocuted."

"If she's dead," Jason continued, pouring wine into both goblets, "she killed herself by walking into the shower holding a running hair dryer. Don't blame my wife. And don't blame Carolyn for Mercedes being shot. Have you checked the gun in Catherine's apartment to see if it—"

"There was no gun," said the inspector. "We checked under the silverware holder, where we were told to look, and there was no—"

"That's not your handbag over there on the floor, is it, Carolyn?" my husband asked.

Of course it wasn't. Mine was on the bed.

"Why don't you look in there," Jason said to the inspector. "Maybe she brought the gun along. She brought a couple of vials of something with her."

"That's another thing we didn't find," said the inspector.

"Well, one's in the wastebasket, and there's another over there on the bathroom floor. You'll want to test those for tetrodotoxin. It's highly poisonous, and she was synthesizing it."

"Maybe you're the person with the gun and the poison," said the inspector. "You or your wife."

"We haven't touched any of those things, and we're not going to. If you're not willing to look at the evidence, I'll call the consulate in Lyon and make a complaint. In fact, I'll do it anyway. I damn near got run over by a car, and my wife has been injured twice, not to mention being accused of trying to kill two different women." Jason picked up the phone.

"Calm down, Professor," said the inspector. "We intend to investigate." He waved another officer over to the handbag, and the man, having pulled on gloves, opened it and found a gun.

"Is it a target pistol?" I asked. "If it is, it's probably the same gun her husband killed himself with. By the way, Jason, the article that Catherine thought killed her husband was one you wrote. Pierre looked it up for me."

"I wrote?" Jason looked astonished. "I don't recall writing—"

"Well, it was fifteen years ago, a letter to the editor of *JACS*."

"Oh." Jason thought about it and looked upset.

Scowling ferociously, the inspector asked, "You are responsible for the death of the deceased's husband?"

"Of course he isn't," I retorted. "Maurice Bellamee, according to other members of the department, was subject to serious depression. He was already depressed before Jason pointed out the errors in his work. Scientists are always finding problems in each other's work and writing letters and papers about the errors, and the scientists who made the mistakes just write a retraction; they don't kill themselves."

Jason smiled at me and poured me more wine. "Why don't you just pack up the evidence and take the body away, Inspector."

"There are fingerprints to gather, and—"

"So do it. Call us when you've discovered that my wife solved your crime for you and that the criminal killed herself. Probably knew she was caught and didn't want to go to jail."

"There are no bullets in this gun," said the officer who had opened the handbag.

"Well, that explains it," I said. "She collected things to kill us when the concierge said the police were in the courtyard, but she forgot to put in bullets. An understandable mistake. Then she walked over here and got into our room somehow so she could wait for our return and shoot us, or me. Perhaps she thought I'd come back first and she'd shoot me and then get Jason with the poisoned wine."

"What poisoned wine?" asked the inspector.

"The bottle's in the wastebasket by the desk. My wife knocked the glass out of my hand and poured the wine over the concrete wall so I couldn't have a drink. Perhaps you should send someone down to get a sample before the puddle dries up."

Inspector Villon shook his head with dismay. Obviously this was all too complicated for him. I almost felt sorry for him, and thought of offering him a glass of wine, but really, he needed all his wits about him to figure out the whole Machiavellian plot that Catherine had concocted against us.

Epilogue

Jason

Carolyn and I took our bottle and glasses to the lounge to watch television while the inspector tried to make sense of the evidence in our room. The news was not good. Rioting had spread across the country, embassies were warning their nationals to stay away from the affected areas, and those included, of course, Lyon and Paris, through which we had to pass to fly home.

Carolyn took the whole thing very cheerfully. She pointed out that the airlines couldn't refuse to change our tickets under the circumstances, and the extra days, however many there were, would allow us to visit all kinds of interesting places in southern France. I would have liked to see Marseilles and Toulouse, but they were out because their youths were torching whatever they could get to. Carolyn wanted to see Albi, which had an "amazing" fortress church and was the seat of the heresy that so intrigued her, not to mention Carcassone, the largest walled fortress in Europe.

What could I say? Obviously, I'd be taking busses and trains all over the area until the French government got the uprising in hand. My department wouldn't be pleased when I didn't arrive back in El Paso for classes, but they couldn't expect us to make our way home through hordes of rioting kids.

At least I was happy to see my wife unstressed and excited about future sightseeing. "Did the doctor say anything about what you could and couldn't do while your ankle is healing?" I asked.

"I told you he said I should walk on it, and I have, and I intend to keep doing so."

"I wasn't thinking of that," I murmured and sent her a look that has passed between us many times over the years.

Carolyn started to laugh. "Oh, *that* won't be a problem, Jason. I'll just wear the boot to bed."

"Really? I've never made love to a booted woman."

"Well, we *are* on vacation," she replied, eyes dancing. "Vacations lend themselves for new experiences. I wonder when they'll get out of our room. Not soon, I'd imagine. Maybe we should go out to dinner while we're waiting. I heard about a wonderful restaurant at the Hotel de la Mirande, very sophisticated."

"What a romantic woman you are," I retorted. "I sometimes think you're more interested in food than you are in me. And just how expensive is this sophisticated restaurant?"

"Very," she replied, "but worth every penny."

Was my Carolyn talking about the food or the dessert she'd promised when we got back? Still, we were both alive and on good terms. Why not? "Let's go."

She gave me a kiss and jumped up. "We'll need to get clothes from the room. We can't go to Hotel de la Mirande dressed in wine-spattered outfits. And goodness, Jason, I wonder if the poison on the fabrics could soak through our skin."

I doubted it, but just to be safe I agreed to a change of clothes.

Then Carolyn bad another thought. "I wonder if my black dress has been repaired yet. I'll have Bridget call the shop and ask."

"Great. Just as a long as you don't wear high heels."

"But, Jason, I could only wear one, and then I'd be un-balanced again. Physically. Did you know that Albertine called me deranged?"

I didn't but had to admit to myself that sometimes my wife, as loveable as she is, does seem a bit deranged. Per-haps *eccentric* would be a better word.

Recipe Index

Penguin Group (USA) Online

What will you be reading tomorrow?

Tom Clancy, Patricia Cornwell, W.E.B. Griffin,
Nora Roberts, William Gibson, Robin Cook,
Brian Jacques, Catherine Coulter, Stephen King,
Dean Koontz, Ken Follett, Clive Cussler,
Eric Jerome Dickey, John Sandford,
Terry McMillan, Sue Monk Kidd, Amy Tan,
John Berendt...

You'll find them all at
penguin.com

*Read excerpts and newsletters,
find tour schedules and reading group guides,
and enter contests.*

Subscribe to Penguin Group (USA) newsletters
and get an exclusive inside look
at exciting new titles and the authors you love
long before everyone else does.

PENGUIN GROUP (USA)
us.penguingroup.com